Later, after Stephen dropped her off at her condo and she prepared for bed, Nina's mind whirled with thoughts of Gwyneth and her planned bell tower performance. Would she succeed in following through? If so, would her appearance result in the hoped-for department chairmanship? What were the troublesome matters she wanted to confide? Despite all the questions, Nina eventually fell asleep.

All too soon, her ringing cell phone awoke her. She reached for the phone and squinted at the screen. Six o'clock. "Wow, Stephen, you're up early. What's happening?"

"Bad news, I'm afraid."

At his serious tone, she gripped the phone and sat up. "What happened?"

"Gwyneth Miller won't be performing from the bell tower."

Her stomach twisted. "Why not? Stephen, tell me."

"She's dead."

Praise for Linda Hope Lee

"A page-turning whodunit as Nina investigates her mentor's death while the murderer tracks her every move."

~Liz Osborne, award-winning mystery author

~*~

"Linda Hope Lee weaves a university campus bell tower, secret student society, and the mysterious death of a popular English professor into a super cozy mystery. Prepare to burn the midnight oil and follow amateur sleuth Nina Foster in DEATH RINGS A BELL."

~Joanne Otness,
co-author of PASSION FLOWERS by Molly Charles

~*~

"I recommend MURDER BETWEEN THE PAGES and look forward to the next in the series."

~Valerie's Musings Blog

~*~

"The mystery kept me hooked."

~The Book Decoder Blog

~*~

"The story's twists and red herrings kept me guessing."
~Book Club Librarian Blog

~*~

"A mystery not easily solved and a saucy, fun romance make this a delightful read."

~ Laura, FUONLYKNEW Blog

~*~

SECRETS TO DIE FOR: "A superb cozy mystery. Highly recommended."

~N. N. Light

Death Rings a Bell

by

Linda Hope Lee

A Nina Foster Mystery, Book 4

Death Rings a Bell

Cover Art by *Kim Mendoza*

The Wild Rose Press, Inc.
PO Box 708
Adams Basin, NY 14410-0708
Visit us at www.thewildrosepress.com

Publishing History
First Edition, 2022
Trade Paperback ISBN 978-1-5092-4553-6
Digital ISBN 978-1-5092-4554-3

A Nina Foster Mystery, Book 4
Published in the United States of America

Chapter One

"Me? A lecturer at Lit Fest?" Sitting in her office at the Richmond, Washington, Seaview Public Library, Nina Foster could hardly believe her caller's request.

"Yes, we want you, Nina."

Gwyneth Miller's emphatic tone rang in Nina's ear.

"You're quite the authority on children's literature. I've read your published articles and also your blog. Besides, we feature PNU alums whenever we can. Bragging about our students' successes is good publicity. So, what do you say? Are you on board?"

Nina tapped her fingers on the desk while considering her former professor's invitation. As a student, she always looked forward to Pacific Northwest University's fall literature festival. Participating as a professional promised a unique experience. "I accept. That is, if Gil gives me the time off." Gilbert Grady, Director of the Manuska County Library System, was Nina's boss.

"I'm sure he'll be as delighted as we are—What? No, not *now*."

Someone responded to Professor Miller, but the words were unintelligible.

"I said, we can't discuss the matter now." The professor's voice rose. "We'll meet later…"

Hearing the distress in Professor Miller's voice, Nina gripped the receiver. She waited, hoping her former teacher would successfully handle the obviously upsetting interruption.

"Are you there, Nina?" Professor Miller came back on the line.

"I'm here. Is everything okay?" Although she didn't want to pry, genuine concern prompted her to inquire.

The professor heaved a breath. "I'm fine. So sorry for the interruption. Where were we?"

"Gil giving me permission to take time off."

"Right. If he gives you any trouble, let me know. He owes me a favor or two. Now, what else do I need to tell you? I'll email you the festival's schedule, which includes meetings with our faculty planning committee. We'll talk on the phone, as well."

Nina relaxed her hold on the receiver. "Thank you again, Professor Miller, for the invitation. I'm honored to be included."

"You're most welcome, Nina, and please call me Gwyneth. We're no longer professor and student—we're contemporaries."

After the call ended, Nina sat back and took a deep breath. Wow. Lit Fest. What a great opportunity to share her love of children's literature. She used her knowledge here on the job, of course, with storytelling programs and assisting patrons. But the festival would be the first time speaking to an audience whose interest ran deeper than just wanting a good story.

She stood and approached her bookshelf. Looking over the framed pictures lining the top shelf, she picked up the photo of PNU's campus. Established in 1895, the university enjoyed a reputation as one of the best in the state. The campus certainly was impressive in appearance, with buildings featuring Tudor-Gothic architecture. Especially notable was the bell tower, with its giant clock on one wall and surrounded by a grassy quad.

Although the university was only a few miles from Richmond, she hadn't visited the campus much since graduation. Her life had moved on, first to graduate school at the University of Washington and then to her job at Seaview. Participating in the festival offered an opportunity to reacquaint herself with her alma mater.

Her thoughts turned to her conversation with Gwyneth and the interruption the woman experienced. Her emphatic dismissal of the person indicated they were not on the best of terms. Why? Something to do with the festival? Or a more personal matter? Nina would admit to suspecting a mystery lurked around every corner. Sometimes, she was proven wrong, but in at least a couple occurrences, her instincts were correct. Which would be the case this time?

****

"What do you think of this arrangement?" Stephen Kraslow made a sweeping gesture to include the entire room. "Bed, chest of drawers, and the table for all his computer stuff."

Nina took a moment to gaze around the spare bedroom in her significant other's house. They met over a year ago and had progressed from dating to spending alternate weekends at Nina's town condo at Edgemont Estates and Stephen's home here on the shores of Puget Sound.

David was his fifteen-year-old son from a former relationship. The teen's mother introduced him to Stephen and Nina on a trip last summer to Stephen's Idaho hometown. Now, he prepared for David's first visit to Richmond, which would occur at Christmastime.

She turned toward him. Standing at six feet, he had brown hair a few shades lighter than hers and, largely due to workouts at the local gym, a slender, though muscular, build. "David should be very comfortable here."

Stephen smiled and patted her shoulder. "Glad you approve. Now, how about some dinner?" Taking her hand, he led her into the hallway and downstairs.

A few minutes later, she and Stephen sat at opposite ends of the dining room table, with its panoramic view of the Sound, including Whidbey Island and the Olympic Peninsula, where snow-covered mountains rose to meet the sky. Shortly after moving to Richmond as the new owner of the weekly newspaper, *The Richmond Review*, Stephen purchased the older, waterfront home in need of remodeling. The renovation was a work in progress, as evidenced by the lumber stacked on the deck and the toolbox occupying one corner of the dining room.

Nina sampled Stephen's chowder, full of succulent clams drenched in a thick, creamy sauce. "Mmmm, your chowder is delicious."

"Thanks. Your tossed salad's a winner, too. We make a good team." Stephen smiled. "But now, tell me about your appearance at your alma mater's Lit Fest."

Nina filled him in on Gwyneth Miller's invitation. "As you can imagine, I'm really pleased—and flattered—to be included. But I do have reservations about being on campus again."

Stephen's brow wrinkled. "Because of Wildeen and Zelma?"

He referred to Wildeen Bergman, whose tragic murder Nina had solved a little over a year ago, and to

Zelma Duke, another friend who had the misfortune to be the prime suspect. "Yes, we roomed together for a semester and remained friends even after we each pledged different sororities. I know returning to campus will remind me of them."

Stephen touched his napkin to his lips. "What about the professor who contacted you today? You said she was your advisor."

"She was a wonderful teacher and counselor." Nina added more croutons to her chowder. "I really liked her...and still do. We had a good conversation today, except for an interruption." She related what she overheard. "When I inquired, Professor Miller—Gwyneth—insisted she was all right, but I could swear someone threatened her."

He tilted his head. "Uh-oh. Now you're into sleuth mode. You think she's in some kind of trouble?"

"I don't know, but I can't help worrying." Nina broke open a roll and spread butter on one portion.

"I'll be on campus from time to time, if my presence will help."

His news brought a smile. "You will? So, you already know about Lit Fest."

He nodded and dipped his spoon into his chowder. "A rep from the university's publicity department already contacted me about coverage."

She raised an eyebrow. "You won't assign the event to one of your reporters?"

"Not now that I know you'll be on the program. I'd like to sit in on your lecture, too, unless my presence would make you uncomfortable."

"Not at all." His thoughtful suggestion brought warmth to her cheeks. "I'd be honored to have you in the audience." Knowing Stephen would be on campus for the festival, at least part of the time, helped Nina to put aside her concerns and concentrate on planning her presentation.

Still, in the ensuing days, her worries about Gwyneth Miller nagged. Nina suspected something serious troubled her. Who had interrupted their initial phone call? The matter must have been serious to warrant so rude an intervention. Ever inquisitive when a mystery presented itself, Nina vowed to find the answers to her questions.

Chapter Two

On Friday morning, having received permission from Supervisor Grady, Nina drove the thirty miles to Pacific Northwest University to attend a meeting of the Lit Fest Planning Committee. Leaving Richmond and the shores of Puget Sound behind, she traveled inland, first on the freeway and then on secondary roads leading through farmlands and small communities. Now mid-September, leaves of gold, red, and orange decorated the otherwise green landscape, while overhead the sun shone from a cloudless sky.

The turnoff to PNU led her through a thick woods, part of the property lumber magnate Jezra Weller deeded to the university. Around a bend, the trees thinned and, as though someone waved a magic wand, the campus popped into view.

Nina drove past the quad, where the bell tower presided, and then on to the visitors' parking lot. A few minutes later, she entered Bannon Hall, home of the English Department—and the Lit Fest Committee. Like all the campus buildings, the interior featured remnants of the Gothic era—high ceilings, dark wood wall trim, and stained glass windows.

The meeting was held in the second floor Faculty Lounge. As she turned toward the elevators, she noticed the wide stone staircase. Memories flooded her, and in her mind's eye, she saw herself once again an underclassman rushing up the stairs, hoping to reach class before the bell in the tower outside chimed the hour.

Eager to relive the memory, she approached the stairs, placed a hand on the stone railing, and began to climb. At the midway landing, streams of sunlight shining through a red-and-yellow stained glass window added warmth to the otherwise gray-and-brown color scheme. She stopped and, still lost in the past, gazed at the window.

A group of students, laughing and talking, clattered down the stairs from above and rushed by, snapping her back to the present. Okay, she was no longer a student but an adult who, with her Lit Fest membership, would be on a par with the faculty. Straightening her shoulders, she marched up the remaining steps to the second floor.

After treading down a long hallway, she finally reached the Faculty Lounge. The door was closed, but through the frosted glass, Nina discerned movement and heard voices. Should she knock? Or walk in? Better knock.

No answer.

She knocked again, this time louder.

The door edged open, and a woman peered out. "Yes? We're having a meeting here."

"I know. I'm attending. I'm Nina Foster—guest speaker at Lit Fest."

The woman's lips curved into a smile. "Well, c'mon in." She opened the door wider. "I'm Jazmine Hibbley. Ethnic Studies. Folks call me Jaz." She patted her black curls and then pulled a shawl in bright shades of blue and purple tighter around her shoulders.

Nina stepped into the room. "Nice to meet you, Jaz. Is Professor Miller here?" She peered over Jaz's shoulder.

"She is." Jaz pointed toward a group of three or four people standing near a window.

One of them, a middle-aged woman with blonde hair, was indeed Gwyneth Miller.

Just then, Gwyneth looked around.

Nina caught her eye and waved.

Breaking away, Gwyneth hurried to her side. "Welcome, Nina." Reaching out, she gave Nina a handshake.

"Thank you." Nina smiled, careful to hide her surprise at how her former professor had changed. Ten years ago, she was a stunning blonde with flawless skin and wide-set blue eyes. Now, her hair had lost its luster, and wrinkles underlined eyes lacking the old sparkle.

Were the changes in her appearance due to normal aging? Or to something else? Something to do with the interruption during her and Nina's initial phone call?

"We're ready to begin our meeting. Help yourself to coffee or tea and then sit next to me at the table." Gwyneth gestured first toward a cart holding urns and cups and then to an oval table near the opposite wall.

Pleased to find her favorite Earl Grey tea, Nina soon settled at the table with a steaming cup of the fragrant brew.

With Gwyneth's call of "Let's get started, people," the others soon filled the remaining chairs.

In addition to Gwyneth, Nina, and Jaz, four other faculty members made up the committee. Two were men Nina recognized from her undergraduate days: Ambrose Grandstrom, who taught Shakespeare, and

Desmond DeSoto, whose forte was Composition. She had fond memories of attending Professor Grandstrom's classes, but Desmond DeSoto's were another matter. Too bad he was on the team.

The two faculty members new to Nina were Vivian Blanchard, who specialized in Popular Fiction, and Eldon Harmsworth, who presided over the Speech classes.

Gwyneth cleared her throat and rapped her knuckles on the table. "I have some exciting news about our keynote speaker, but first let me introduce another presenter and new member of our committee." She gestured toward Nina. "Nina Foster, Managing Librarian at Richmond's Seaview Library, will lecture on children's literature." She turned to face Nina. "Can you share some details of your presentation?"

"Thank you, Gwyneth." Nina straightened her spine and took a deep breath. "My talk will be illustrated with a slideshow, books from my personal collection, and handmade puppets I use in storytelling at the library. I'll include well-known authors, of course, but also a few lesser-known writers I consider worthy."

Vivian Blanchard, who wore her dark, wavy hair in a chignon, regarded Nina over the top of her black-framed eyeglasses. "Are you including graphic novels? With the help of the Art Department, my students have produced some clever takeoffs of several children's classics."

Eldon Harmsworth frowned. With his broad shoulders and thick arms, he appeared more suited to teach physical education than speech. "Do we want comic books in our program?"

Nina hadn't considered graphic novels, but neither would she rule them out. She looked to Vivian to see her response.

Vivian stuck out her pointed chin. "Graphic novels are quite acceptable as part of today's popular fiction."

"Uh-huh." Eldon snorted.

"I'll have to go with Eldon on this, Viv." Desmond DeSoto flattened his narrow lips and shook his head. "This is a Lit Fest—for *literature*."

"Wait a minute, Des." Ambrose Grandstom straightened his shoulders. "Some critics still maintain Shakespeare wrote his plays for the illiterate rabble. Do you recommend cancelling my talk, too?"

"People, people." Gwyneth spread her hands. "Nina has the final say. We'll let her decide."

Nina blew out the breath she'd been holding. While she would have defended her choices, as a brand new member of the committee, she was glad not to become involved in their argument.

Gwyneth waved a hand. "Now, I must share my news. I have just contracted our keynote speaker, Alexander Brightly."

Looking as proud as though she'd just won a Pulitzer, Gwyneth gazed around the table. Nina was familiar with Brightly's work and was curious to know what the others thought of him.

"Brightly?" Desmond DeSoto wrinkled his nose. "He writes porn."

"Yeah, but it's *literary* porn." Jaz sent him a sly smile.

Desmond shook his head. "No such thing. Porn is porn."

"I thought we all had a say in who would be

keynote." Vivian removed her glasses and tapped one stem on the table.

Several others echoed her protest.

Nina heaved an inward sigh. Did these people ever agree on anything? Her staff at the library sometimes clashed during meetings, too, but they always managed to work out their differences. She hoped an amicable resolution would be the case with this committee.

"Quiet, please." Gwyneth rapped the table again. "You all gave me the authority to make the final decision. Your agreement is in our meeting notes. Alexander is signed, sealed, and delivered, so to speak, because he's already arrived. He'll be on campus, so you'll have plenty of opportunities to meet him. Now, I have other news about my poetry presentation. Instead of giving my reading in the auditorium, I will lecture from a new place."

Jaz raised a hand. "I bet I know—the StuU."

"The Student Union Building?" Gwyneth frowned. "How mundane. No, my reading will be from—ta da"—she wiggled her shoulders and beamed a smile—"the bell tower."

Silence greeted her announcement, then several people spoke at once.

"Are you serious?"

"Crazy idea."

"Dangerous."

Gwyneth frowned and shook her head. "Not crazy and not dangerous. I'll be inside looking out the window at the top, so those assembled in the quad can see me. I'll begin with a short talk about the importance of poetry in our lives and then recite poems, including a few I've written especially for the occasion, 'Ring the

Bells,' 'Brazen Bells,' 'Billy's Bells…' "

"How about 'Hell's Bells'?"

Desmond DeSoto's comment drew a round of titters from the group.

Gwyneth pursed her lips. "I've already received permission from President Hollivera. She thinks my idea is wonderful."

"She would," Desmond muttered.

More grumbling echoed around the table.

Although Nina also had misgivings about Gwyneth's plan, as a newcomer, she refrained from commenting.

Gwyneth succeeded in moving on, and the meeting soon ended.

Along with the others, Nina rose and, teacup in hand, headed for the coffee cart.

Ambrose Grandstrom stepped close. "How nice to see you again, Nina. Welcome to Lit Fest."

Up close, she saw how much he'd aged in the past ten years. He was thinner, more stoop-shouldered, and his hair had turned from gray to almost white. But his smile was as warm and friendly as she remembered.

"Thank you." Nina placed her cup on the cart. "You're still teaching Shakespeare, I see, and on the festival program."

"I have students in costume reading from *Hamlet* and *Othello*. Their performances should be well received." Ambrose put his cup beside hers.

"I'll be sure to attend. I remember how entertaining your Lit Fest presentations were when I was a student.

Desmond DeSoto joined Nina and Ambrose.

Unlike his colleague, who had let nature take its course, DeSoto dyed his hair a shiny black. Dressed in jeans, a sports shirt, and a leather vest, he looked more like a student than a professor.

"You look familiar." DeSoto craned his neck toward Nina. "Were you in any of my classes?"

"I was one of your Freshman Composition students." Nina gritted her teeth and struggled to keep her tone neutral. Now was not the time to let bad memories take control.

"So you're a librarian now. How nice. Have you visited our library yet? We've done some upgrading. I was on the committee." He puffed out his chest.

"I haven't stopped in yet, but of course, I plan to."

"Well, I must get to class. Students waiting." With a nod toward Nina, Professor DeSoto swiveled on his heel and, head high, strode out the door.

"I'll be on my way, too." Professor Ambrose nodded to Nina. "See you at the next meeting."

Gwyneth approached. "Nina, can you stay on campus awhile? I'd like to talk to you. I don't have a class until eleven, and it's just ten now." She pointed toward her wristwatch.

"I can stay." She would like private time with Gwyneth, as well. They'd had several phone calls and emails, but being in each other's company would add another dimension to their new relationship. Plus, from what she'd observed, the woman was under stress. Was her discomfort due to her leadership role in Lit Fest? Or to something else?

"Just let me gather my papers." Gwyneth turned toward the table where a scattering of papers lay next to a large tote bag. As Gwyneth stuffed her papers into her tote, a small book tumbled out and fell onto the floor. She retrieved the book, which had a pink plastic cover decorated with a spray of red roses, and held it up. "My jottings. I never know when a poem will bloom. Sometimes they come full-blown, like Venus from the head of Zeus. Other times, fragments float through my mind. I find pen and paper work much better for recording my inspirations than punching a keypad." She ran a forefinger over the small pen attached to the book's spine.

Nina recalled seeing Gwyneth write in a small notebook when she was a student. "I know what you mean. I carry pen and paper, too." She patted her purse. Her paper was a plain spiral notebook, though, and her writing instrument a pencil nub usually buried in the purse's bottom.

Out in the hallway, Gwyneth waved toward the stone stairway. "Do you mind the stairs? The elevator makes me claustrophobic."

"The stairs have always been my preference, too. As I came up them on my way to the meeting, I felt as though I were stepping back in time."

"Hmmm, stepping back in time, dreaming of my love sublime…" Gwyneth laughed. "There I go again." Pulling out her pink journal, she opened it and made notes. Once outside, Gwyneth stopped, placed her hands on her hips, and gazed around. "We could go to the StuU, but I've had enough coffee. Why don't we walk to the quad instead?"

Nina nodded. "Good idea."

On the way to the quad, Nina and Gwyneth passed the residence halls. The three-storied buildings housed the Independents, while the smaller, two-storied homes belonged to the Greeks.

"Are you planning to visit your sorority?" Gwyneth

slowed her steps to turn a corner. "You're a Mu Omega Mu, aren't you?"

Nina followed Gwyneth's lead along the sidewalk. "Yes, and I do plan to visit. Not today, though."

The Mu house came into view. Seeing the vine-covered cottage with its gabled roof and mullioned windows brought a flood of memories and mixed emotions—making new friends, adjusting to the rules and regulations of communal life, and learning how to combine the social and the academic obligations. Gwyneth's voice brought Nina back to the present.

"I'm a Zeta Zeta Beta." She pushed a windblown lock of hair into place. "At the U of Caldonia—in Illinois."

Gwyneth's admission reminded Nina how little she knew of her professor's background. "You came all the way across the country to teach here?"

Gwyneth shrugged and looked away. "Well...I was also following someone. A man. What a mistake..."

Wanting to hear more about the relationship, Nina waited, hoping Gwyneth would continue.

Instead, Gwyneth smiled and straightened her shoulders. "Now, I have other goals in mind. Like Lit Fest. I want this year's occasion to be the biggest and the best ever."

"You do have ambitious plans."

"Ah, you're thinking of my performance in the bell tower. Come on, let's take a closer look." She led the way past the Admin, Science, and Math buildings to the quad.

Gazing around the familiar area brought another rush of memories—hurrying along the paths to reach a class on time, taking a leisurely stroll with a friend, or sitting alone on one of the benches while studying an assignment. Today, though, the bell tower was the focus. Standing beside Gwyneth in the garden surrounding the structure, Nina looked first at the clock, then at the narrow ledge above, and, finally, at the arched opening where, like a king in a castle, the bell held court.

Gwyneth turned to Nina. "I suppose you've been in the tower."

"Just during Freshman Orientation." The tower was off-limits to unsupervised students. Still, accessing the structure was often part of sorority and fraternity initiations or the rites of the secret society rumored to be active on campus. "How about you? Doesn't being inside bother your claustrophobia?"

Gwyneth lifted her chin. "Not at all. I've managed my phobia just fine."

"I understand your performance is really important." The woman's determination intrigued Nina, and she hoped to learn more.

"Very important. I'm hoping—" Gwyneth waved a hand. "Oh, I can tell you. Everyone else knows, and you're one of us now."

Nina doubted her spot as guest lecturer truly made her "one of them" but refrained from protesting and instead waited to hear Gwyneth's explanation.

Gwyneth took a few steps forward then turned and placed both hands on her hips. "You see, Nina, I want to be named department chair. Dr. Ogilvie is retiring—finally. Oh, he's a dear, but way past his prime. Being department head has been my dream since I came to PNU."

"Do you think a poetry reading from the bell tower

will achieve that goal?" Nina glanced again at the tower. Surely, other abilities such as organization and leadership were involved in being named department head.

"The reading is just one way to show Dean Hargrove—she's the person who appoints chairs—that I will bring a fresh approach to the job."

"You're sure to attract a lot of attention. Is anyone else in the running?"

Gwyneth frowned and pursed her lips. "Desmond DeSoto is my main competitor. Even though he's been passed over for years, he still lobbies for the job. But he's so—so boring."

Other, less flattering adjectives sprang to Nina's mind, but not wanting Gwyneth to ask for an explanation, she chose a new topic. "Has Professor DeSoto published anything?"

Gwyneth snorted. "His book on composition just came out, but I've already published several booklets of poetry. All are from the university press, granted, but I have a longer manuscript I intend to submit to a major publisher."

Nina stepped aside to allow several students to pass by. "Good luck with that. But tell me more about your reading in the tower. Will you be speaking 'live,' or will the poems be prerecorded?"

"Live, except for the taped music background. I'll stand inside the tower using a microphone connected to a speaker placed outside on the ledge." She pointed toward the top of the tower.

Following her gesture, Nina focused on the ledge, which, although it extended along all four sides of the tower, appeared no more than a few feet wide. "Is everything all set up?"

"Oh, no. I'm still practicing and working out the details. My performance must be perfect." She ran a hand over her wrinkled brow. "Unfortunately, I've run into a couple of…distracting problems."

"Anything I can help you with?" Nina took a step closer. "I've had experience setting up recordings at the library. I'm no expert but—"

Gwyneth waved a hand. "Not those kinds of problems. I've learned things that are, well, disturbing. I don't quite know what to do. I thought of you and how you solved the mystery of Wildeen Bergman's tragic death. I'm hoping you might have advice for my dilemma."

The promise of a mystery captured Nina's interest. "I'm intrigued, Gwyneth. Why don't you tell me exactly what has upset you?"

"We need to sit for some serious talk. Let's find an out-of-the way bench." Just then, a chime sounded from the depths of her purse. "Oh, my phone." She pulled out the phone, looked at the screen, and frowned. "Sorry, but I need to take this."

"Of course." Disappointed at the interruption, Nina stepped away.

Gwyneth turned aside, too, putting the phone to her ear. "What? I told you I haven't made a decision yet…. Can't you wait? I'm busy now. You…"

A group of students passed by, laughing and chatting, which drowned out Gwyneth's words. She slipped the cell into her purse and turned toward Nina. "I'm sorry, but I must postpone our discussion. I can't wait too long, though. I really need your help. Can you come to campus on Monday afternoon?"

"I'm sure I can. I've allowed a lot of free time to devote to Lit Fest."

Gwyneth frowned and bit her lower lip. "I hate to inconvenience you or get you in trouble with Gil."

"Don't worry." Nina waved a hand. "My staff is supportive, and Gil loves the publicity my appearance at the festival brings to the system. A meeting with you will also give me a chance to visit the new library and visit the Mu house."

"All right. Come to my office at one o'clock. We'll have privacy there."

Later, on the drive to Richmond, Nina reviewed her visit to PNU. Despite the occasional disagreements, the Lit Fest Planning Committee meeting went well. Her private time with Gwyneth was another matter. Gwyneth began on a positive note but soon confessed her distress. Did the problem have to do with Lit Fest and her performance from the bell tower? Perhaps the opposition expressed at today's meeting disturbed her. Maybe someone threatened to sabotage her program.

Or was her distress due to the phone call interruption? Perhaps the two issues were related. But, if so, how? Oh-oh, she slipped into sleuth mode again, thinking up scenarios that probably had no basis in reality.

Still, she wished she'd found out more today. Monday was three days away. A lot could happen in three days. Well, she'd just have to wait. Once she learned the problem, she would do her best to help Gwyneth find a solution.

****

"Number five in the side pocket." Nina gripped her cue stick and leaned over the pool table. Squinting an eye, she took aim and sent number five on its way. But, instead of dropping into the hole, the ball veered off course and lodged against the table wall. Nina straightened and shook her head. "Another miss. My game today is really off."

Nina and Stephen were spending their usual Sunday afternoon with her grandmother, Jessica Bingham, and Jessica's friend, Joe McGarrity, both of whom resided at Marley Manor, Richmond's elegant retirement home. After enjoying a buffet dinner, the four adjourned to the basement recreation room for a game of pool.

Stephen slipped an arm around Nina's waist. "Not to worry. The game's not over yet."

"Plenty of time to gain points." Joe stepped to the table to line up his next shot.

A recent addition to the group, Joe moved into Marley last spring. In his seventies, he had gray hair with a slight curl that gave him a boyish look. Workouts at the gym kept him fit and trim. Although he and Jessica maintained separate apartments, they were considered a couple.

"I think you're preoccupied." Jessica straightened the collar of her print blouse, a combination of red shades that matched her hair.

Nina sighed. "You know me too well, Gran."

"As soon as our game's over, we want to hear what's troubling you." Jessica raised a forefinger.

Her grandmother's sympathetic, yet adamant, request brought a smile to Nina's lips. "All right. I'll tell all."

Although Nina did her best for the remainder of the game, she pocketed only a few of her shots.

In the end, Jessica and Joe emerged the winners.

After putting away their equipment and racking the balls for the next players, Nina and the others took the elevator to Jessica's third floor apartment. Once inside, Nina spent a few moments enjoying the view from the living room window. The residence bordered Lake Mead, and on this sunny autumn day, people strolled the paths or sat on benches facing the water. Several rowboats were lined up at the dock, while farther out, a sailboat swept by, sails billowing in the brisk breeze.

Leaving the window and moving to the kitchen, Nina filled a teapot with hot water and took teabags from the cupboard.

Jessica arranged a plate of her freshly baked chocolate chip cookies.

Once they all were settled in the living room, Jessica turned toward Nina. "All right, dear, let's hear your dilemma. Hopefully, we can help."

Nina sipped her tea, savoring the spicy blend. Then she told them about Gwyneth's plan to give her poetry reading from the bell tower.

"Why use the bell tower?" Jessica touched a napkin to her lips.

Nina set her cup in the saucer. "She thinks the unique location will help her to gain the appointment as department chair, a promotion she's wanted for a long time."

Joe helped himself to another cookie. "If she can pull off her performance, she's certain to make the local news, anyway."

"News...hmmm." Stephen frowned and stroked his chin. "I'm reminded of another story out of PNU that made the news."

Her eyebrows peaked, Jessica turned toward him. "Oh? Tell us."

Stephen placed his cup on the coffee table. "While doing research for the feature we're running on Lit Fest, I came across an article about a student who went missing last summer. A week later, his body was found in his car, at the bottom of a ravine near Sattoo Pass."

"I remember the unfortunate incident." Nina nodded and sat forward. "I didn't know him, but his being a PNUer caught my attention."

"His parents were quoted as saying he never would have been drinking and driving"—Stephen's gaze encompassed the group—"especially not at the pass."

Nina sipped her tea, thinking what a terrible time that must have been for the parents. "I wonder if Gwyneth knew him. I'll ask her when we meet on Monday." She filled in Jessica and Joe on Gwyneth's request for her help. "I'm really worried about her. Something serious troubles her. I just wish I could've found out more today, before a phone call interrupted us."

Joe's eyebrow quirked. "Sounds like you're involved in a new mystery."

"Maybe." Nina reached for another cookie, bit into it, and savored the rich chocolate flavor. "Of course, I want to help Gwyneth, if I can. She mentored me when I was a student. Despite our age difference, we have a lot in common. We are no long teacher and student, she said; we are contemporaries. But, anyway, thanks for listening. What would I do without all of you?" Warmth filled Nina as she looked from one to the other.

"We're here for you, Nina." Jessica patted Nina's shoulder.

Joe nodded and raised a forefinger. "Keep us posted."

Later, after Stephen dropped her off at her condo and she prepared for bed, Nina's mind whirled with thoughts of Gwyneth and her planned bell tower performance. Would she succeed in following through? If so, would her appearance result in the hoped-for department chairmanship? What were the troublesome matters she wanted to confide? Despite all the questions, Nina eventually fell asleep.

All too soon, her ringing cell phone awoke her. She reached for the phone and squinted at the screen. Six o'clock. "Wow, Stephen, you're up early. What's happening?"

"Bad news, I'm afraid."

At his serious tone, she gripped the phone and sat up. "What happened?"

"Gwyneth Miller won't be performing from the bell tower."

Her stomach twisted. "Why not? Stephen, tell me."

"She's dead."

Chapter Three

Two hours later, still reeling from the news of Gwyneth's sudden death, Nina entered the glass double doors to the Seaview Library. Passing the display of new books and then the checkout desk, she followed the path to the staff room.

Larry Hardisty, Myo Chung, and Arlette Robbins soon joined her. Other part-time employees made up the staff, too, but these three formed the core group. They were like family. Of course, they had their differences, but whenever trouble occurred, they closed ranks.

Larry, Nina's assistant manager, peered at her through his black-framed eyeglasses. "You've heard about Gwyneth Miller?"

Nina shed her jacket and hung it on the coat tree. "Stephen called me, and then I turned on the TV news. I'm in shock."

"So are we." Myo Chung handed Nina a cup of tea and then smoothed shiny black hair from her forehead.

Nina accepted the offering, inhaling the Earl Grey aroma. "Thank you. This hits the spot."

Arlette Robbins, who towered over both Myo and Larry, stepped forward. "I brought sweet rolls." She held out a tray of small, round rolls, each with a different jelly center. "I was saving them for later, but would you like one now?"

Nina had eaten a light breakfast and still was not hungry, but she appreciated Arlette's thoughtfulness. "Yes, thank you. They look delicious." She selected one with an apricot center, and when she took a bite, the pastry melted in her mouth. Arlette's baked goodies never disappointed.

"So what do you know about Ms. Miller's death?" Larry leaned against the counter and folded his arms.

Nina finished chewing a bite of roll. "Probably no more than you know. The news said she fell from the bell tower." A shudder rolled through her at the thought of poor Gwyneth hurling through space from the top of the tower to the quad below.

"Uh-huh, at midnight." Myo sipped her tea.

"What on earth was she doing in the bell tower at that hour?" Arlette shook her head and pursed her lips.

Nina saw no reason to keep secret what would soon be general knowledge. "My guess is she was practicing the poetry reading she planned to give for Lit Fest."

Larry snorted. "Reading poetry from the tower? That's nuts."

"Not to say dangerous." Myo rolled her eyes.

"Why would she want to put on such a show?" Arlette set the tray on the counter.

Nina spread her hands. "She wanted to present something spectacular."

"What will happen to Lit Fest?" Myo stepped to the sink and rinsed her teacup under the faucet.

"I don't know. I've been wondering that myself." Nina looked at her wristwatch. "Almost time to open. We'd better get busy."

Larry straightened and gave a salute. "Right, madam librarian. All hands on deck."

Arlette covered the plate of rolls with foil. "These goodies will be in the fridge for anyone who wants them."

"The pot has more tea, too." Myo nodded toward the stove.

"Thank you all for your support." Nina placed a hand on her chest. "What would I do without you?"

"Oh, I expect you'd find another crew to command." Larry grinned and wiggled his eyebrows. "But, yeah, I'm off to the reference desk."

"I'm on check-out this morning." Arlette gestured toward the semi-circular counter outside the office.

Myo grasped the handle of a book truck loaded with books. "I'll sort these new arrivals."

Nina took a last sip of tea and placed the cup on the counter. "I'll make my rounds." She liked to check the library before opening to make sure everything was ready to receive patrons. Exiting the office, she began with the children's wing, stopping at the aquarium to watch goldfish, swordtails, and neon tetra catch light rays from the nearby window. At the story area, in addition to comfortable chairs and cushions, a puppet theater invited animated storytelling.

A nearby wall displayed the works of local artists. This month featured an oil painter's autumn scenery. Nina straightened a couple pictures and then moved to the stacks, pausing here and there to rearrange untidy shelves or to pull out a book so that the cover would be on display.

At the end of the shelves, a large seating area faced a picture window offering a view of downtown Richmond, the ferry dock, and Puget Sound. Across the water, the Olympic Mountains, often obscured by clouds, today presented a sharp outline against the clear sky.

Usually, Nina enjoyed the cruise through her domain. The library, where order reigned, brought her comfort. But today, Gwyneth's death threw Nina's world out of order. True, nothing in the morning news indicated the woman's demise was not accidental. But Nina knew she wouldn't rest until she found out for certain what led to Gwyneth's tragic fall.

****

Stephen's second call that morning came at 9:30, half an hour after the library opened, when Nina was at her desk reviewing the week's schedule. "I'm driving to PNU," he told her, "to cover Professor Miller's accident. I thought you might like to go along."

Nina welcomed the opportunity. "I would. She's been on my mind. I was to meet with her on campus today, so I already have the time off reserved."

"Okay. I'll pick you up in half an hour."

Stephen arrived as planned, and soon he headed north on the freeway and then traveled on the secondary roads through the countryside.

On any other occasion, Nina would enjoy the autumn scenery, but today, the purpose of the trip preoccupied her. Would she learn more about what happened to Gwyneth?

"That road leads to Sattoo Pass." Stephen slowed the car and pointed out the window.

His comment captured Nina's attention, and she looked up in time to glimpse the sign directing travelers to the popular pass. "I'll bet the area is really beautiful now the leaves are turning." Then another thought occurred. "Isn't the pass near where they found the

PNU student whose car went into a ravine?"

Stephen nodded and pressed the accelerator. "Right. I read the report again to refresh my memory. His name was Benjamin Logarth."

"Such a terrible accident. I wonder if Gwyneth knew him. Guess I'll never know now."

After reaching the campus and parking the car, Nina and Stephen walked to the quad. Not surprisingly, a crowd gathered at the bell tower. Sheriff's deputies guarded the yellow-taped boundary, while photographers cruised the area snapping pictures.

Words floated to Nina's ears. "Professor Miller...what a tragedy...such a loss..." Gazing at the tower, Nina had a sudden vision of Gwyneth falling with arms outstretched, her eyes wide with terror. "Oh..." Nausea gripped her, and she clutched her stomach.

Stephen put an arm around her waist. "Are you okay? Would you rather return to the car?"

Nina took a deep breath and straightened her shoulders. She could do this. If she wanted to discover the truth, she *must* do this. "No, I'll be fine."

Taking her hand, Stephen led her along the walk, stopping next to two young men at the edge of the crowd. "Hey, guys, are you students here?"

The two nodded.

Stephen pulled a notebook and pen from his coat pocket. "We're from *The Richmond Review*. Mind if we ask you a few questions?"

The taller student ran a hand through his bleached blond hair. "Sorry, can't help ya. I didn't know the professor."

"Me, neither." His companion touched the bill of

his baseball cap. "But those two were eyewitnesses." He pointed toward a young man and woman standing a few yards away.

"Thanks." Stephen gave them a salute and then guided Nina toward the couple.

The two stood close together, holding hands. The man wore jeans and a plaid flannel shirt, while the woman was more formally dressed in an ankle-length skirt and a wool jacket.

Stephen stepped forward and introduced himself and Nina. "We heard you witnessed the professor's fall."

The man frowned and stroked his bearded chin. "We've already told the police everything we know."

The woman smoothed a lock of blonde hair from her forehead and smiled at Nina. "I know you. You're a Mu alum, and you came to our Christmas party last year."

As recognition dawned, Nina returned her smile. "I'm back on campus this year presenting at Lit Fest."

"I saw your name on the program. I'm Cara O'Meary, and my friend is Diego Ortez." She gestured toward her companion.

Diego nodded but continued to frown.

"Professor Miller was a special friend." Nina hoped her relationship to Gwyneth would prompt the couple to share their experience. "I was so saddened to hear of her accident, but to be a witness must really have been traumatic."

Cara's mouth turned down. "I'll never forget looking up and—"

"Let me tell them." Diego placed a hand on Cara's shoulder and then turned toward Stephen and Nina.

"We were out walking, taking a break from a party, and came by the tower. We heard a scream, looked up, and saw her flying out the window."

Flying out the window. At the image, Nina inwardly shuddered.

Cara tugged Diego's arm. "Don't forget about the bell."

"Oh, yeah." Diego nodded. "The bell rang. The sound was what made us look up."

Stephen wrote in his notebook. "You didn't see her when she was in the tower?"

"Or on the ledge?" Nina added, hoping for more specific details.

Diego shook his head. "Nope. We had no clue anyone was in the tower."

"Did anyone else from below see her fall?" Nina looked from Diego to Cara.

Cara raised a hand. "I thought I saw—"

"You didn't see anyone, Cara." Diego's brows folded into a deep frown.

"R-right. I didn't." Cara bit her lower lip and looked away.

Stephen made another note. "Then what did you do?"

Diego turned back to Stephen. "Called 911 while we were running to where she fell." He shrugged and stroked his beard. "She was gone. Head at an odd angle and lots of blood."

Cara's eyelids closed, and a moan escaped her lips.

"What about—" Stephen held his pen poised.

"I think we've talked enough." Diego stuck out his chin then slid an arm around Cara's shoulders and pulled her close.

"Sure." Stephen tucked his notebook and pen into his coat pocket. "Sorry, Cara. We didn't mean to upset you. You take it easy, now. You've had a bad shock."

Nina put out a hand toward the young woman. "I plan to visit the Mu house while I'm on campus working on Lit Fest. How about getting together for tea?"

Cara looked up, and her lips wobbled into a smile. "That would be great, Nina."

Nina took her card from her purse and handed it to Cara. "In the meantime, feel free to call me and just chat. As soon as I know when I'll be at the Mu house, I'll let you know." She waited until the couple was out of earshot and then turned toward Stephen. "Poor Cara."

Stephen nodded. "I hope she gets help. I'm glad you knew her, though. Otherwise, we'd have met with another dead end."

Nina stepped aside to allow a group of students to pass by. "She didn't tell us much. Diego did most of the talking."

"She's traumatized."

"Maybe so, but he insisted on being the one to describe what they saw."

Stephen's eyebrows peaked. "Why? A control issue?"

Nina shrugged and pulled her jacket tighter against a sudden breeze. "Hopefully, I'll learn more about their relationship when I visit her at the Mu house." She gazed around. "What's next? Can we find someone else for you to interview?"

"I see a deputy I know, Brett Adams." He gestured toward a man wearing the brown uniform of a Manuska

County lawman. "Hey, Brett."

The man waved and headed in their direction.

Stephen introduced Brett and Nina. "Nina was a friend of Professor Miller."

"You on the faculty here?" Brett tipped up his hat with a thumb.

Judging from his piercing gaze, Nina would bet he didn't miss much. "No, I'm Richmond's librarian. But I knew Gwyneth from when I attended here. Plus, I'm part of the upcoming Lit Fest."

"So, what's the verdict?" Stephen took out his notebook and pen again.

Brett propped his hands on his hips. "Nothing's official yet, but I'd say either an accident or a jumper. No evidence of foul play or that anyone was up there with her."

"Did she fall from inside or from the ledge?" Nina pointed toward the top of the tower.

"Again, we don't know. Possibly from the ledge. We found electrical cords and a couple loudspeakers there. But don't quote me on that." Brett pointed a finger. "Wait until the word's official. My boss wouldn't like me spoutin' my own conclusions."

After finishing their conversation with the deputy, Stephen took a few photos, and then he and Nina headed back to Richmond.

"So, what are your thoughts?" Stephen asked when he had them underway. "Any theories on exactly what happened to Gwyneth?"

Nina turned from gazing out the window. "I'd rule out suicide. Gwyneth looked forward to being named department head. She was enthusiastic about having her poetry published. She had a lot to live for." A lump formed in her throat. *What a tragedy.*

Stephen slowed to negotiate a turn in the winding road. "Do you think she fell from the ledge?"

"I suppose she could have, since speakers were found there. I just don't know." She frowned and shook her head.

"Why would she be in the tower so late at night?"

Nina shifted in her seat to face him. "The late hour does seem odd. Again, I don't know. So many unanswered questions."

"All we know for sure is that she fell either from inside the tower or from the ledge."

"Or someone pushed her from either location."

He shot her a glance. "I figured you'd throw that possibility into the mix. Does this mean you'll do some serious investigating?"

She gave a solemn nod. "I owe it to Gwyneth—and to myself—to discover for certain what happened. My involvement in Lit Fest gives me the perfect opportunity to discover the truth."

They reached the freeway, and Stephen accelerated to enter the on-ramp. "Do you have a specific plan?"

"First, to gain access to the bell tower. I need to experience the place for myself to judge the potential hazards."

"Well, I'm here to help. In the meantime, I'll put my research skills to use and see what I can find out about Gwyneth's past."

She laid a hand on his arm. "You're the best, Stephen. Thank you."

He smiled and nodded. "We make a good team." Then his brow wrinkled. "But you know I'll worry about your safety."

"I promise I'll be careful." She meant the vow, too. But at the same time, she knew from past experience that solving a murder carried risks. What challenges would she face while investigating Gwyneth's death?

Chapter Four

On Tuesday morning, the Lit Fest Planning Committee held an emergency meeting. Nina drove to campus with butterflies in her stomach. Would Lit Fest proceed as planned? Or would Gwyneth's untimely death result in cancellation? She hoped the program would go forward, especially since she had a plan to investigate Gwyn's death.

Thinking she might also use the occasion to check on Cara O'Meary, Nina called the Mu house and left a message.

Cara texted a reply that she would meet Nina at the house that afternoon.

Without Diego present, Nina hoped Cara would be more forthcoming about what she witnessed at the bell tower. Arriving on campus, she parked in the visitor's lot, hurried to Bannon Hall, and slipped into a seat at the table just as Vivian Blanchard, the new chairperson, called the meeting to order. Vivian appeared very official today in a conservative blue suit and with her long black hair corralled in a tight knot at the nape. Her eyes were serious behind her black-framed glasses.

"We come here today saddened by the death of our esteemed colleague." Vivian gazed around the table. "While we mourn, we also must determine the fate of our festival. Admin will have the final decision, but they want our input. Opinions, anyone?"

Desmond raised a hand. "I say we go ahead as planned. I've invested too much work in my 'Don't Be Comatose About Commas' presentation to let it languish until next year."

"Des has a point." Eldon Harmsworth folded his hands on the table and leaned forward. "My students are all prepared with their speeches. Be a shame to scrap the event."

Vivian made a note on her agenda and then looked up. "I'm inclined to agree, but if we do proceed, will people think we're regarding Gwyn's death as trivial rather than tragic?"

Vivian's wrinkled brow indicated her concern about public opinion.

Ambrose waved a forefinger. "Here's an idea. We'll dedicate the event to Gwyneth and honor her throughout. All the programs will go forward as scheduled, including her poetry reading."

"I'm on board with that plan." Jaz nodded and sat straight. "But not with reading her poetry from the bell tower. Who would want the risk? Not me." She shivered and pulled her shawl closer around her shoulders.

Nina silently thanked Jaz for the perfect opening to propose her plan. Taking a deep breath, she raised a hand. "I'll present Gwyn's program from the tower."

Everyone stared, wide-eyed. Then they all spoke at once.

"Why would you—"

"Crazy idea."

"Too dangerous."

"Never be allowed."

"Quiet, please." Vivian raised both hands. "Let's

take comments one at a time. Des?"

Desmond pursed his lips and shook his head. "An absolutely insane idea. If you must read her poems, go stand under a tree somewhere."

"Ambrose?" Vivian nodded in his direction.

"Such a generous gesture, Nina." Ambrose tilted his head and smiled. "I admire your loyalty to your teacher, but using the bell tower is so unnecessary. We have other, safer venues."

Eldon leaned around Ambrose to face Nina. "The drama department's stage would work."

"Jaz?" Vivian pointed a pencil.

Jaz made fists with both hands and turned thumbs down.

Not ready to give up, Nina straightened her spine. "I appreciate all your concerns, but I really want to use the tower, just as Gwyneth planned." She turned toward Vivian. "Would you ask Admin what they think of my idea?"

"Who cares what they think?" Desmond snorted.

Striving to maintain her patience, Nina faced him. "Vivian just told us they have the last word on whether or not the festival goes forward. Why can't they make the final decision on whether or not I use the bell tower for Gwyn's poetry?"

Jaz sipped her coffee. "She has a point, Des."

Vivian made a note on her agenda and then looked over the top of her glasses. "We wouldn't want to veto Nina's idea and then have Admin learn we'd gone over their heads."

Desmond rolled his eyes. "God forbid."

"All right." Vivian sat back and folded her arms. "I'll present your proposal to Admin, Nina, and we'll abide by what they say."

Nina breathed a sigh of relief. "Thank you, Vivian. I appreciate your effort on my behalf—and on Gwyneth's."

Vivian moved on to other topics and half an hour later declared the meeting adjourned.

Everyone gathered papers and belongings, placed tea and coffee cups on the cart, and then left the room.

Nina headed for the door.

Vivian approached. "Oh, Nina, may I speak to you a moment?"

"Of course."

Vivian slung her purse over her shoulder. "Actually, I'd like more than a moment. Are you free for lunch?"

"I am. I'm not due at work until later this afternoon." Nina welcomed the invitation. Sharing lunch would give her a chance to become better acquainted with the new chairperson.

"Good. How about the StuU?"

"Sure. I haven't been there yet, and as I recall, they serve good food." She followed Vivian out the door, wondering what the woman wanted to talk about. Had she changed her mind about advocating for Nina's performance in the bell tower?

****

The StuU hadn't changed much since Nina's days at PNU. The building was still the hub of student activity. Front and center on the first floor were the cafeteria and coffee shop, set with tables seating both small and large groups. Branching off were meeting rooms, and two staircases, one on either side, leading to the second floor balcony.

Nina and Vivian joined the line at the buffet.

Several people stopped to talk to Vivian, expressing shock and sadness at Gwyn's death.

"I'm sure Gwyn will be the talk of campus for quite a while." Vivian filled a plate with turkey, mashed potatoes, and gravy. "Try some of this turkey, Nina."

Nina picked up a plate. "No, thanks. I'll have a salad." She'd already spotted the bowls of greens and fresh veggies.

Vivian looked her up and down. "Not watching your weight, are you?"

The personal comment jolted, yet she kept her reply matter-of-fact. "No, I'm just not very hungry." True enough. Since Gwyn's accident, Nina's appetite had shrunk.

"I'm the one who should be weight watching." Vivian patted her stomach. "But teaching makes me hungry."

By the time she reached the end of the selections, in addition to the turkey, Vivian's tray included a piece of apple pie, a roll, and several pats of butter. In contrast, Nina's held only a bowl of salad and a small dish of sliced cantaloupe.

"Let's sit in the staff lounge where we can talk." Vivian led the way to a large room under the staircase.

After stopping at several tables to exchange more comments about Gwyn, Nina and Vivian settled at a corner table for two.

"Mmmm, delicious," Vivian said after a bite of her turkey and mashed potatoes. "How's your salad?"

"Very tasty." Nina added more dressing from a plastic packet. She let a couple minutes elapse while they ate. "I'm guessing you want to talk about Gwyn's poetry presentation. Are you having second thoughts about taking my request to Admin?"

Vivian touched her napkin to her lips. "No, but I want to know more about your motivation. I think you're sincere about honoring Gwyn's memory, but are you also hoping to find out exactly what happened in the tower?"

Taken aback by Vivian's question, Nina frowned. "What do you mean, 'exactly what happened'?"

"Oh, come on, Nina." Vivian's eyes narrowed. "You think Gwyn may have been—okay, I'll be blunt—*murdered*, and you want to investigate."

Nina put down her fork and shook her head. "Despite what I might think, I have no authority to investigate."

Vivian snorted and stabbed another forkful of turkey. "Amateur sleuths don't need authority. Besides, I know you've solved murders before. Wildeen Bergman's...Ellie Larkin's."

"You knew Ellie?" Ellie was a friend of Jessica's. When she'd mysteriously drowned in Lake Mead, Nina had taken it upon herself to find out the truth.

"Not personally, but my aunt, Cynthia Dowling, lives at Marley Manor." Vivian leaned forward. "So, are you investigating Gwyn's death?"

Vivian's interest in Nina's future course of action intrigued her. What was her motive? "Well, if she was murdered, of course, I want to see justice done. What about you? Do you think her fall was accidental?"

"I do. I know she's been upset lately. The stress of chairing Lit Fest, I suppose. She was in the tower late at night, setting up her equipment, and was undoubtedly tired to begin with." She shrugged. "Gwyneth became confused and disoriented and tumbled out the window."

Nina had to admit Vivian's explanation contained logic. "Do you know what she might have been upset about, besides the pressures of chairing Lit Fest? Was she worried she'd lose the department chairmanship to Desmond DeSoto?"

Vivian mopped up gravy with her roll. "So, you know about their competition?"

"Gwyneth mentioned it, yes."

"Did you take any classes from Des?"

"Composition 101." Nina grimaced.

Vivian peered at her. "Bad memories?"

"I'll admit his class wasn't my favorite."

"You probably committed his egregious comma sins, or maybe you hyphenated too often?" She laughed. "Ah, yes. Dear Dezzy, such a perfectionist."

Dezzy? Nina couldn't imagine the man approving such a frivolous nickname. But then, perhaps he had a playful side she was not aware of. Or perhaps he and Vivian were on more intimate terms than just colleagues. Nina waited while Vivian took a few bites, closing her eyes while she chewed. "Did Gwyneth have family?"

Vivian's eyes opened. "What? Oh, yes, she had a younger sister, Cassandra Lightship, or so she calls herself. She'll be here in a few days and will visit one of our committee meetings." She picked up her coffee cup, took a long swallow, and then pointed toward the wall clock. "I see the time is nearly one. I'd better get to class."

Nina folded her napkin and laid it on her tray. "So, let me get the purpose of this conversation straight. You're against my doing any so-called investigating into Gwyneth's death."

Vivian crumpled her napkin and tossed it onto her plate. "Only because of the futility of such action. But I can't stop you. If you get into trouble, the responsibility is yours. I have my hands full taking over the committee leadership."

With Vivian at her side, Nina left the StuU.

A man on his way in waved. "Vivian!"

A smile lit Vivian's face. "Hello, Linc."

"Terrible news about Gwyneth. Just terrible." He frowned and shook his head.

"Her death is a shock to us all. We had a special Lit Fest committee meeting today to regroup." Vivian gestured toward Nina. "This is Nina Foster. She's an alum and presenting at the festival. Lincoln Hopkins is president of our board of directors," she added to Nina.

Nina accepted his firm handshake. "I remember seeing your name when I attended here. We never met, though." Although in his fifties and with gray hair, he had a youthful face with eyes a deep blue and the tanned complexion of someone who spent considerable time outdoors.

He tilted his head and studied her. "No, I don't think so. Did you know Professor Miller?"

"Oh, yes. She was one of my favorite teachers."

"Tsk, tsk. Such a loss. My son had a class from her this year. I'm meeting him here." He looked around. "Ah, there he is. Jason! Over here."

Nina followed Mr. Hopkins' wave to where two young men stood near the building's door. One was Diego Ortez, whom she met yesterday, while the other, who with his tall stature and square-jawed face was obviously Mr. Hopkins' son, Jason.

Jason nodded and gave his father a salute. He turned and spoke to Diego. Then each made a fist and exchanged the traditional fist bump, except upon withdrawing, they linked forefingers.

Maybe. The added gesture happened so quickly Nina couldn't be sure.

Jason hitched up his backpack and, with long-legged strides, joined his father. "Hey, Dad, you're right on time. Me 'n Diego just finished lunch." He turned toward Vivian. "Hello, Professor. Terrible about Dr. Miller."

"We're all in shock." Vivian extended a hand in Nina's direction. "Please meet Nina Foster. She's a Lit Fest speaker."

"Lit Fest is still on?" Jason's eyebrows peaked.

Vivian tilted her head and nodded. "As of now, it is. Admin will issue a formal statement soon."

"Well, if we get the go-ahead, I'll be working with you, Ms. Foster. I'm a student assistant, and I'm pretty sure your name is on my list."

"Having your help would be great, Jason." Nina warmed to the young man and his friendliness.

"Have to give back." Jason ran a hand through his thick, black hair. "PNU has done a lot for me."

"Volunteering looks good on your resume, too." Lincoln Hopkins laid a hand on his son's shoulder. "Jase enters Harvard Law School next year."

Unmistakable pride rang in his voice.

Jason met his father's gaze. "Yep. I got the news last week."

"Good for you." Vivian clapped her hands.

"Congratulations," Nina added, impressed with Jason's accomplishment.

"We'd better be on our way, son." Lincoln looked at his wristwatch. "We're due at the club in twenty minutes. Your mother's picking up Dr. Mortimer and his wife."

Jason tipped his head toward his father but kept his gaze on Vivian and Nina. "He always has someone *important* for me to meet."

Nina joined Vivian in polite laughter and then echoed the other woman's goodbye. Watching father and son walk away, she was stuck by their resemblance to each other. They were the same height and had the same swing to their shoulders. But for the difference in hair color, they could have been twins.

"Lincoln sure dotes on that boy." Vivian pursed her lips and shook her head.

"Is he an only child?"

"They have a daughter who's a freshman here. Both are really good kids." Vivian pointed toward her wristwatch and frowned. "I must run, now, too, or be late to class. I'll be in touch as soon as Admin rules on your proposal."

"I look forward to hearing from you."

"You'll know as soon as I do." With a wave, Vivian turned and hurried along the sidewalk toward Bannon Hall.

Nina headed for the Mu house, mulling over her lunch with Vivian and the woman's disapproval of Nina's investigation into Gwyn's death. Was her reason only because she felt Nina would be wasting her time, or did she have another, more personal motive? What about Desmond DeSoto? Were Vivian and Dezzy more than colleagues?

Her thoughts turned to meeting Lincoln Hopkins

and his son, Jason. Interesting that Jason and Diego Ortez were friends. Maybe more than friends, considering the special hand gestures they exchanged. When Nina attended PNU, that fist bump and forefinger link had a certain meaning. Was that still the case?

Ah, there sat the Mu house up ahead. Time to turn her attention to her visit with Cara O'Meary. Would their meeting prove fruitful to Nina's inquiries into Professor Miller's death? Or would Cara exhibit the same reticence she showed yesterday?

Chapter Five

Upon reaching the Mu house, Nina stopped at the top of the walkway and gazed at the familiar two-story, concrete structure with its mullioned windows and lattice of ivy framing the door. Entering would be like stepping back in time, and she must be careful not to let the past dominate. She needed to concentrate on the present and solve the mystery of Gwyn's death. Would she learn something useful from Cara? Taking a deep breath, Nina continued down the walk, stepped onto the porch, and rang the doorbell. After a short wait, the door opened, and Nina at once recognized Midge Cornell, the Mu House Mom.

A grin lit Midge's face. "Nina Foster! Come in, come in."

Nina stepped into the foyer and received Midge's warm hug. With a rush of affection, she returned the gesture. "You're looking good, Midge."

Although now in her fifties, the house mom maintained a youthful appearance with her auburn hair shoulder-length and brushed back from her face, emphasizing prominent cheekbones and large brown eyes.

"Thanks," Midge said. "So are you."

"Are the girls treating you well?"

Midge tossed back her head and laughed. "They're a challenge—some more than others. Of course, *you* never caused any trouble." She rolled her eyes.

"I was a model sister." Nina matched Midge's teasing tone. Noticing Midge's outfit of slacks, T-top, and sweater tied around her neck reminded her of the housemother's involvement in sports, especially tennis. "How are the tennis matches going?"

"Very well. I've added a few more trophies to my cache. I saw your name on the Lit Fest program and hoped you'd stop in to see us... Oh, so sad about Professor Miller." Her mouth turned down, and her brows drew together.

Nina nodded and stuck her hands in her jacket pockets. "Quite a shock. She was one of my favorite teachers, and I looked forward to working with her on the program."

"One of ours witnessed her fall. Cara O'Meary."

"I know. I stopped by today to see her. Is she in?"

"I don't think so, but let's check." Midge led Nina from the foyer into the Greeting Room where guests were entertained. Approaching a desk in the corner, she bent over an open book. "She hasn't signed in yet. How about a cup of tea while you wait?" She gestured across the room to a table holding urns and cups.

"Tea sounds good."

Soon Nina and Midge were settled in front of the fireplace where a cheerful fire blazed. The décor was as Nina remembered, with chairs and sofas upholstered in the sorority colors of turquoise and magenta. Above the fireplace hung an oil painting of Chessy Chipmunk, the Mu mascot, painted by a sister artist. Conversation centered on the sorority, including the record number of new pledges and remodeling the kitchen. Then, after a brief lull, Midge narrowed her eyes and leaned toward

Nina. "Do you think Professor Miller's fall was an accident?"

Caught off guard, Nina struggled with her reply. "The authorities are calling her death accidental, aren't they?" She sipped her tea, watching over the rim of her cup to catch Midge's reaction.

"As far as I know." Midge gave a tight-lipped nod. "But the 'M' word has been whispered."

" 'M' meaning…"

"You know"—Midge's gaze shifted in one direction and then the other—"Murder."

"Really?" Nina leaned forward. "What exactly are people saying?"

"That her fall wasn't accidental."

That others also held this opinion filled Nina with satisfaction. "I'll admit my suspicious mind has been at work, but I know nothing conclusive. What about you?"

"I know one thing she was upset about. My friend Ericka overheard her say she was sorry she invited that big-name writer to be a featured speaker."

"Big-name writer?" Nina wrinkled her brow. "Oh, Alexander Brightly. Did Gwyn say why?"

"Ericka didn't hear the reason. They were in the ladies' room at Bannon Hall, and just then, somebody flushed."

"Hmmm." Nina rubbed her chin. "I haven't met Mr. Brightly yet. I heard he's here, though."

"Uh-huh." Midge's eyelashes fluttered. "Whenever he's on campus with his *entourage*, he draws a crowd—mostly female."

The door from the foyer opened, and Cara stepped inside. She stopped and turned to someone.

The person was hidden from Nina's sight.

"No, I don't want to go out tonight. I don't feel well. I—I have a headache." Cara ran a hand over her forehead.

The reply was unintelligible but definitely male and carried an impatient overtone.

Cara shut the door, crossed to the desk, and signed in.

"Hello, Cara." Nina rose and went to meet her.

"Oh, Nina, you're here." Cara pressed a hand to her chest. "Sorry I'm later than I expected."

With her red-rimmed eyes and down-turned mouth, she appeared even more distressed than when Nina and Stephen first met her. "If you're not up to a visit, I'll come another time."

Cara put out both hands. "Please stay. I've looked forward to seeing you. We'll go to my room and talk."

Midge stepped up beside Nina. "If you two need anything, just give me a call."

"Thank you, Midge." Cara's lips wobbled into a smile.

"Thanks for the tea and the visit," Nina said. "So good to see you again."

Cara led Nina through the Greeting Room and into a hallway that soon opened out to a large, square sitting room. While the Greeting Room was for visitors, this area was reserved for the Mu residents. Several young women were present—one sitting at a small table with her laptop, another curled up in an overstuffed chair reading a book, and two more chatting in a corner.

Recalling her favorite place was a corner surrounded by bookshelves, Nina let her gaze rove the room, finally landing on her spot. The same chair still sat there, today occupied by a young woman taking a nap.

Nina and Cara passed the chapter meeting room, the dining room, and then the kitchen, where the aroma of baked chicken drifted out the open door, indicating dinner preparations were underway. Just beyond the kitchen, a staircase led to the second floor. Nina followed Cara as she climbed the stairs. At the top, Nina had time to glance toward the left hallway, which led to her old room, but before memories had a chance to surface, Cara veered off to the right.

After passing the bathrooms and study area, Cara stopped at a door. "Here's my room." She unlocked the door and then stepped aside, allowing Nina to enter.

A quick glance around told Nina the sleeping quarters were still the same as when she'd lived there. Twin beds, one stood on either side of the room, each with an adjacent overstuffed chair. A built-in desk and a storage and clothes closet completed the furnishings. Dividing the two areas were a counter with a sink, a small refrigerator, and a hotplate. All the comforts of home compressed into a cozy space.

"Have a seat." Cara pointed toward one overstuffed chair and then crossed the room and tossed her backpack on the bed. "My roommate is out for the afternoon, so she won't interrupt us."

Nina sank into the chair, and although memories still colored the edges of her mind, she also felt far removed from the life she led while a student here. So much had happened since then—attending graduate school for her master's degree and then securing a job as librarian. Undergrad days were long gone, and while she was thankful for them, she was also glad to put them to rest. She must do that now, especially, and concentrate on Cara and Gwyn and Lit Fest.

Cara kicked off her shoes, flopped on her bed, and leaned against a pile of pillows. "Do you want tea, Nina? Coffee? I have some made from this morning." She waved toward the counter with the hotplate.

"No, thanks. I had tea with Midge. But how about you?"

Heaving a deep sigh, Cara shook her head.

"You're having a difficult time, aren't you, Cara?"

The young woman's lips flattened. "I keep seeing Professor Miller fall...even when I close my eyes."

"Yet, if no one had seen her, the authorities wouldn't know her fall was accidental."

Cara bit her lip and lowered her gaze.

Suspecting Cara hadn't told her everything she knew, Nina sat forward. "I don't mean to pry or make you feel any worse, but is something else bothering you, besides seeing Gwyn fall?"

Cara's brow wrinkled. "Yes, and if I don't tell someone, I'll burst."

"Would you feel comfortable telling me?" Nina's heart beat faster. Was Cara about to share important information about that fateful night? Information to confirm Gwyn's death was not accidental, after all?

Long moments passed while Cara stared at the ceiling. Finally, she turned toward Nina. "If I tell you, you have to promise not to tell anyone else."

Nina gave an inward sigh. Cara's request wasn't the first time she was asked to keep to herself information that might need to be passed on, especially to the authorities. Such a situation always created a dilemma. However, if she wanted to conduct her own investigation, she needed all the information she could gather. "I will keep your confidence."

Cara took a deep breath and propped herself up against the pillows. "That night, right after we saw Professor Miller fall, something near the tower's door caught my eye I turned to look and thought I saw someone running away."

Nina took a moment to digest the startling news. "Did Diego see the person, too?"

"I grabbed his arm and told him to look, but he said he didn't see anyone and that I only imagined someone was there."

Cara sharing her secret encouraged Nina to continue probing. "Did you tell the police?"

"Diego said not to, because I couldn't be positive. I'm so confused." She pressed both hands to her cheeks.

"Even if the person had nothing to do with Gwyneth or what happened, don't you think the authorities should know?"

Cara folded her arms over her chest. "I really don't want to talk to them again, especially when I'm uncertain. But holding in what I saw—or thought I saw—makes me want to burst, which is why I had to tell someone—who turned out to be you."

She offered Nina a wan smile.

"Thank you for taking me into your confidence."

"I don't know why—when I hardly know you. Maybe because you're a Mu sister." She waved a hand. "Plus, you were Professor Miller's friend."

"Can you tell me anything more about the person you saw? Man or woman? What they wore?"

"I saw only the person's back before he—or she—disappeared into the shadows."

How much more should she question Cara? While reluctant to cause her any more distress, she might not have another chance to learn all the details. Strike while the iron was hot, as her Grandmother Jessica would say. "I saw Diego today at the StuU," Nina said, "with Jason Hopkins. Are they frat brothers?"

"Uh-huh. They're Omicron Alphas."

"I was thinking of another fraternity—or society." Nina studied Cara, eager to see her reaction to the word "society."

"What do you mean?" Cara's eyes narrowed.

"I saw them exchange a fist bump and a forefinger link. When I was a student here, the gesture belonged to members of a secret society. The Spearheads, if I recall correctly."

Cara turned away her face. "I wouldn't know anything about a secret society."

Nina gripped the arms of her chair. "You've shared a confidence, and now I'll share one with you. I'm suspicious Gwyn's death wasn't an accident. I'm not alone. You've undoubtedly heard the rumor. So, if foul play was involved, wouldn't you like to see whoever's responsible caught and punished?"

"I have heard what people are saying." Cara's voice lowered. "But what makes you think Jason and Diego, or the Spearheads, have anything to do with Professor Miller?"

Cara's confirmation sent a ripple of excitement through Nina. "So the group is still active on campus?"

"I don't know anything about them." Cara twisted away and rolled toward the wall.

Nina stood and walked to the window. Below was a courtyard, featuring a fountain surrounded by walkways, flowerbeds, and wrought iron benches. The familiar sight brought a sigh to Nina's lips. Many a time when something upset her, she found solace in the courtyard. Pushing away the memories, she turned back to Cara. "I'm sorry, Cara. I didn't want to upset you. I've been worried about you and wanted to see how you're doing."

"I know. I'm sorry I'm not better company."

Looking around, Nina spotted hanging on the wall a framed watercolor painting showing a path covered with autumn leaves leading into a woods. Stepping closer, she saw the artist's initials in the lower right corner: C O'M. She turned toward Cara. "Did you paint this picture?"

"Yes, in art class."

"It's very good. I love the colors and the perspective of the path winding through the trees."

Cara sat up, and a smile lit her face. "I do like to paint. One of my pictures is in the exhibit our class is having at Lit Fest."

Glad to find Cara engaged in conversation again, Nina returned her smile. "I'll be sure to visit the show and look for your picture." Nina and Cara talked about art for a while, with Nina sharing stories of artists her Seaview Library had featured. Then, feeling she had stayed long enough, Nina reached for her purse. "I need to be going. I still have a few hours to put in at my library. But I hope we can visit again."

Cara slid to the edge of the bed and stood. "I'd like that. I'll try to be better company next time."

"Let me know if you need anything, and if you just want someone to talk to, I'm here."

"Thanks, Nina."

On the way to the door, Nina spotted framed photos sitting atop a bookshelf. One that caught her eye showed three young men sitting on a sofa with their arms stretched across one another's shoulders. The two on the ends were Jason Hopkins and Diego Ortez. Who was the youth in the middle? He had sandy-blond hair, a mischievous grin, and wore an oblong, silver medal around his neck. She peered closer, but the printing on the medal was too small to discern. Should she ask Cara to identify the young man? No, better not risk churning her distress. Leave well enough alone—for now.

Downstairs in the Greeting Room, Nina found Midge sitting at the desk, punching computer keys.

Midge looked up. "Did you and Cara have a good visit? How is she?"

Nina approached the desk, standing across from Midge. "Still upset, and I'm afraid I'm partly to blame."

"She's a very sensitive young woman, especially so since the accident."

"Witnessing Gwyn's fall must have been traumatic. Have she and Diego been together long?" Nina hoped her question sounded casual.

Midge sat back and folded her arms. "Since last year." Her nose wrinkled. "I think he controls her, sometimes."

"I had the same impression when my friend interviewed them about the accident."

"But he's good to her, too, and to us. At this year's pledge party, he and his Omi brothers helped us set up and then clean up afterward."

"Good to know. Well, please look in on Cara. I'll contact her again in a day or so."

"You bet." Midge stood and stepped around her

desk to give Nina a hug. "We'll take good care of her. I'm looking forward to your next visit."

On the drive to Richmond, Nina reflected on her time with Cara. The young woman was still in distress from what she witnessed at the bell tower. Had she really seen someone leaving the tower after Gwyneth's fall? Or, as Diego insisted, was she mistaken? Also, Cara denied knowing about the Spearheads. True? Or, again, had she been instructed to display ignorance when asked?

What about the photo Nina spotted upon leaving? Who was the third young man shown with Jason and Diego? What role, if any, did he play in the mystery? Nina shook her head and heaved a sigh. So many questions to keep her busy searching for answers.

Chapter Six

That evening after dinner, Nina retreated to her second floor office to work on her Lit Fest presentation. In addition to the customary desk, worktable, and file cabinet, her office included an overstuffed chair with a reading lamp where she could relax. Bookshelves filled the wall space from floor to ceiling. Part of her collection was on open shelves, while other, more fragile volumes were protected behind glass. She felt comfortable and at home here, surrounded by her much-loved children's books.

Sitting at the worktable where she had already gathered some of the chosen stories, she opened her laptop and accessed the program file. Computer visuals, as well as actual books, would illustrate her presentation. Sometime later, as she composed a story about meeting a favorite author in person, her cell phone rang.

Stephen's name appeared, and soon, his smiling face lit up the screen. "I see you're working tonight."

"On my Lit Fest presentation." Nina propped the phone on the tabletop and settled into her seat. "What are you up to?"

"Kicking back after a busy day. I attended a City Council meeting this afternoon with lots of issues on the agenda. I had time to research Gwyneth, though, in preparation for writing my article."

Nina leaned forward. "Did you find anything I might be interested in?"

"I hope so. Let me get my notes." He pulled his laptop into view. "She was born in Chicago. Attended Caldonia University, majoring in English. Taught at a girls' school for a few years then hired on at her old alma mater, Caldonia. She taught there for several years before moving here to take a position at PNU."

"She hinted she came here because of a man. No indication in your research who he was?"

"No, but I'll do some more digging. Meanwhile, I'll send over my notes and sources. Maybe you'll discover something I missed. Now, tell me about your day on campus."

She described the Lit Fest meeting and Vivian's agreement to ask Admin about her plan to present Gwyn's poetry.

"Sounds like you have an ally."

Nina frowned. "I'm not sure, because when she and I had lunch afterward, she accused me of wanting to present Gwyn's program so I could investigate her death, and that such a goal might be dangerous."

"Sounds kinda like a warning." Stephen's eyebrows peaked. "Better put her on your suspect list."

"I will." Nina continued to bring Stephen up to date with the events at PNU.

His eyes widened. "Wow, I'd say you had quite a productive day. Anything you need my help with?"

"Hmmm." Nina propped her chin in her palm. "I'd like to know more about the Spearheads. When I was on campus, I was aware of them but too busy with classes and with being a Mu to pay much attention. But since they're a *secret* society..."

"Hey, I was an investigative reporter, remember?" He shrugged. "We have our ways. Plus, as you've been talking, I've also made notes for other subjects to research."

"I really appreciate your help, Stephen…and your just being there."

"I could be there more…" His voice dropped a notch. "Or you could be here. By the way, did you catch the sunset tonight? Spectacular."

"When I came upstairs, I saw the last rays. Yes, beautiful." She turned toward the window. Edgemont Estates sat on a hillside overlooking Richmond's downtown. Now, although twilight darkened the sky, lights twinkled up from the streets below and from a ferryboat on its way to the Olympic Peninsula.

"You could have a front and center seat at my place." He gave a broad wave. "You wouldn't have to go upstairs to catch a sunset."

"Uh-huh…" She cleared her throat. "I'll watch for the notes you're sending." Then she held her breath. Would he accept her change of subject, or would he continue to talk about their relationship?

A frown creased his forehead, but then the lines cleared, and he smiled. "Sure, I'll finish organizing my notes tonight. What's next on your agenda?"

Nina exhaled a relieved breath. "Only a few weeks until Lit Fest, so I'll be on campus often. I hope to know more when I gain access to the bell tower."

"You think Admin will grant your request?"

"If they won't, I'll find some other way to get inside the tower."

One eyebrow quirked. "Knowing you, Nina, I bet you will."

After the call ended, Nina sat for a moment, staring at the blank cell phone screen. Stephen never missed an opportunity to remind her he wanted to make their relationship more permanent. She sighed. She wanted to, also. She really did, but she just couldn't take that step.

Her reluctance centered on her father abandoning her and her mother when Nina was only five years old. After that, her mother had vowed never to trust again. She concentrated on her career in real estate, and although she was quite successful, her dedication created another type of abandonment for Nina. Now, her mother was gone, too.

Gran arrived as a presence in Nina's life after she was grown, and Nina was thankful for her. But relationships were still a problem. Not that she hadn't tried. She'd had two, both of which ended unhappily. Then she met Stephen, whose wife passed away several years earlier from cancer. Despite her fears, Nina fell in love. Her therapist of the past year helped to sort out her feelings, but she still had more work to do.

Now, she had Gwyneth's death to investigate. Plus, her presentation needed attention. Setting aside her cell phone, she turned to her laptop. *Let's see, where was I? Ah, yes, in the middle of an anecdote...* She continued where she left off but was still aware of Stephen's image hovering in the background.

****

" '*Under the budding birch, we sat that April morn, inhaling Nature's sweet perfume, while watching Spring be born....*' " Larry Hardisty stopped reading and looked over the top of his eyeglasses. "Seriously? This is your esteemed professor's poetry?"

"The book has her name on it." Nina pointed toward the cover of the book Larry held, which had in fancy cursive writing, *The Seasons of Our Lives*, and underneath, *Poems by Gwyneth Miller*.

Nina, Larry, Myo, and Arlette were in the Seaview Library staff room, having just finished their morning meeting. The aromas of spicy tea, strong black coffee, and cinnamon from the rolls Arlette brought filled the air. Earlier, Nina pulled from the shelves three of Gwyn's poetry booklets and brought them to the office, intending to read them later.

Larry spotted the books and sampled the contents.

Nina turned toward Myo. "What do you think?"

Myo sipped her tea and put down the cup. "Did she write any haiku? That would be my choice."

"I haven't run across any haiku, but I'll be on the lookout." Nina leaned forward to address Arlette. "What's your opinion?"

Arlette finished a bite of roll and patted a napkin to her lips. "I'm not much for poetry of any kind. But if I had to name a favorite, I'd say nursery rhymes."

"Interesting choice." Nina gave her an encouraging smile. "Tell us more."

"I read so many to my kids that the verses still rattle around in my head. 'Little Jack Horner sat in a corner…' "

"Spare us, please, Arlette." Larry held up a hand. "I'd rather hear Ms. Miller's rhymes."

Arlette folded her arms. "Okay, let's forget about the poems and talk about her. My neighbor, whose son goes to PNU, says he heard the professor's death might not have been an accident."

Seeing no reason to exclude her staff from the

latest developments, Nina nodded. "Some indications lead to that conclusion."

"What do you think?" Myo took another sip of her tea.

All three gazes focused on Nina.

Not wanting to fuel the rumors when she had no proof, Nina took a moment to weigh her words. "I'm keeping an open mind."

"Yeah, right." Larry chuckled. "You're investigating, I can tell."

"You don't need to be in denial with us, Nina." Arlette reached for another cinnamon roll. "You've already proven to be quite the sleuth."

Nina sighed. "I'm not sure I want that reputation. I just want to see justice done." She grinned and turned up her hands. "Well, okay, I love a mystery. What can I say?"

"So do we." Behind his eyeglasses, Larry's eyes lighted. "You'll let us know if we can help."

"Of course." Nina swept a smile over the group. "What would I do without all of you at my back? I'll try not to be too preoccupied or absent too often."

Myo shook her head. "Not to worry. We've got you covered."

The meeting soon ended, and the library opened for business. Nina's next opportunity to examine Gwyn's poetry booklets occurred during her break when she retreated to her office for a cup of tea. Sitting at her desk, she reached for the top book, titled *Searching for Beauty and Other Poems*. Riffling through the pages, she read at random, sometimes smiling and other times cringing. How could Gwyn be so talented at putting words together in some poems and so clumsy in others?

According to the copyright page, the booklet was published twenty years ago. Ah, perhaps that explained the disparity in quality. Gwyn was a novice then and still learning. But, like so many poets and prose authors alike, she was eager to achieve the enviable status of "published."

The dedication page read "To T.L., with love forever and a day." Hmmm, who was T.L.? A colleague at PNU? Reviewing the male members of the English department revealed no one with those initials. "Love forever and a day," despite being a cliché, certainly sounded serious. Was the person someone she was still in love with at the time of her death? An unrequited love?

So many questions. *Will I ever find the answers?*

****

"Admin will allow you to present Gwyn's poetry from the bell tower during Lit Fest," Vivian told Nina in a phone call at the library the following morning. "They think your program a fitting tribute."

Yes! Nina made a fist and pumped the air. "I'm so glad they agreed."

"They laid down rules, though. They don't want to risk any more accidents."

"What are the rules?" Vivian's serious tone put Nina on alert.

"No walking or standing on the ledge or placing any equipment there."

"Not a problem." Nina relaxed her tense muscles. "I will play the portion of the recorded program from inside the tower. I need to visit the tower ahead of time, though."

"Admin okayed that, too, but only during daylight

hours. Why Gwyn was there at night will remain a mystery."

No, it won't, because I intend to find out. "Tell Admin not to worry—I have no plans to be in the tower at night." *Right now, I don't, but soon, I might.* "When can I make my visit?" Nina reached for her desk calendar.

"Following our committee meeting on Monday," Vivian said. "Someone from Maintenance will meet you at the tower and let you inside."

After the call ended, Nina sat back with a smile. Hopefully, examining the tower would reveal clues to what happened that fateful night. Had Gwyn been alone? Or was someone with her? If so, was Gwyn's companion the person Cara saw running away? Eager to share her news with Stephen, Nina picked up her phone again and made the call.

"I'd like to go with you," he said when he heard her plans. "I have an appointment in Seattle that afternoon, but I'll reschedule."

"No, don't, Stephen. I'd love to have your company, but I'll be fine. Plus, Admin might not okay you being in the tower, too."

Stephen frowned. "I don't like the idea of you alone in that tower, even in daylight."

"I won't be by myself. A person from Maintenance will be there, too. I won't stay long, and I'll call you as soon as I leave."

After ending the call, Nina continued to think about her upcoming visit to the tower. What would her search uncover? She could hardly wait until Monday to find out. Now, though, she'd best attend to her job here at Seaview. Stepping from the office, she gazed around.

At the checkout desk, Arlette processed a stack of books for an elderly couple.

Near the front door, Myo placed new books in the glass display case.

Several patrons sat at the computers, while others browsed the stacks.

Ah, a nice, quiet day at the library. Nina gave herself a mental thumbs-up.

Just then, loud voices shattered the peace. A sweeping look around revealed three men and a woman crowded around Larry at the reference desk. Who were they, and what did they want? Well, she'd better find out. Turning on her heel, Nina marched toward the disturbance.

Chapter Seven

Reaching the reference desk, Nina stood next to Larry, facing the noisy group. "May I help?"

Larry waved a hand. "This is—"

"I'm Alexander Brightly." One of the men stepped forward and extended a hand. "You must be Nina Foster." His gaze swept her from head to toe.

Nina accepted his handshake but quickly disengaged her fingers from his firm grip. "Oh, yes, Mr. Brightly. You're appearing at Lit Fest."

"Right. I'm the featured speaker."

He looked exactly like the photos on his book jackets: in his thirties, dark-haired, and with a teasing glint in his eyes.

"Alex, over here!" someone called.

Inwardly cringing, Nina turned to find that one of the other two men had left the group and now stood in the middle of the children's story pit.

"What do you think of this spot?" The man waved long arms.

The third man, standing behind Alexander, cupped his hands around his mouth. "Forget it, Cab. That's where the kiddies hang out."

"Bleah." Cab's nose wrinkled. "Okay, Otis, then maybe we don't wanta be here at all."

"I think we do." Alexander smiled at Nina.

The woman tugged Alexander's arm. "I know just

the spot, Alex."

No more than five feet tall, she gazed up at him with eyes that appeared owlish behind round, black-framed glasses.

Alexander finally tore his gaze away from Nina and turned to his associate. "I'm, sure you do, Porsh."

Needing to establish order, Nina made her tone firm. "Mr. Brightly, let's all go to the conference room, and you can tell me what your visit is about."

"Good idea, Ms. Librarian." He turned toward the others and waved a hand. "Come on, gang."

Cab climbed from the story pit and joined Otis, who when paired with the tall Cab, resulted in a couple that reminded Nina of the old comic strip characters Mutt and Jeff.

Mumbling to one another—or perhaps to themselves—the Brightly entourage fell into line.

Nina led them to the conference room, closing the door to shut out their noise, which she expected to continue.

However, once seated, the group fell curiously quiet.

Cab leaned back in his chair, arms folded, long legs outstretched.

Otis, whose thinning gray hair pegged him the oldest, studied the bulletin board on the opposite wall.

The woman Alexander called Porsh tapped her cell phone with pink-painted fingernails that exactly matched the color of the phone's case.

Alexander kept his gaze on Nina.

Not about to let the brazen man unnerve her, Nina sat tall. "So, Mr. Brightly, tell me why you and your *people* are here today."

Alexander beamed a grin around the table. "Hear that, everybody? You're my *people*." He turned again to Nina. "Let me introduce these fine folks." He gestured toward the woman. "This lovely lady is Portia Quinlan, my publicity director."

Peering through her eyeglasses, Portia offered a smile that looked pasted on.

"Pleased to meet you, Nina."

Nina returned a smile she hoped appeared sincere. "Nice to meet you, too."

Alexander turned toward the two men. "These dudes are Cab Feraro, my manager..."

"Howdy." Cab made a salute.

"And Otis Lindstrom, my literary agent."

Otis nodded. "Good to be here."

Nina let her gaze rove over the group. "First of all, you've heard about Gwyneth Miller's tragic death..."

"Yes, what a shock." Alexander's mouth turned down. "She's an old friend, especially to me and Porsh." He turned toward Portia.

Portia looked up from her phone. "But she would want us to carry on with our plans."

The others murmured their agreement.

Nina sat back and folded her arms. "All right. How can I help you?"

Cab raised a hand. "We're looking for a venue in your fine city for Alexander to talk about his latest book. He's already scheduled at the Center for the Arts..."

"And we want something cozier." Otis used hand motions to indicate a small box.

Nina tilted her head. "How about a bar? We have several on the waterfront."

"No, too noisy, too…" Portia's nose wrinkled.

"Seedy." Cab rolled his eyes.

Nina wanted to say that their waterfront bars were quite elegant, but arguing was probably useless. Still, the thought of this noisy, disdainful group invading her peaceful domain distressed her. "I doubt we have what you're looking for here in the library."

"Yes, you do." Portia's eyes widened along with her vigorous nod. "I saw the perfect place when I searched for better phone reception. I tried to tell you, Alex, but you were…busy." She looked pointedly at Nina.

Alexander leaned forward. "Let's hear whatcha got, Porsh."

"A seating area is located by a big window." She nodded toward the door. "Comfy chairs and nice tables."

Nina's brain spun to come up with an excuse for denial. "I know where you mean. But I'm not sure what you've planned is possible."

"Not possible?" Otis's jaw dropped.

"I'm assuming you want to meet after hours, and we'd have to get my supervisor's permission."

Cab spread his fingers and slapped the table. "No one's ever turned down an Alexander Brightly event yet, regardless of size or location."

"I want to see the place Porsh recommends." Alexander shifted in his chair to face the door.

"Certainly. I'll be glad to show you." Nina pushed back her chair and stood. "Although, please be aware we have other patrons who value the library's…*peaceful* atmosphere."

Cab chuckled behind his hand. "She means keep

your big mouths shut."

Otis pursed his mouth into a smirk. "I remember how our librarian at school went around with a finger to her lips going 'Shhh.' "

Upon hearing the outdated complaint about her profession, Nina gritted her teeth. She made no comment, though. She'd long ago learned ignoring the stale joke was the best response. Intending to take the lead, she crossed the room and opened the door.

Stepping in front of Nina, Portia rushed ahead.

The men fell into line behind Portia.

Left to bring up the rear, Nina followed the group through the stacks to the seating area Portia described.

Several patrons appeared comfortably settled with their reading material. Others contemplated the view of downtown buildings, Puget Sound, and the Olympic Peninsula, visible from the large picture window.

Hands on his hips, Alexander gazed around. "Hmmm. I see what you mean, Porsh. This spot is cool."

A smile lit Portia's round face. "I knew you'd like my choice."

Cab shook his head. "Uh-uh, Alex. You got competition here. Between you and the view, the view wins, hands down." He made a sweeping motion toward the window.

Otis plopped into one of the overstuffed chairs. "Not if he sits here. Then everyone has their backs to the window."

"Yeah." Alexander's eyes shone. "After I'm done mesmerizing everyone with my—what did that one critic call my last book, Porsh?"

" 'Full of scintillating prose.' You're *such* a good

writer, Alexander."

Alexander's chest expanded. "'Of course, I am. And you're *such* a good PR person."

Portia smiled and fluttered her eyelids.

Cab stepped forward. "All right, you two, enough already. We're on a time schedule here." He tapped his wristwatch with a forefinger.

Portia's smile faded. "Right. Okay, we'll put the coffee and cake cart there." She pointed toward a corner by the window. "The table with your books will go on the other side." She swung an arm around toward the window's far end.

Otis rubbed his chin and jumped to his feet. "I'm seeing a plan that could work."

"Done." Cab made a fist and pounded his palm. Pulling out his phone, he danced his thumbs over the screen. "My calendar says the Tuesday after your presentations at the Lit Quest."

"Lit Fest," Nina corrected automatically.

Still focused on the phone's screen, Cab waved a hand. "Whatever."

Alexander high-fived with Otis and then turned to his publicity director. "Porsh, you can work on the invite list."

Feeling out of control, Nina raised a hand. "Now, wait just a minute. You might have decided, but we haven't."

Cab's bushy eyebrows drew together. "We? Who?"

"Me." Nina pointed a forefinger toward her chest. "And my supervisor, Gilbert Grady."

"Okay, just let us know when all the red tape is rolled up." Cab pulled a business card from his shirt pocket and handed it to Nina.

Otis waved his arms. "Hey, we gotta make tracks. We're due at KATW in twenty minutes."

"Let's go, guys." Portia turned and headed toward the front of the library.

One by one, the men fell into line behind her.

Nina followed in their wake, stopping at the checkout desk to watch them leave through the front door. Then, with a relieved sigh, she approached her office.

"Nina! Wait!"

She turned to see Alexander waving a book and running toward her. *Oh, dear, what now?*

Reaching her, he stopped at her side. "I almost forgot to give you my latest." Placing the book on the counter, he took a pen from his shirt's breast pocket then opened the book to the title page.

His gesture brought a smile to her lips. "Oh, how thoughtful. Our patrons do like autographed books."

"This book is not for the library; it's for you." He wrote, finishing with a flourish. Then he closed the book and thrust it into her hands.

"I, ah, thank you…Alexander."

"Thank *you*, Nina Foster, for your hospitality and for convincing your boss to let me have my little party here."

"I can't make any promises." She felt guilty accepting the book without yet receiving permission for the event.

"But I know you'll put in a good word for us. Contact Cab about the details. But if you want to reach me for any other reason, here's my personal email and phone number." Pulling a business card from his shirt's pocket, he tucked it into the pages of the book. "Oh, by the way, I hear you'll be visiting the bell tower, where poor Gwyneth met her tragic end." He pressed his lips together and shook his head.

Nina dropped her jaw. "How do you know about my going to the tower? I received the word only this morning."

He laughed and patted her shoulder. "Let's just say I know people in high places. Anyway, how about letting me tag along?"

The unexpected request was another surprise. "Why would you want to?"

"Just curious. Like I told you, Gwyn and I go way back."

"She mentioned you were a student of hers at Caldonia."

"Right. Portia, too. I kinda owe my career to Gwyn. She liked one of my stories and recommended I send it to *Upcroft,* the fancy literary magazine. They bought it, and the rest, as they say, is history. Gwyn and I became friends and kept in touch. Anyway, about me going with you…"

"Despite your relationship, I don't have the authority to include you. Why don't you have your people arrange a visit?" She nodded toward the group waiting near the door.

Alexander stroked his chin. "Hmmm, I suppose I could. I just thought going with you would be cool. Since we both were Gwyn's friends, and all." His brows drew together. "Are they still calling her death accidental?"

"As far as I know." Her suspicion aroused by his question, she studied him. "Do you think otherwise?"

His eyes widened. "Why, no. I just can't help

wondering, though."

"Alexander! Get a move on." Cab hissed from the doorway.

"Gotta go. Call me." Alexander turned away and, broad shoulders swinging, joined the others.

Nina waited until the group was out the door and out of sight before retreating to her office. Then, exhaling a breath, she laid the book on the desktop and dropped into a chair.

Larry burst in. "So, what did Alexander the Great want?"

Before she could respond, Arlette joined them, her eyes wide. "Wow, he's so handsome."

Myo stuck her head in the door. "Was that man who I think he was? Alexander Brightly? Oooo." She clasped her hands and rolled her eyes.

"Did he give you a book for our collection?" Larry nodded toward the book.

Nina ran a hand over the book's cover. "Not for us—for me."

"Ah, personalized." Behind his glasses, Larry's eyes glinted. "But, anyway, what was all their flap about?"

"He wants to do a reading here, with a few select people."

"Are you letting him peddle his porn in our library?" Larry stuck out his chin.

Nina kept her tone patient. "First of all, Larry, this library isn't *ours*."

He folded his arms. "You know what I mean."

"I'm obligated to pass along his request. Gil will make the decision."

"Hmpf. Well, I sure won't be here." He shook his

head.

"You won't be invited." Arlette sent Larry a sly smile. "Only women will receive invites." She pressed a finger to her chin. "Hmmm, I wonder how *I* can get on the list?"

When her staff finally left, Nina closed the door behind them. Then she sat at her desk again and stared at Alexander's book. *Island Dreaming* was the title. The cover showed a body of water with an island and mountains in the background. A man and a woman sat facing each other in a canoe—the man with an oar raised, the woman trailing a hand in the water. She'd read about this latest book in review journals and, anticipating its popularity, had ordered several copies for the library.

She opened the book and read the blurb and the copyright and printing data, purposely avoiding the page he autographed. Finally, she read the inscription:

"For Nina, a most charming librarian, who I hope will join me in Island Dreaming. All the best."

His signature was a mass of whorls and lines bearing no resemblance to letters of the alphabet. Well, at least, the inscription wasn't too personal, although she wasn't sure what he meant by joining him in Island Dreaming.

He wanted to visit the bell tower with her, which of course was out of the question. Why he desired to be in the tower still puzzled her. Then she recalled that Midge Cornell had told her Gwyn was overheard saying she regretted inviting Alexander to speak at Lit Fest. Why? Had she discovered something that tarnished his reputation? How could she find out the reason for Gwyn's change of heart?

Thinking of the tower turned her thoughts to the upcoming visit—but not until Monday, and today was only Thursday. Three more days to wait. Too bad she had no reason to be on campus tomorrow. The more time spent there, the more opportunity to discover something important about Gwyn. But wait. She had a reason to visit, after all. She'd better check on the man's availability, though. Picking up her phone, she made the call.

Chapter Eight

The following morning, Nina mounted the steps to enter PNU's Herkimer Memorial Library. Today's visit with Leopold Manus, head librarian and a personal friend, provided a reason for her presence on campus, as well as the opportunity to learn information helpful to her sleuthing. As always happened when she entered a library, a sense of peace washed over her. Here was a refuge, an escape from the often-chaotic world outside.

Like many of the campus buildings, the structure had a high ceiling and several stained glass windows. Staircases and elevators, similar to those in Bannon Hall, led to the second and the third floors. Looking around for the upgrading Desmond DeSoto had mentioned, of which he was so proud, she saw that more computers for individual use had been added, as well as a self-service checkout facility.

She focused on finding Leo, and just as her gaze swung to his office, the door opened, and he appeared. Catching her eye, he hurried to her side. "So good to see you, Nina." He grasped her extended hand in both of his.

In his fifties, Leo was a portly man with thick, white hair and a neatly trimmed mustache and beard. He tended toward formal dress, as evidenced by today's gray suit and blue bowtie. "Nice to see you, too, Leo." Nina returned his hearty handshake. "I'm sorry I haven't visited sooner, but between Lit Fest Committee meetings and my own job, I just haven't had the opportunity."

He nodded and ran a forefinger along his mustache. "I've been busy with Lit Fest, too. Besides helping others, I'm working on my presentation."

"I saw on the program that you're showing off something new you've acquired." Leo was known for his personal collection of manuscripts from the Middle Ages.

"A treasure I recently found. Come take a look." He gestured toward his office.

Nina followed him into the room where, not surprisingly, the walls were lined with bookshelves.

Leo closed the door and led her to a table where a large book rested on a stand under a lighted magnifying glass. "A monk wrote these poems. Very, very rare."

Nina stepped closer and peered at the book. Although wrinkled and stained, the pages showed verses written in pen and ink. She pictured the long-ago poet in his dark and cold monastery, laboriously recording his creations by candlelight. She straightened and turned toward Leo. "This book was quite a find. How do you plan to use it in the festival?"

"I'm featuring the poems in my lecture on religious writings of the Middle Ages."

"Sounds interesting. I'll plan to attend."

"Love to have you in the audience. But now, sit and bring me up to date on life in a public library." He waved toward several chairs and then settled behind his desk. "Are you keeping your patrons supplied with the latest books?"

Nina took a seat. "I'm doing my best."

"Have you gathered tales of rabbits and squirrels and such for our festival participants?" His eyes twinkled.

His good-natured teasing brought a smile to her lips. "Oh, yes. Like you, I have a rare book or two to share. Just lately, though, I've been reading Professor Miller's poetry booklets."

Leo's brows drew together. "Poor Gwyneth. Rest her soul."

"Did you know her well?" His comment piqued her interest.

"I like to think so. We both had an interest in poetry."

"One of her books was dedicated to a 'T.L.' Do you have any idea who that is?" Anticipating his answer, Nina leaned forward.

Leo frowned and stroked his beard. "I can't think of anyone with those initials. They probably belong to someone in her life before she came here. But, speaking of her poetry, I hear you're taking over her bell tower presentation."

"I thought honoring her plans would be a fitting tribute."

His forehead wrinkled. "Maybe so, but that tower is a pain, if you ask me."

"Why?"

"Don't you remember from when you were a student that frats and sororities use the place for initiations and parties? No matter what kind of lock Admin uses, someone always manages to get in."

"The tower does have a reputation. But, speaking of fraternities, I also recall as an undergrad hearing rumors about a secret society. The Spearheads, I think was their name. Do you know if such a group still exists?"

He laughed and shook his head. "Secret societies are never secret. I don't know why they bother. The membership might be under cover, sometimes, but the existence of the group is a known factor. But to answer your question, let me show you something." He stood and beckoned her.

Leo led her from his office through the checkout area and then to the stacks. Despite the renovations, the route was familiar. How many times had she trod the same path, first researching on the computer and then off to search for the books?

The rows of shelves opened to a large area, also familiar, where students sat at tables or cubicles reading or using their personal computers.

Leo followed the room's perimeter, stopping in front of a large aquarium.

Nina widened her eyes. Here was something she didn't recall ever seeing in the library.

"What do you think of this addition to our building?"

She shifted her gaze from the angelfish, tetras, and swordfish swimming in and out of seaweed and coral reefs, to Leo. "What a beautiful aquarium, and it fits perfectly in this room." She nodded toward their surroundings.

Leo ran a hand along the tank's metal rim. "I'd been wanting one for a long time. The faculty and students also expressed their interest. So, a few months ago, this aquarium and all the fish were delivered—a gift from an anonymous donor, the card said. But rumors suggest the Spearheads are responsible."

"The secret society."

"Uh-huh. This isn't the first anonymous gift bestowed upon our campus. Last year, a new bench for the quad appeared, and before that, a flagstone walk at the StuU."

As a thought occurred, Nina nodded. "When I was a student, a new podium suddenly appeared in the auditorium. Rumors credited the secret society with that gift, too."

Leo took the handkerchief from his jacket's breast pocket and wiped away a spot on the tank's glass. "We don't know for sure. But I suspect all these anonymous deeds are the work of the Spearheads."

"So, they do good for the university."

He held up a forefinger. "Most of the time. Rumor also has it they're a bit rowdy, too. The trampling of flowers in the greenhouse garden was blamed on an initiation ceremony when they had too much to drink. But no one has proven anything, one way or another." He studied her. "But why your interest?"

Nina kept her tone casual. "Oh, I just like to know what's happened since I've been here. Being a part of Lit Fest has stirred up many memories."

On the way back to the main reading room, a young man approached Leo. "'Scuse me, Dr. Manus. Professor Desmond checked out a bunch of books and forgot this one." He held up a volume. "Want me to run it to him?"

Leo reached for the book. "*Writing the Modern Composition.* Ah, yes, one he requested we purchase." He frowned and stroked his beard. "Hmmm, I don't know about making a special delivery. We're a bit understaffed today."

Nina put out a hand. "I'll deliver the book. Bannon Hall is on my way to the parking lot."

Leo frowned. "You're sure?"

"No trouble at all."

"Well...all right." He handed her the book.

Nina left the library, shaking her head. What was she thinking? Visiting Professor Desmond's classroom would surely revive painful memories. Then she reminded herself she was investigating and must take advantage of every opportunity to garner clues and valuable information.

Desmond DeSoto's classroom was at the end of a second floor hallway. To save time, Nina took the elevator. Passing students, none of whom she knew, made her recall the stranger she'd been ten years ago. She hadn't known anyone then, either.

She reached the closed door to Desoto's classroom. No movement was visible through the frosted glass. She could leave the book outside the door and make her escape. But what if someone stole the book? Leo had entrusted her with the errand. She wouldn't let him down. Still, when she put out a hand to the knob, she drew back.

Stop being such a chicken.

Taking a deep breath, she grasped the knob, opened the door, and stepped into the room. Looking around, she saw no one. She moved her gaze over the rows of empty seats, landing on the spot she occupied while taking Desoto's Composition 101 class. Focusing on the front of the room, she visualized him sorting through a stack of papers on his desk, assignments the class had turned in. He pulled out a paper and held it up. "Here's an example of the bad writing I've been talking about." He turned toward the blackboard, picked up a piece of chalk, and wrote. She could still hear the scratch of the chalk and see the words that appeared. Her words.

Finished writing, he then criticized the prose, using negative words such as "trite," "bland," and "pedestrian." Certain everyone knew she was the author, Nina sank in her seat.

True, he also picked on others, but Nina's work turned up more often—or so it seemed. Now, she wouldn't be so sensitive. But then, she was a scared freshman, and he'd been the teacher, the authority. Nina's stomach churned.

"Hello. Are you here to see me?"

The voice jolted her back to the present. She turned to find the man who'd just trashed her writing standing in the doorway. But no, that was then, and this was now. She'd been in a time warp. She shook her head to clear the memories.

Desmond DeSoto shut the door and peered at her. "You are? Oh, yes, Nina…" He snapped his fingers.

"Foster."

"Yes, yes, from the committee. Gwyn's former student. Did you want to talk to me about something?"

Now fully returned to the present, Nina took a deep breath. "While I visited Leo Manus at the library, one of his staff found a book you checked out and forgot." She held out the book.

He took the volume and studied the title. "Ah, yes, a good treatise on composition but lacking in some important areas. My book will replace this one as the favored college text."

So, as Gwyn mentioned, he was writing a book. Of

course, he was. All college professors were under pressure to publish or perish, as the old aphorism warned. "Gwyneth published poetry," she said. "I've been rereading her books."

He snorted and waved a hand. "Her pamphlets from Universo Press? I suppose they have a certain appeal to the undiscerning ear. Now, my book will be forthcoming from Rudders & Tiff, a very prestigious firm."

"Of course." Nina inwardly rolled her eyes.

He studied her with narrowed eyes. "Were you in my composition class? Don't think so."

So, although her experience was burned into her memory, he didn't remember her. She was tempted to say no, she hadn't been in any of his classes. But what would that accomplish? She lifted her chin. "I was in your freshman comp class."

"Really?" His eyes widened. "I don't recall you. But then, I've mentored hundreds of students."

The door again opened.

"Dezzy?" a female voice chirped. "Are you ready?"

"Ah, someone's here." DeSoto tilted his head in Nina's direction.

Vivian Blanchard stepped into the room. Her gaze landed on Nina. "What are *you* doing here? Our next committee meeting isn't until Monday."

Nina wanted to counter with, "What are *you* doing here? And why are you calling him Dezzy?" Instead, she explained her errand. "Professor DeSoto and I were discussing his new book."

"Oh?" Vivian's eyebrows shot up, and her gaze flitted from Nina to DeSoto.

"I was just leaving." *I'm not your competition.*

"Thanks for delivering the book." Desmond strode to the door, opened it wider, and waved to Nina.

Nina stepped out, and, with a swish, the door shut behind her. She turned to see DeSoto's and Vivian's heads outlined in the frosted glass, but then they disappeared. Was *Dezzy* escorting Vivian to his private office for their meeting…or whatever?

Were they having an affair? If so, would they worry about Nina seeing them together, or did everyone know, anyway? Did his wife know? Did their relationship have anything to do with Gwyneth? Perhaps she had had an affair with him, too, arousing Vivian's jealousy. Jealousy could be a motive for murder… *Wait. You're letting your speculations run wild.* Still, she'd learned from her past sleuthing experiences to explore all the possible scenarios.

Whatever, today's visit to campus had been well worth the drive and the time. Even though she had no conclusive answers to Gwyn's death, she had new information to add to her investigation. The challenge would be to put together all the clues to determine exactly what had happened that fateful night in the bell tower.

Chapter Nine

" 'Charming librarian.' Well, I certainly agree." Stephen looked up from reading the inscription in Alexander Brightly's *Island Dreaming*.

Sitting next to him on the sofa in her condo, Nina lightly slapped his shoulder. "You have to agree. Otherwise, you're stuck making breakfast."

"Hmmm, isn't breakfast kinda my job, anyway?" Stephen's eyes teased.

She folded her arms. "Okay, I'll think of some other punishment."

Today was Saturday, and she and Stephen relaxed, drinking their coffee before tackling breakfast. While shuffling through the latest edition of *The Richmond Review* scattered about the coffee table, he spotted Alexander's gift.

Stephen turned back to the book. "So, what's this about joining him in Island Dreaming?"

"I don't know." Nina shrugged. "I haven't had a chance to read the story yet."

Stephen turned the pages, stopping here and there to read. "Well, if this is what he means, I'll have to keep an eye on you two." He pointed toward a passage and handed her the book.

Nina read the words, and her cheeks heated. "I, ah, no, of course, he doesn't mean *that*. We hardly know each other, and even if we were better acquainted, we wouldn't—I wouldn't…" She waved a hand. "Would you put down the book, please, before I fall into the hole I'm digging."

With a chuckle, Stephen shut the book and replaced it on the table. "All right. He has a reputation for burning up the pages, though. Have you read any of his other books?"

"I've read a couple and browsed the rest as they came across my desk at the library. Has he contacted you about publicity?"

Stephen sat back. "I had a call from one of his minions, Cab somebody."

"Cab Feraro. Otis Lindstrom and Portia Quinlan are the rest of his crew."

"He'll be included in the feature we're doing on Lit Fest. Anything else will come from whomever hosts his other events. That includes you, if he gets permission to use the library."

Nina folded her section of the newspaper and added it to the stack. "Even if he does, he'll be too busy basking in the glow his fans radiate to pay much attention to me."

"Do you *want* him to pay you attention?" His eyebrows peaked.

"Only if he can tell me something about Gwyn. He knew her years ago when he was her student. In fact, he credits her with giving him his start in the writing world. She liked a story he wrote for a class assignment and recommended he send it to a magazine. They published it, which launched his career."

Stephen stroked his chin. "Hmmm, I'll run a check to see if he has any skeletons in his closet." He turned toward her with a grin. "Now, how about that omelet we planned?"

Nina picked up her coffee cup and drained the last drops. "I'm ready. I stopped at the market yesterday and bought the crab meat and cheese." She looked at her wristwatch. "We have time for a nice, leisurely breakfast before we're due at Marley." Today was the retirement home's Fall Collectibles and Crafts Show.

"We don't want to miss the big event." Stephen stood and held out a hand.

Accepting the gesture, Nina stood and followed him into the kitchen. After the stress of preparing for Lit Fest and the trauma of Gwyn's death, she looked forward to spending a relaxing and enjoyable afternoon with Jessica and Joe and their friends. Maybe she'd even find a treasure or two to bring home.

****

"This is quite a show." Stephen stopped inside the door to Marley Manor's Activity Center and gazed around.

"The event grows in popularity every year." Standing beside him, Nina also marveled at all the tables displaying handmade items and collectibles. The show was open to the public, which brought people of all ages. Music from the string quartet on the stage blended with the buzz of conversation, while the aroma of popcorn from the old-fashioned machine floated along the airwaves. Spotting the table her grandmother shared with Joe, Nina led the way. "Hey, Gran, Joe. We found you."

"Hi, honey. Hi, Stephen." Jessica waved from her seat behind the table.

Sitting beside her, Joe smiled and nodded. "Good to see you two."

"Your scarves look beautiful, Gran." Nina gestured toward the colorful knitted scarves arranged on the table. Next to them were wooden boxes with designs carved on the lids. "These boxes are interesting. Are they yours, Joe?"

"Yep. I made 'em in wood class. Good for jewelry or other trinkets."

"Or just to admire," Jessica said. "Like the one you gave me to put on my dresser."

Nina picked up a box featuring a rose blossom. "These will make great gifts for my staff."

"My employees would like them, too." Stephen fingered a box with a poinsettia on the lid.

Nina and Stephen both made their selections, then added several scarves from Jessica's display.

"You two are our best customers. Right, Joe?" Jessica reached for tissue paper to wrap the scarves.

Joe looked up from his calculator. "You bet. Many thanks."

The next sellers Nina and Stephen visited were Lily Ciliano and Wally Anders, also Marley residents and friends of Jessica and Joe. Lily had short, curly white hair and wore thick-lens eyeglasses attached to a gold chain. She and Wally, a widower, had been special companions for the past year, having met and bonded at the annual Games Galore Night, when she beat him at checkers.

Their table was a jumble of, well, *stuff* was the only word Nina could think of to describe the assortment. The items included a sugar and creamer that appeared to be sterling silver, a jar of assorted buttons, a teacup paired with an unmatched saucer, and a pillowcase embroidered with *Sweet Dreams*.

"We cleaned our closets." Lily folded a cloth napkin and added it to a stack. "Seein' as how I'm not talented."

"You are talented." Wally patted her shoulder. "You make the best noodle soup I ever tasted."

"Aw, isn't he sweet?" Lily fluttered her eyelashes. "Anyway, maybe we have something you two can't live without."

After a few moments perusing the items, Nina found a set of coasters, each featuring a different lighthouse.

Stephen dug into a box of kitchen utensils and pulled out an old, hand-operated eggbeater. "I have an electric beater, but I like these, too."

Lily took their money and added it to the pouch at her waist. "I hear you're solving another murder, Nina." Her magnified eyes gleamed.

Nina took her wallet from her purse. "Where did you hear that?"

"You know word travels faster than lightning around here." Wally placed their purchases in a paper bag.

"I can't recall just where I heard the news." Lily frowned. "But I'm with you, Nina. Your friend didn't fall from the bell tower by accident, and she didn't commit suicide. She was pushed, just like in the movie. You know, the one Alfred Hitchcock made."

"She's a Hitchcock movie fan." Wally handed Stephen the bag. "Scares her, but she watches 'em anyway."

Nina arched an eyebrow. "So, Lily, just because the woman in the movie was murdered, you think Gwyneth met that end, too."

Lily nodded and shook a finger. "So do you, Nina. Don't deny it."

Lily was right—no use in denial. If Nina continued her investigation—and she knew she would—people would soon realize what she was up to. Nina heaved a sigh. "I do find Gwyn's death very suspicious."

"So you're on the job?" Lily straightened and clasped her hands.

"Let's just say I'm open to learning more about the incident."

Lily placed a hand on Wally's arm. "See? Told ya she was investigating. We'll keep our eyes and ears open, won't we?"

Wally nodded and laid his hand over hers. "You bet. Count on us, Nina."

Other customers approached the table.

Nina and Stephen waved goodbye to Lily and Wally and continued on. The next stop was the book sale managed by Selma Belari and Mabel Whiteside, also special pals of Jessica. When the two helped Nina establish the home's lending library, they became her good friends, too.

Selma turned from arranging books on a portable shelf, and her eyes lighted. "Hey, Mabel, guess who's here."

Mabel looked up from sorting a stack of magazines. A grin split her lips. "Hello, Nina and Stephen. We heard y'all were comin'."

"So good to see you two in charge of the books." Nina looked from one woman to the other.

Mabel pulled her shawl tighter around her slim shoulders. "We caught the book bug when we helped set up our library. Right, Selma?"

"We certainly did. So here we are." Selma made a sweeping gesture to include the display.

"We'll take a look and see what we can find." Nina stepped to one of the shelves. After several minutes of perusal, she discovered a children's story to add to her collection.

Stephen's simultaneous search uncovered a book on home remodeling.

"Here's a book we thought you would be interested in." Selma pulled a thin paperback from underneath the table and handed it to Nina.

"*A Summer to Remember* by Gwyneth Miller." Nina paged through the booklet. "The poems appear to be all about a relationship." She turned to the front. "Ah, it's dedicated to T.L., the same as the other books she wrote."

"How romantic." Mabel pressed both hands to her chest. "Ah've never had anyone write poems to me."

"My husband used to write 'I love you' on the bathroom mirror," Selma said. "Somebody told him to do that—I forget who. But, Nina, you will find out exactly what happened to your old professor, won't you?"

Mabel's brows knit. "You know we're here to help you."

"Thanks, ladies. I appreciate your support. You can start by telling me who donated this book." Nina tapped the cover with a forefinger.

Selma and Mabel looked at each other and shrugged.

"People put their donations in a big box in the lobby." Selma's sweeping arm gestures indicated the size of the receptacle.

"Unless they include a note, we don't know who gives what." Mabel shrugged.

Nina reached into her purse for her wallet. "Well, if you do find out, I'd appreciate knowing."

"We'll ask around," Selma said.

Nina raised a hand. "Don't mention me when you do, please."

"We won't." Selma and Mabel spoke in unison.

Nina and Stephen visited the remaining sellers, making a few more purchases. Lastly, they stopped at the baked goods table. While inhaling all the enticing aromas, Nina studied the selections of cookies, breads, pies, and cakes. After some discussion, she and Stephen settled on an apple pie, a loaf of cranberry bread, and a variety of muffins. Tucking the goodies into her tote, she turned away from the table and came face to face with—of all people—Desmond DeSoto. "Professor DeSoto? What are you doing here?"

He stuck out his neck and squinted. "And you are? Oh, yes, Nina Foster, from Lit Fest. Our alum recruit."

Just then, a woman appeared at his side. "I'm ready to go, Desmond." She frowned at Nina. "Who's this? Another of your students?" Dressed in a gray jacket and slacks that matched her gray hair, and with her face devoid of makeup, she brought to mind the term Plain Jane.

"Not anymore. Now, she's a Lit Fester." Desmond turned toward Nina. "This is my wife, Jane."

"Hello." Nina nodded and smiled.

The woman's thin lips barely turned up at the corners.

Stephen joined them, and Nina introduced him.

"What brings you to Marley's show?" Stephen

looked from one to the other of the couple.

"Jane's mother lives here." Desmond tilted his head toward his wife.

Nina nodded. "So does my grandmother, Jessica Bingham. Who is your mother, Jane?"

"Sonia Harding."

Jane's flat tone told Nina she found the question—and perhaps the entire conversation—annoying.

"I haven't heard the name, but I'll bet Gran knows her. She knows everyone." Nina laughed.

"Really." Jane gave Nina another wintery smile and looked at her husband. "Are you ready to go, Desmond? I think we've seen everything."

"More than ready." Desmond tipped his nose into the air. "These amateur craft shows can be quite tedious."

Nina watched the two walk away. Meeting Desmond's wife introduced yet another person to consider in her investigation. Had Jane been involved in Gwyn's death? If so, with or without her husband's knowledge?

****

Later that evening, after dinner at a favorite waterfront restaurant, followed by a walk on the beach, Nina and Stephen returned to her condo. After settling on the sofa with a cup of tea, Nina reached for her computer and switched it on.

"No relaxing with TV tonight?" Stephen sat beside her and held up the TV's remote control.

As she brought up a blank screen, Nina shook her head. "I need to organize my thoughts about Gwyn's death."

"Aha. A suspect list?"

"I want to start one, even though we don't know for sure Gwyn was murdered. Just in case, though, I want to be prepared."

He put down the control and took out his cell phone. "I'll make a list of my own to help with your research."

"Thanks, Stephen. You know I appreciate your interest—and your help."

He put an arm around her shoulders and gave her a hug. "Of course. We're in this together, and, like I've told you before, we make a good team. Okay, who's first?"

"Desmond DeSoto." Nina typed her old professor's name.

"That was quick. Do you have a motive?"

"Gwyn told me she and Desmond were competing to be named department head, so maybe he decided to get rid of her. Or maybe I want him to be the one because I just don't like him." She told Stephen how DeSoto criticized students' writing, including hers, in front of the entire class. "Today I would brush off his criticism, but as a green freshman, I was crushed."

Stephen tapped his cell phone screen. "He did seem a bit full of himself."

"I've never met his wife, Jane. I wonder why she puts up with him."

Stephen put down his phone and turned toward her, his brow wrinkled. "Wouldn't being a professor's wife give her a certain status in the university community?"

"I suppose so."

Stephen snapped his fingers. "Here's a thought. What if Jane got rid of Gwyn to clear the way for Desmond to get the promotion?"

She flashed an appreciative smile. "Good thinking, Mr. Kraslow. Let's add her to the list.

Nina and Stephen spent a few silent minutes updating their lists.

Stephen looked up. "Okay, who's next?"

"What about Vivian Blanchard? If she and Desmond are having an affair, maybe she eliminated Gwyn to help him get the promotion. Another long shot, but let's include her."

"From what you've told me and from what I saw of him today, I'd say an affair is likely."

Nina also listed the other members of the Lit Fest Committee, even though she had no motives.

Stephen finished adding the names to his list. "Who else?"

"Alexander Brightly, although I have no motive. The only clue I have is that Midge Cornell talked to someone who overheard Gwyn say she was sorry she invited Alexander to Lit Fest. I have no idea why or if the reason was serious enough to warrant murder."

"We'll add him, anyway. Should we include his 'people,' as you call them?"

"Yes, although again, I have no motives." She typed *Portia Quinlan*, *Cab Feraro*, and *Otis Lindstrom*, and then turned her computer so that Stephen could copy the names to his list.

He finished typing and sat back. "What about the person Cara O'Meary thought she saw running from the bell tower the night of Gwyn's fall?"

"Good reminder. We'll call him—or her—*Person Running From Bell Tower*." The next suspect, who also had no name, she entered as *Person Who Interrupted Gwyn's and My Phone Call*. The anger and the fear she heard in Gwyn's voice indicated the mystery person posed a threat. Nina folded her arms. "Can you think of anyone else?"

Stephen tapped his cell phone screen with a forefinger. "Hmmm, how about the 'T.L.' dedication in Gwyn's poetry booklets?"

"Ah, a man from her past." Nina raised her eyebrows. "Might as well add him, too." She scrolled through the list. "I see that only two people have possible motives. I have a lot of work to do." Turning off her computer, she set it on the coffee table. "But Monday is my visit to the bell tower. I hope I find something there."

"Wouldn't the police have searched the place?" Stephen laid his phone next to her computer and then put an arm around her shoulders.

"I'm sure they have, but I have a feeling the tower hides secrets. If I'm to solve the mystery, I need more clues, and fast. My time on campus is already running out."

"Just let me know how I can help."

Warmth filled Nina. "You're a dear, Stephen. I'm so glad you're on my side."

"Me, too. Now, how about moving on to another activity?"

"You mean watching TV?" Her lips twitched with teasing.

"No, I'm now in the mood for something else." Cupping her chin, he guided her face to his and, in the next moment, closed his lips over hers.

Nina sighed and gave herself up to the kiss. Right now, she wanted nothing more than to be in Stephen's arms. Tomorrow, though, she'd be back on the job solving the mystery of Gwyn's untimely death.

Chapter Ten

Promptly at ten o'clock on Monday morning, Nina joined the Lit Fest Committee members in Bannon Hall's faculty room. Although she looked forward to the meeting and being brought up-to-date on the festival activities, her visit to the bell tower dominated her thoughts.

Smiling and nodding her greetings to the others already assembled at the table, she slipped into the empty seat next to Jaz. Focusing on Vivian, anticipating her call to order, Nina noticed a woman she did not recognize sitting beside Vivian. She turned toward Jaz. "Who's the newcomer?"

"Don't know," Jaz whispered behind her hand. "She came with Vivian."

Vivian tapped her gavel on the table. "Good morning, everyone. Some of you have already met our visitor, but for those who haven't, this is Cassandra Lightship, Gwyneth's sister."

Sister? The news jolted Nina. She recalled Vivian telling her Gwyneth had a sister, but she wouldn't have guessed her relative to be this woman. The two were vastly different—in appearance, anyway. While Gwyneth had worn her silver-blonde hair in soft waves framing her face, Cassandra's stark black hair was piled atop her head in a mass of curls. Gwyn's makeup had been subtle, quite the opposite from her sister's heavily outlined eyes, obviously false eyelashes, and dark red lipstick.

Vivian turned toward the woman. "Cassandra, we are so sorry for your loss. Gwyneth was a valued faculty member, as well as a good friend."

Cassandra dipped her head, revealing tiny, star-shaped ornaments embedded in the curls. "Thank you all for your kindness." She placed a hand to her chest, fingers spread. "I am devastated, as you might imagine. Gwyneth and I had no other family, only each other."

"We're here for you," Vivian said. "Just let us know how we can help."

"I will. I must apologize for taking so long to arrive. When I heard the news, I was on a ship in the Caribbean, with my group, the Stellar Stargazers. I came as soon as I could."

"Will you stay for Lit Fest?" Vivian asked. "Nina Foster has taken over Gwyn's presentation." She nodded toward Nina.

Cassandra beamed Nina a smile. "How kind of you. Yes, I believe I will be here. Settling Gwyn's estate, with her home and all her belongings, will take a while." After a few minutes of conversation with the rest of the group, Cassandra took her leave.

Vivian accompanied Cassandra to the door and when she returned to her seat, she slowly shook her head. "So sad, so sad." Then she straightened her shoulders and tapped her agenda with a forefinger. "Let's move on. We need to decide who gets the StuU conference room Saturday morning, Alphabet Soup, or Hieroglyphics Galore…."

Nina listened, but soon her mind wandered, first to the surprise appearance of Gwyn's sister and then to her upcoming visit to the bell tower. When the meeting was finally over, she was the first to head for the door.

"Nina!" Vivian called. "May I see you a moment?"

What now? "Of course, Vivian."

"About your visit to the tower…"

"I'm on my way there now." Fearing a last-minute cancellation, Nina tensed.

"I just wanted you to know you don't have to go through with the performance. We can do something else to honor Gwyn."

Nina made her tone firm. "I appreciate your concern, Vivian, but I'm all set to do the program."

Vivian pursed her lips and shook her head. "Be careful, Nina. The tower has its dangers."

Just then, Eldon interrupted with a question, and Vivian turned away.

Outside Bannon Hall, instead of heading directly to the bell tower, Nina turned her steps to the visitor's parking lot. Reaching her car, she transferred her phone and a notebook and pen from her purse to her jacket pocket, then locked her purse in the trunk. A piece of paper wedged in the top of the driver's side window caught her eye. Thinking it to be a bit of trash that had somehow stuck there, she reached for the paper, intending to throw it away. Pulling it free took a couple yanks. The paper was folded, with writing visible on the inside. Opening the note, she stared at the crude printing:

Keep away from the bell tower!

Nina pursed her lips and shook her head. Honestly! Did anyone really think she would pay attention to such a childish and cliché prank? Stuffing the note into her jacket pocket, she headed for the tower. She hadn't let

Vivian's warning deter her, and she certainly wouldn't let this anonymous message stop her, either. Besides, someone from the university's maintenance department would be with her.

Still, she wondered who had left the note. Glancing around, she spotted Cara and Diego on the next block. Were they responsible? Nina kept her gaze on them, thinking that if they looked her way, she would wave. They were deep in conversation, though and, without giving her a glance, disappeared around a corner.

Passing the Admin building, Nina glimpsed Gwyn's sister, Cassandra Lightship, climbing the steps.

Reaching the door, she stopped to pat her curls and straighten her black jacket then disappeared inside.

Could she have left the note? Hardly. She didn't know about Nina's planned program until this morning. Or had she just not acknowledged she'd learned earlier? Nina continued on to the StuU. Here, too, familiar figures caught her eye.

Desmond DeSoto, briefcase slung over his shoulder, stood outside talking to a student.

Had Desmond stuck the note in her car window? He'd been vocal in his opposition to her bell tower presentation. The student with Desmond was Jason Hopkins, the young man who had exchanged the fist bump, forefinger link with Diego Rivera. Jason's father was university board president, Lincoln Hopkins. She couldn't think of any reason why Jason would care about her visit to the tower. But, then, she'd only recently met him. She recalled the photo in Cara's room, showing Diego and Jason with a third young man, whose identity she didn't know.

Reaching the bell tower, Nina approached the door

and grasped the handle. Perhaps the person who was to accompany her waited inside. The door handle did not yield. Turning away, she spied a nearby bench. She sat and took a deep breath, hoping to relax, but her nerves tingled with anticipation.

She gazed at the clock and then the arched opening, which allowed a glimpse of the bell, and immediately thought of Gwyn's fall. The mental image of her body hurtling through space brought a shiver, and she hugged her arms. Would she ever look at the tower without a reminder of Gwyn's fate?

A man in his forties—tall and wiry, and wearing a PNU Maintenance parka—strode along the sidewalk. Reaching the tower's door, he stopped and looked around.

Hoping he was the person to admit her, Nina stood and hurried to his side. "I'm Nina Foster. Are you looking for me?"

He peered at her and thumbed over his shoulder. "If yer the one going in the tower."

"I am."

"Okay, let's do it. I'm Wildon." Pulling a ring of keys from his pants pocket, Wildon selected one and stuck it into the lock. He turned the handle, and the door swung open.

Here goes. Taking a deep breath, Nina stepped over the threshold. After the bright sunlight, the tower's dim interior brought momentary blindness. The air was musty and stale, too, as though bottled up too long. But then Nina's vision adjusted, and her surroundings materialized. Not that there was much to see. Two square, wooden tables and several chairs occupied one corner. On the other side, an open wooden staircase led to the tower.

"You gonna be long?"

Wildon's question drew her attention. "Oh, half an hour or so. I need to get the layout of the place so I can plan the program."

"Yeah, I heard about yer program. I'm supposed to stay with you. They don't want you climbin' up to the tower by yerself. Maybe you don't need to climb up there at all?" He tilted his head and eyed her.

Nina straightened her shoulders. Now that she'd finally gained entrance to the tower, she wasn't about to forego the rest of her plan. "The top is where the recorded program will be broadcast, so, yes, I must climb up there today. You don't have to go with me, though. I'm sure I'll be fine." In fact, she didn't want him to accompany her. How could she investigate with him watching her every move?

Wildon folded his arms and spread his feet. "I don't make the rules, but I get into trouble if I don't enforce 'em."

"All right." Nina approached the bottom step and gazed upward to where a shaft of light illuminated the platform underneath the bell. "Does anyone come here besides maintenance?"

He laughed. "Oh, yeah, even though we change the locks. We even tried puttin' a bar at the bottom of the stairs but that didn't do no good."

Just then, a garbled voice came from the phone attached to his belt. He freed the device and pressed it to his ear. "Whatcha got, Clem?"

The only words Nina made out were "water" and "now," the latter spoken emphatically.

Wildon glanced at Nina. "I got a babysittin' job

here in the bell tower." He listened. "Okay, okay, I'm comin'." He fastened the phone to his belt and turned. "We got a broke water pipe in Hervey Hall basement. I need to go. You done?"

Done? She'd barely started. "No, I'm not. You go ahead with your emergency. I'll be all right by myself." *Please go.*

Wildon stuck both hands on his hips and frowned. "Don't like to skip out on ya. Got my orders, but—" He looked from her to the door and back again.

"I'll be all right. Really."

"Okay. When you leave, just pull the door shut. It'll lock by itself. I'll come back later and check."

After he left, Nina breathed a sigh of relief. The man was a distraction she didn't need. However, the quiet that settled over the tower soon proved as unsettling as Wildon's unwanted presence. Did she really want to explore on her own? Then she thought of Gwyneth. She'd been here alone...well, unless someone else was with her the night she met her death. Nina needed to know if that were the case. So, she'd better get to work—before her "babysitter" returned.

She approached the tables and finding drawers, opened them, but they all proved empty. Shadows lurked in the corners, but she found nothing hidden there, either. Placing her hands against the cold stone, she searched the walls but discovered no hidden crevices. Her examination eventually brought her to the bottom of the circular staircase.

Looking up, she glimpsed a part of the bell's curved shell and a bit of the underside. According to the orientation booklet she'd saved from her freshman days, the tower was 650 feet in height. Climbing these stairs would be similar to trudging up the stairs in lighthouses she'd visited along the coast. But on those occasions, she'd been with a group and a guide. Now, she was alone. A little shiver rippled down her spine. Perhaps she should wait until another time and let Stephen accompany her, after all.

She thought of the note stuck in her car window: *Keep away from the bell tower*. Rather than laughable, the words now carried a power that gave her pause. She glanced at the door. She could wait outside for Wildon's return.

Come on! This opportunity had been difficult to arrange. Refusing to explore the tower now would be a huge waste of time and effort. Stepping forward, she placed a hand on the railing and a foot on the bottom step.

As she climbed, she studied her surroundings for anything that might relate to Gwyneth. She found nothing to indicate she—or anyone else—had been there. Halfway up, she reached a landing with a locked cupboard she guessed housed the clock mechanism. With the absence of human bell ringers, the clock now provided the bell that sounded the hour.

Resuming her climb, she reached the landing underneath the bell. The clapper and dangling rope hung motionless, surrounded by the thick hood. She approached the open window and looked out, feeling the cool autumn breeze wash over her. She moved her gaze past the campus to houses and farmlands and then on to the snow-capped mountains.

Looking down, she focused on the ledge surrounding the tower. The stone was about four feet wide, barely enough to stand on. Surely Gwyneth hadn't planned to give her presentation from the ledge. More likely, she would set up a loudspeaker there and remain inside.

Peering over the ledge, Nina viewed the quad below, where students walked the paths or crisscrossed through the grass on their way to classes. No one looked up to witness her presence in the tower. Leaning just a bit more enabled her to locate the spot where Gwyneth's fatal fall ended. One quick look and then, her heart pounding, she drew back inside.

She focused again on the bell. Diego and Cara said the ringing had initially drawn their attention. Then, when they looked up, they saw Gwyn fall. Had she rung the bell as a plea for help? Or had her assailant, to announce the success of his or her crime?

Reminding herself of her other reason for being in the tower, that of planning her presentation, Nina took out her notebook and made notes on the equipment placement. She listened for evidence of Wildon's return, but all below remained silent.

Finally ready to leave, she returned to the top of the stairs, grasped the railing, and started down. Descending wasn't as easy as going up. The stairs seemed steeper, and more than once, she lost her balance and had to grip the railing with both hands.

At the middle landing, she stopped to catch her breath. Then, as she looked down to secure her footing, she spotted something pink against the wall. Clutching the wooden frame for support, she leaned to capture a closer look. The object was a small book that looked familiar. Then realization dawned. Gwyn's book, which she carried everywhere, had a pink cover. Could this one be hers?

Nina reached for the book, but her fingers fell a few inches short. Still holding on to the frame, she leaned farther but still failed to grasp the book. Her heart racing, she stepped closer to the edge of the landing and contemplated her next move. If she slipped, she could tumble all the way down the stairs and break a leg—or worse. Was claiming the book worth the risk?

She chuckled to herself. Of course, it was. Sucking in a deep breath, she leaned over the railing and this time wrapped her fingers around the book. Yes! It was tightly wedged, but, with more pulling, finally came free. Slipping it into her coat pocket, she took a deep breath and prepared to descend the rest of the stairs. A noise from below caught her attention. She leaned over the railing but had no view of the door. "Wildon? Is that you?"

No answer, and yet she sensed a presence. "Wildon?"

Another sound came, like a door clicking closed.

Nina descended the rest of the stairs. At the bottom, she looked around, expecting to see her guide, but no one was in sight. She swung her gaze to the door.

The door was closed.

Wildon had told her that when shut, the door would self-lock. It wouldn't be locked from the inside, though…would it? She ran to the door and grasped the handle. It was loose in the socket. She pushed the handle back into its slot, but it still wouldn't turn. Repeated tries brought no success. Finally, the truth dawned: she was locked in the tower.

Her heart pounding, Nina stared at the closed door. Had the handle malfunctioned by accident? Or had someone deliberately sabotaged the mechanism? She thought of the note stuck in her car's window. Was being locked inside the tower her punishment for ignoring the warning?

Chapter Eleven

Nina had no time to worry about how she was imprisoned. She must deal with the problem. The logical solution would be to call someone. But who? She didn't have Wildon's number. She had Vivian's, and she could look up others associated with the school. But she hesitated to ask any of them for assistance. Revealing her dilemma might make Admin change their mind about allowing her to use the tower for Gwyn's presentation.

She hurried to the bottom of the stairs and looked up. She could climb to the top, stick her head out the window, and call for help. Yeah, that response to her dilemma would be as bad as phoning. Turning away, she slumped into a chair. This outcome was not what she'd planned for her visit. She'd wait awhile longer, counting on Wildon's return.

She checked her cell phone and saw half an hour had passed since he left. She considered looking around more but didn't want to stray too far from the door. Another half hour crept by. Taking Gwyn's journal from her coat pocket, she opened it, but knowing she couldn't concentrate on its contents, she quickly closed the book and tucked it back into her pocket. She was about to give in and phone Vivian when footsteps sounded outside the door. Jumping up, she ran forward just as the door opened. She held her breath. Wildon?

Or someone else?

In the next moment, Wildon pushed wide the door and stepped inside.

Nina exhaled a whoosh of air and offered up a prayer of thanks.

He peered at her. "You still here? When I saw the door closed, I figured you were gone. Thought I'd better check to make sure."

"I'm glad you did. I would have left, but the door handle wouldn't turn." She pointed toward the handle.

"Huh? Not working?" Frowning, he examined the handle. "I see the problem. A coupla screws are missing. Should be around here somewhere."

For the next few minutes, Nina helped Wildon search the floor for the missing screws, but neither found any.

Wildon straightened and propped both hands on his hips. "Kinda odd we didn't find 'em. Nobody's cleaned up lately, that I know of... But, anyway, are you finished doing whatever?"

"For today, I am, but I'll need to come back at least once more before the presentation." Actually, what she really wanted was to do more investigating.

His nose wrinkled. "I got a busy schedule."

"I'm sure you do. Maybe you have an extra key?" Obtaining a key would save asking Admin for one.

Wildon stroked his chin. "Not sure givin' you a key's a good idea. I could get in trouble."

She held up a hand. "I promise I'll return it as soon as Lit Fest is over."

"But you'd be here alone." He made a sweeping gesture.

"I was alone today, and nothing bad happened.

Well, except for the door. I'll be fine, really. Besides, I have a friend who will come with me."

Several seconds elapsed while Wildon frowned and scratched his head. Finally, he nodded. "Okay, deal. I'll fix the handle so you won't have no more trouble. Now, let's get outa here."

Nina stepped outside and took a deep breath of fresh air.

Wildon shut and locked the door. Then he removed the key from the ring and handed it to her. "Don't lose this key, and don't give it to anyone."

Nina gave a solemn nod. "I'll take good care of it, I promise."

Wildon headed down the walk.

Nina fell into step beside him. "Did you get the broken water pipe fixed?"

He snorted. "False alarm. We didn't find any burst pipe at Hervey Hall. Don't know who phoned, either."

Nina widened her eyes. Had Wildon been called away so that someone—say, the person who left her the note—could break the tower's door handle and trap her?

At the end of the walk, he stopped and raised a hand. "I'm goin' back to my office. You mind that key now."

"I will, and thank you, Wildon. I appreciate all your help." She gave him her best smile.

"Aw, no problem."

He actually returned her smile. Maybe she'd made a friend, after all. Just in case anyone was watching, on the way to her car, Nina kept her head high and her step firm. Reaching the vehicle, she scanned the windows to make sure no more notes had been left. The windows, including the windshield, were all clear.

On the drive to Richmond, she mulled over her visit to the tower. With all the excitement of finding Gwyn's journal and then the door malfunction, she'd all but forgotten she had achieved her goal of examining the area for the Lit Fest program. Discovering Gwyn's book was an exciting bonus. She could hardly wait to get home and explore her professor's personal writings.

The warning note and the broken door handle were not anticipated, although not altogether surprising. Were the two related? First, the note, then the fake call to Wildon, to remove him from the scene. Then, to trap her in the tower. Surely, the person—or persons— would know any imprisonment would be only temporary. They had to assume she carried her phone and could call for help. They would know that eventually Wildon would return and free her.

These events were meant to scare her rather than cause any real harm. Someone didn't want her in the tower. Why? Did he or she—or they—know about Gwyn's book and want it for themselves? Was something else in the tower yet to be found?

If the perpetrators of today's events expected to scare Nina, they were sorely mistaken. What happened only served to prove a mystery surrounded Gwyn's death, which fueled Nina's resolve to discover the truth. She would not back off but instead forge full steam ahead.

As Nina pulled into her parking spot at the Seaview Library, she realized she forgot to call Stephen to tell him she finished her trip to the tower.

"I've been thinking about you," he said, when he answered her call. "Everything okay? How'd the tower visit go?"

"Very…interesting." She hadn't thought through just how much she would tell him.

"You climbed to the top safely?"

"With no problem. Oh, and I found Gwyn's journal." Nina patted her jacket pocket, feeling the book through the fabric.

"Her diary?"

"Sort of, but mostly for jotting down poetry. The book was wedged between the stairs and the wall. I haven't had a chance to read it yet, but since I just arrived at the library, the book will have to wait. I'm excited to look at what she wrote, though. Hopefully, I'll find clues."

"Sounds like a good find. So, your trip went off without a hitch, otherwise?"

"Well…the maintenance man met me as scheduled. The tower was…tall…and big." Would he see through her evasive rambling? "I'd better sign off now and report to work." Nina straightened and grasped the door handle.

"Wait. Come to my place for dinner tonight. Bring Gywn's journal. We'll look at it together."

"All right. I was planning to share it with you." After the unsettling events of the day, being where she felt especially safe and secure held a strong appeal.

"I'll pick up some Chinese at Wink's Wok."

She laughed. "That clinches the deal. I'll be there."

He matched her laugh with a chuckle. "I know how to get my way with you. See you later."

Nina looked forward to discussing her trip to the tower with Stephen, but would she share all the details?

****

At six o'clock, Nina arrived at Stephen's house, parking her car next to the garage. A covered walkway led to the back door and the kitchen. The door was open with Stephen's outline visible in the growing darkness.

"Hey." He took her hand, drew her inside, and pulled her into an embrace for a long, lingering kiss.

"What a greeting," she said, when at last they broke apart.

"I've missed you." He led her through the kitchen and down a hallway to the living room, where a fire blazed in the arched fireplace.

Slipping off her coat, Nina laid it over the back of a nearby chair and then turned to the picture window, where the view always drew her attention. Beyond the deck, a path led through his front yard to the beach and a boat dock. Out on the water, lights glowed from several boats, including a ferry headed for the peninsula.

Stephen picked up two glasses of wine from the coffee table and held out one. "Here you go."

She sipped the wine, recognizing at once a favorite Chablis. "You're pretty fancy tonight. What's the occasion?"

"You. Us. Being together." He gave her a lingering look.

Just then, a buzzer sounded.

"Uh-oh. The food's ready." He set his glass on the coffee table.

"I'll help." Placing her wine next to his, she followed him into the kitchen where trays of food waited in the oven. All her favorites, she soon saw, from wonton soup to sesame chicken to sweet and sour prawns. The aromas filled the room, making her mouth water.

She helped Stephen carry the food into the living room and arrange it on the coffee table. Settling next to him on the sofa, she loaded her plate with servings. Then, picking up her chopsticks, she eagerly sampled each dish, savoring the various flavors. The wonton dumplings were juicy with ginger and soy sauce, the sesame chicken crisp and crunchy, and the prawns enhanced with sweet and sour flavors. "Mmm, everything's delicious."

Stephen reached for another piece of chicken. "I agree. Wink's is the best."

After awhile, Nina sat back and patted her stomach. "That was wonderful, Stephen. Thank you so much."

"My pleasure." Stephen refilled her teacup. "Now, let's hear about your trip to the tower and take a look at the book you found."

"I'm eager to examine it, too." Nina reached for her coat and pulled the journal from the pocket. Placing the book on her lap, she stared at the bright pink cover decorated with purple flowers, and suddenly the excitement of her discovery faded, replaced by a new dilemma.

"What's wrong?" Stephen's brow wrinkled.

She turned toward him. "I don't know if I should keep this book or not. Legally, it belongs now to her sister, Cassandra."

"Cassandra?"

She nodded. "I met her today at the committee meeting. I'll tell you more about her later."

"I understand how you feel, but what if the journal holds the answer to the mystery of Gwyn's death?" He sipped his tea and set the cup on the coffee table.

Nina ran a forefinger over the book's embossed roses. "You make a good argument."

"The decision is up to you, of course, but why not read the entries and then give the book to her sister?"

"Okay, here goes." She opened the book. Gwyn's name on the inside cover confirmed the ownership. The first page was dated six months ago, and the writing—some in pen, some in pencil—featured phrases such as *"a song springs forth," "the earth's awakening yawn,"* and *"thunder explodes,"* with *"explodes"* crossed out and *"bursts"* written in its place. Perusing several more pages revealed the same pattern.

"What are you finding?" Stephen leaned to look over her shoulder.

"Just jottings, nothing put together, and nothing really personal. Not yet." She read more pages and then looked up. "This journal is disappointing. I expected to find clues to what troubled her. Tell me what you think." She handed him the book.

Stephen sat back and, brows knit, focused on the book. Then he looked up. "I see what you mean."

As he returned the book, the back cover fell open, revealing a glued-on piece of cardboard stuffed with something solid.

"What's this?" Nina pulled out a metal disc attached to a chain. "A medal, engraved with '*First Place, Drag Dusters.*' " Under the inscription was the outline of a racecar and then the date. "Whoever this belongs to won a car race two years ago."

"I wonder why Gwyn had it. Something she found, I suppose, but why would she keep it, especially in her journal?"

"It must be important..." Nina fingered the medal. "Look, the chain is broken, with only one half of the clasp remaining." She pointed toward the chain's broken end. "We need to know the medal's owner."

"I'll take on that assignment." Stephen picked up his cell phone from the coffee table and punched the keyboard. "Finding out who won that race two years ago should be easy enough."

"All right. Meanwhile, I'll give the book more study." She tucked the medal into the book's makeshift pocket.

He replaced his phone and turned toward her. "Were you comfortable enough in the tower to go ahead with the Lit Fest program?"

Nina's stomach tensed, and she looked away. "Well... Something else happened..."

"What? Tell me."

"I found a note stuck in my car's window." Nina dug the note from her coat pocket and held it out.

Stephen unfolded the paper and read aloud: "*Keep away from the bell tower*." He looked up, his brow wrinkled. "Did you discover this before or after you went into the tower?"

Nina took a deep breath. She wished she didn't have to tell him about the disconcerting experience, but he needed to know. Trust was important in a relationship. "Before, but I wasn't about to cancel my visit, not after all the trouble I had obtaining permission. I knew the maintenance man would be with me, so what could happen?" She shrugged and turned up both palms.

"Nothing came of the note, then?" He tapped the paper with a forefinger.

"I'm not sure…" She told him about the broken door handle and waiting for Wildon to return. "I don't know whether the note and the problem with the door are connected or not. Or if the warning is just a prank."

Stephen straightened and handed her the note. "Do you plan to go back to the tower before the program?"

"I'd like to. I talked Wildon into giving me a key."

"I'll go with you for sure, next time."

Nina put out a hand. "You don't have to."

"Oh, yes, I do." He reached for her hand. "I want to help."

"I know, Stephen, and you are helping." She gave his fingers a reassuring squeeze. "Coming here tonight was just what I needed. But about your going with me next time, let's wait and see. Now, I'd better go home. Besides being full of delicious food, I'm beat."

"Stay here tonight." He put an arm around her shoulders and drew her close.

His nearness stirred her senses. Spending the night would be so easy… "Thank you, Stephen, but I need to sleep in my own bed tonight."

He heaved a deep sigh. "Okay, I hear you. Let me get your coat, and then I'll walk you to your car." Before tucking her into her car, he took her in his arms and kissed her. "Goodnight, Nina," he whispered in her ear. "I love you."

Warmth filled her. "I love you, too, Stephen." She really did love him, she thought as she drove away. If only their lives weren't so complicated. Especially now, with this mystery to solve… Nina straightened her shoulders and gripped the steering wheel, renewing her vow to continue her investigation until she discovered the truth about Gwyn's last night in the bell tower.

Chapter Twelve

At the Seaview Library the following morning, Nina guided a book truck around the stacks, choosing books for an autumn-themed display. She had a list from their catalog, but she also kept an eye out for any titles she might have missed. Finished with her task, she returned to her office.

Her computer pinged, indicating a new email. The message was from Gil Grady, her supervisor:

Alexander Brightly's book talk confirmed. Send pertinent details for our newsletter.

So, Alexander would have his wish to use Seaview for his gathering. She must give him the news, but before she could look up his email address, her office phone rang. The number displayed was unfamiliar. She picked up the phone. "This is Nina Foster."

"Hello, Nina."

Although she recognized Alexander's deep, sexy voice, she couldn't resist asking, in her most professional tone, "Who's calling?"

"Alexander."

"Mr. Alexander?" Nina pressed her fingers to her lips to suppress a laugh.

"No, no. Alexander *Brightly*."

"Oh, of course, Mr. Brightly. From Lit Fest."

"Alexander, please. I think we've passed the mister and ms. phase of our relationship."

Relationship?

"I called to find out if you've received a go-ahead for my event."

She'd best stop teasing and give serious attention to his question. "As a matter of fact, a moment before your call, my supervisor sent an email."

"Good. Now, we need to discuss the details."

She held up a hand. "Wait. Don't you want to know what the email said?" Did it occur to him his request might be refused? Apparently, not.

"All right. What was in the email?"

Ignoring his impatience, she kept her tone cheerful. "That your book talk is confirmed."

"Of course, it was. I'm sure George—"

"Gil."

"Whoever—realizes the publicity value of a Brightly event. Now, we need to meet and work out the details. I've heard the Blue Heron is one of your best restaurants. Friday night fits my schedule. My associates have other plans, so we'll be free of distractions."

Nina shifted in her chair. "Oh, no, Alexander. I, no…"

"Are you telling me the Blue Heron is not a good place?"

"The food is excellent. But I have…other plans for that evening." True enough. Friday nights were spent with Stephen.

"But I must see you. We need to talk about my program."

He was right; she did need to do some planning. But best keep their meeting during business hours and in a public place. She didn't want anyone to think she and Alexander had personal reasons for getting together. "I can meet you tomorrow for lunch at Tilly's Café. It's on Pine Street, a few blocks from the ferry terminal."

"Tilly's *Café*?"

His tone reeked of derision. Nina suppressed a chuckle. "Famous for their halibut burgers."

"Well...all right."

After hanging up, Nina returned to planning the book display. Still, a part of her mind lingered on Alexander's invitation to dinner and her immediate refusal. She had no trouble squelching his attempt to turn their business meeting into something more personal. Despite his handsome looks and his seduction skills, she wasn't attracted. She was with Stephen now, even if she couldn't take the next step in commitment. What was the next step, anyway? Living together twenty-four/seven instead of only on weekends? Wearing his engagement ring? Which he hadn't actually offered but had hinted at often enough.

Nina sighed. Relationships could be so complicated and so *troublesome*. Solving mysteries was easier. She'd concentrate on the mystery of Gwyn's death and leave relationships for another time. Still, when she settled on the sofa that evening for a phone call with Stephen, she looked for an opening to casually mention her lunch appointment—she would not use the word *date*—with Alexander.

"I'm attending a city council meeting tomorrow morning, just a couple blocks from Seaview," Stephen said. "How about meeting for lunch?"

Ah, here was the perfect opportunity. "I'd love to, but I'm already having lunch with Alexander."

"Who? Oh, the writer with the big nose."

Picturing Alexander's handsome face, Nina frowned. "Really? I hadn't noticed the size of his nose."

Stephen laughed. "I didn't mean literally. I meant figuratively."

"Oh." She waved a hand. "Well, anyway, we're meeting at Tilly's Café to work out the details of his talk at the library. So you don't need to worry that..." She swallowed hard. What was she getting herself into?

"That's he's personally interested in you? I already know he is. But I'm not worried."

"You're not worried about him? Or about me responding?"

"Neither."

Nina narrowed her eyes "So you take me for granted?"

"Nina, what's going on?" Stephen's tone deepened. "Are you upset about something?"

"No, yes..." She ran a hand over her forehead. "I just have a lot on my mind right now—Gwyn's death, the festival, keeping up with my work at the library."

"I know you have a lot on your plate. But, look, if something about our relationship bothers you, wait until we're together to talk. Over the phone's no good."

"I guess I'm just tired. A good night's sleep should help." She offered a wan smile.

"All right, honey. I'll call you tomorrow night."

"Thanks, Stephen. I should be home by six." Disgusted with herself, Nina sat back and folded her arms. She'd wanted to discuss her lunch with Alexander calmly and matter-of-factly. Instead, as usual, her emotions bubbled over. Would she ever learn how to be successful in a relationship?

She dropped her gaze to the two books lying on the coffee table. One was Alexander's *Island Dreaming*. The other was Gwyn's pink journal. She wanted to explore both, but which one first? In case Alexander asked if she'd read his book, she'd better at least take a look tonight.

After making a cup of tea, she sat again on the sofa and opened the book. The dedication was to Portia, his public relations agent. *"To the best darn PR person ever,"* the line read. Not exactly a poetic or sophisticated dedication, but the words sounded like something he would say.

The story began with the heroine, Delia, who, while recovering from a broken love affair, travels to a Caribbean island resort. She meets dive master Jaret, a free spirit who's refreshingly different from the made-in-a-mold executives she's used to. The story line was not one she would select on her own, but the opening pages drew her into the narrative. The writing proved to be a cross between "literary" and "commercial." Some of the descriptions, especially, were evocative.

At the end of the first chapter, Jaret had just approached Delia with an invitation to a party given by one of his diver friends. Would she fall for his blatant flattery, or would her rational self prevail? Nina chuckled. No mystery there. But, okay, she wanted to find out what happened next. She read on, continuing to be impressed. Alexander might be clumsy in his speech, but he certainly could write.

****

"How many guests did you say you've invited?" Sitting across from Alexander at a window table in Tilly's Café, Nina held her fingers poised over her tablet, ready to record his answer.

Alexander tilted his head, and one eyebrow quirked. "Guests? I thought we were talking about sightseeing."

Nina sighed. Keeping him focused proved challenging. "If we have time today, I'll be happy to make suggestions, but I'm on a tight schedule. I'm sure you are, too."

He sat back and folded his arms. "I have the entire afternoon free. But, all right, business it is."

"Good." Nina consulted her tablet's screen. "Now, if we rearrange the furniture and add a few more chairs, we can accommodate about thirty guests. We'll need a table for posters and handouts, and a cart for coffee and tea…"

"How about some goodies, too?

Actually, she hadn't thought of refreshments. But, of course, people would expect to be fed. "Our Friends of the Library will take care of treats." She hoped.

Their meals arrived. At her suggestion, he ordered the halibut burger. After taking a bite, he turned toward her and grinned. "Hey, this burger is pretty darn good."

Nina enjoyed her crab salad, especially the tangy dressing, a Tilly's favorite. She and Alexander managed to keep to the subject of his event during the course of the meal.

Finished with his burger, Alexander swiped his napkin over his lips. "You sure you're not available this afternoon? I could use a little R and R."

Maybe so, but, thankfully, his entertainment was not her responsibility. "Sorry, I need to return to work." She waved a hand. "I've been gone a lot for Lit Fest. Which reminds me, I met Gwyn's sister the other day on campus. Cassandra Lightship. Do you know her?"

"I've met her. Ding-a-ling." He twirled a forefinger next to his ear.

"She *is* different. But tell me about you and Gwyn."

He turned up both hands. "Not a whole lot to tell. She followed my career and loved to tell folks she discovered me."

"You must have been flattered when she invited you to Lit Fest." She waited, hoping he would reveal something to indicate why Gwyn made the remark about being sorry she'd included him.

He shrugged. "Gotta keep my face in front of the public. If my sales figures fall, nobody's happy."

She studied him. "So that's all your books are to you, sales figures?"

"Hey, staying at the top is hard. My next book has to be as good or better." He made a fist and pounded the table.

"Speaking of your next book, what do you plan to write?"

He shook his head. "Won't know until the words appear."

"I started reading *Island Dreaming* last night. I'm really enjoying it." She meant the compliment, too. "Your descriptions, especially, are very good. What island did you have in mind when you created your fictional one?"

He frowned. "What island? Why, ah, I don't know." He waved a hand. "I made it up. That's what fiction is, right? Made-up stuff."

His vague response seemed odd, but perhaps he had a personal reason for not being more forthcoming.

"Yes, but because your setting seemed so real, I thought it probably was." A knock on the window drew her attention. She looked around to see Portia standing outside on the sidewalk, beckoning to Alexander.

"Oh, geez. I told her to take the day off." Alexander pursed his lips and shook his head.

Portia frowned and pointed toward her wristwatch.

Alexander continued to shake his head.

Portia finally wheeled around and stomped off.

Nina faced Alexander. "I think she wants you to go somewhere." She hoped they could finish their conversation first, though.

He shrugged. "Aw, she's always got an agenda. Now, where we were?"

"You were telling me about your relationship with Gwyn."

"Oh, yeah. We kept in touch and got together whenever convenient... Why are you so interested in her and me?" His eyes narrowed. "Wait a minute. Word's going around her fall wasn't an accident." He pointed a finger. "You the one spreading that rumor?"

She frowned and straightened her shoulders. "I don't spread rumors, but I do have concerns about her death."

"Based on what?"

"Things she told me—her behavior right before she died."

"Did she mention me?" Gripping the edge of the table, he leaned toward Nina. "Did she say anything about my books or my writing?"

His sudden intensity took her by surprise, and she drew back. "Well...she told me you were coming."

"Alexander, you need to leave—right now!" Portia

stood over the table, her eyes blazing behind her glasses.

Alexander looked up, brows furrowed. "What are you talking about, Porsh? I have the afternoon free."

"No, you don't." She stuck a hand on her hip. "You have an appointment with Tonya Heyden in exactly ten minutes."

"Who the hell is she?" Alexander wrinkled his nose.

"She's the mayor's wife, and she's starting a fan club for us—er, *you*. She's not someone you should ignore."

Alexander turned toward Nina. "Do you know her?"

Nina nodded. "I've met Tonya on occasion. She's quite personable and very supportive of the library."

"I spent all morning setting up the meeting." Portia waved her cell phone. "You really need to go." She looked at Nina. "So sorry."

Her condescending tone sounded anything but sorry. "Of course. I think we're finished here." Nina turned off her tablet and tucked it into her purse. Then she took out her wallet.

Alexander put out a hand. "Lunch is on me." Leaning forward, he pulled a billfold from his back slacks pocket. He opened it and then looked up at his assistant. "Porsh, you'll have to get this. I seem to have left my cash and cards at the motel."

Portia smirked. "Of course, you did. Good thing I happened by, isn't it?"

Portia and Alexander took the lead exiting the restaurant with Nina following in their wake. Once outside, though, Alexander stepped to Nina's side.

"Great lunch, Nina. You were right. Tilly's burgers are awesome. I'll be in touch."

"Have a good meeting with Tonya." Nina watched them walk away, deep in conversation. What a strange relationship. Portia was his employee, but at times like today, she appeared to be the boss. Oh, well, as the saying went, "it takes all kinds…"

Chapter Thirteen

At home that evening, after a light dinner of chicken soup and a tossed salad, Nina settled on the sofa. *Island Dreaming* still lay on the coffee table. Picking up the book, she ran her fingers lightly over the cover, her thoughts not on the story but instead on today's lunch with the author. She hadn't learned much about Alexander's relationship with Gwyn, other than he was her student at Caldonia U and that she was responsible for his entry into publishing. He asked if Gwyn mentioned anything about his writing. What did that mean? Was he particularly sensitive to criticism from his former teacher and mentor? But before Nina could pursue the subject, Portia had interrupted.

Theirs was an odd relationship. Of course, keeping her job depended on his success, which might account for her assertiveness. Meeting with the mayor's wife certainly took precedence over lunch with the town's librarian.

Her intuition told her, though, that something wasn't right with those two. Nor was Alexander as happy about his success as one would expect. Perhaps worry about staying at the top took away the joy of being there in the first place.

Okay, enough speculating about Alexander. Nina put down *Island Dreaming* and picked up Gwyn's journal. Her perusal of the book at Stephen's the other night left her disappointed. She had hoped to discover a clue to what happened to Gwyn or to what bothered her. Before her death, she reached out to Nina, indicating she wanted her help. But for what?

Nina began at the book's opening, taking more time than she had at Stephen's. That night, although eager to read Gwyn's words, she was tired and distracted by what occurred at the tower. Tonight, she could focus. However, the first few pages still yielded nothing she could relate to any problems Gwyn might have had. Much of her poetry dealt with nature: trees, flowers and other plants, and the weather. Some lines she recognized from the finished poems Gwyn included in her Lit Fest program.

She skipped to the latter part of the book, where the dates indicated more recent entries. One verse caught her eye.

Climb to the top
And then take a fall
Down to the bottom
With witnesses all.
Whisked away in the dead of night
Leaving behind a cherished prize
To later be found
And expose the lies
That you perished elsewhere.

Climb to the top of what? A mountain? Stairs? If stairs, those in a house or other building? What about the stairs in the bell tower?

Was the poem about a real person? Or just a made-up fantasy, like Gwyn's other verses?

Nina's phone chimed, and soon, Stephen's picture on the screen brought a smile to her lips.

"How was your lunch with Mr. Brightly?" he asked, after they exchanged greetings.

"I learned a few things about his and Gwyn's relationship, but then we were interrupted." She gave him the details of Portia's demand.

"Sounds like she's the boss," Stephen agreed.

"Have you found out who owned the medal?"

"I have. His name is Benjamin Logarth."

The name jogged her memory. "The student who was killed when his car went into the ravine at Sattoo Pass."

"Right. Here's his picture." He held up a newspaper photo.

Nina peered at the black-and-white image. "Wow. I'm pretty sure he's the guy with Diego Rivera and Jason Hopkins in the photo I saw in Cara's room. He wore a medal around his neck, too."

"He obviously wasn't wearing it when he went over the cliff." Stephen shook his head.

"He must've lost it somewhere, and Gwyn found it. I have the feeling the medal plays an important role in her death."

"If she knew the medal was Benjamin's, why didn't she return it to his parents? I'll bet they would want it."

"Unless she kept it for some other reason."

Stephen leaned forward. "What will you do with it?"

"Keep it, for now."

Stephen put aside the photo and then folded his arms. "Are you having any luck reading Gwyn's journal?"

"I found a curious poem. Hang on, and I'll share

it." She picked up the journal, read aloud the poem, and then looked up. "What do you think?"

Stephen rubbed his chin. "Hmmm, climbing to the top of what? A mountain?"

Nina nodded. "I thought of that."

He held up a forefinger. "Or the tower?"

"That occurred to me, too." She loved how their thoughts were often in sync.

"Let's say the tower. Someone climbed to the top and then fell. There were witnesses. Or maybe Gwyn was foretelling her own accident."

Nina narrowed her eyes. "Or did she witness someone else's fall? Not from the tower, but from somewhere else."

"Okay, what about 'cherished prize'?"

"I don't know." She slowly shook her head. "I'll keep reading, and maybe I'll find the answers."

"I'll keep digging, too. Meanwhile, I'm looking forward to our weekend together. Joe and Jessica want us to join them at his club for a round of golf on Sunday morning. I'm in favor." A smile tilted his lips. "How about you?"

"Sounds like a good diversion. The grounds are beautiful this time of year, too." Cheered by Stephen's call, Nina turned back to the journal. Was this book the only place Gwyn recorded her poetical musings? Surely not. She undoubtedly had other writings stashed away in her home. If only Nina had access… Then an idea occurred. Cassandra Lightship stayed at Gwyn's home, settling her estate. Maybe she would appreciate help. Nina checked her wristwatch. Seven thirty. Still early enough to phone.

She could access Cassandra's number on the

Internet—privacy was an obsolete concept in this day and age—but surfing various sites would take time. A much quicker way would be to ask Vivian. Surely, she had established lines of communication with Gwyn's sister.

Nina soon had Vivian on the line. A moment of silence greeted her request.

"Why do you want Cassandra's number?" Vivian asked.

Anticipating the question, Nina had her answer ready. "I thought she might contribute to the biography on Gwyn that I'm preparing for Lit Fest." True enough.

"Biographical info is in the faculty section on our website."

"I know, but I'd like something more personal."

Vivian heaved a sigh. "All right. I don't think Cassandra would mind if I gave you her number. Let me consult my address book."

A few minutes later, Nina had Cassandra on the line.

"Oh, Nina, you're the one giving Gwyn's program at Lit Fest. How nice of you to take on the project. What can I do for you?"

Nina explained the biographical sketch. "I'd also like to give you Gwyn's journal I found in the bell tower."

"Her journal? I don't know when I'll be on campus again before the festival. I'm swamped here."

Ah, here was the opening she'd hoped for. "I'd be glad to help."

"Really? Hmmm, help might be nice. You're a librarian, right? How about sorting through Gwyn's books?"

Nina made a fist and pumped the air. "I'd love to."

Nina and Cassandra settled on the following afternoon at 1:00 p.m.

After hanging up, Nina picked up the journal. She meant what she'd said about turning over the book to Cassandra. However, before it left her possession, she had a plan. Book in hand, she went upstairs to her home office and turned on the copy machine. The machine hummed out the pages, and a few minutes later, Nina had her own copy of Gwyn's journal. Now, she was assured of having more time to discover its secrets.

****

The next day, after leaving Larry in charge of the library, Nina headed out of town for her visit with Cassandra. The first part of her trip followed the familiar route to PNU. Reaching the cutoff to the campus, she wished she had time to stop and call on Cara. The how-are-you-doing texts she sent were answered with a brief *okay*. Especially, she wanted to ask Cara about Benjamin Logarth and his apparent friendship with Diego and Jason. But that conversation would have to wait until another day.

Leaving the campus behind, she relied on her car's GPS for guidance. She'd been on this road for rides in the country, but she never followed the exact route to Gwyneth's home. Nina looked forward to the visit. Would she discover something of importance?

Gwyneth lived in Sunset Hills, a community of cottages with the Cascade Mountains providing a picturesque backdrop. Although the English architecture invited conformity, the owners individualized their homes with gardens, fences, arbors, and other outdoor embellishments. Gwyn's had a white picket fence with an ivy-entwined arbor. No one answered her doorbell ring, although she heard the sound reverberate inside the house. She rang again.

Finally, the door opened, and Cassandra peeked out. "Yes?"

Nina offered a smile. "I'm Nina Foster. We had an appointment today."

"Oh, yes, Nina." Cassandra consulted her wristwatch. "Is it that time already? I've quite lost track. Well, come in." Opening the door, she stood aside and made a sweeping gesture.

Instead of the upswept hairdo she wore to Monday's Lit Fest Committee meeting, today, Cassandra left her hair loose. Tendrils curled around her face, giving her sharp features a softer look. In addition to jeans and athletic shoes, she wore a green sweatshirt embellished with the picture of a flying saucer and the headline: *We know you're out there!*

Nina followed Cassandra through a short entryway to a living room. Piles of clothing, dishes, pots and pans, and other household items covered the furniture and much of the floor, while taped cardboard boxes filled one corner. "You have a big job here."

Cassandra ran a hand over her forehead. "Yes, and I'm already exhausted. I should have hired help, but I didn't, and I'm on a deadline. Our ship sails on another star search right after Lit Fest."

Nina dug into her purse and pulled out Gwyn's pink notebook. "Here's the book I told you about." She held up the journal.

Cassandra's nose wrinkled. "Oh, Gwyn's scribble book. She carried one everywhere. Always jotting down whatever. Why she couldn't jot on her phone, I never could understand. Well, yes, I could. Gwyn was old-fashioned in so many ways. That's why she's the past, and I'm the future."

"I'm sure there's a place and a purpose for both." Nina strove to be diplomatic.

"Hmm, I suppose." Cassandra took a step closer and peered at the book. "You said you found this in the bell tower."

"I went there to plan my presentation. I climbed to the top and, on my way down, I spotted the book wedged in the framework. I'm guessing she lost it the last night she was there."

Cassandra frowned and hugged her arms. "You're not afraid to go up in the tower?"

"Well…I admit it's not my favorite place, but I really want to honor Gwyn by giving her program. Anyway, I brought the book today, thinking you would want it. Although, if you don't need it now, I might find something appropriate in it for the presentation." Nina held her breath.

Cassandra shook her head. "Keep the book as long as you want." She gestured toward the room. "I've enough here to deal with."

Nina exhaled her relief and sent Cassandra a grateful smile. "Thank you." She slipped the journal into her purse. "Now, where are the books you need help with?"

Cassandra led Nina through the living room and down a short hallway to Gwyn's office.

Nina swept her gaze over an oak desk, a worktable with a printer, and a file cabinet to settle on the floor-to-ceiling shelves filled with books. Excitement filled her. "Gwyneth had quite a library."

Cassandra nodded and folded her arms. "She was an avid collector. Mostly books on poetry and teaching English, neither of which I know anything about. Feel free to choose some for your library or for your personal use. The rest I'll take to a used bookstore or donate to thrift stores."

"Sounds like a good plan." Nina shrugged out of her jacket, hanging it and her purse on Gwyn's desk chair.

"You can use those boxes for packing." Cassandra pointed toward a corner filled with empty cardboard boxes. "If you need me, I'll be in the living room." With a wave, she turned and left.

As expected, most of Gwyn's library contained volumes relevant to her teaching. Nina found several reference books to add to Seaview's collection, as well as some she wanted for herself. The majority, however, went into donation boxes.

Sometime later, Cassandra poked her head in the doorway. "How're you doing?"

Nina straightened from perusing books on a bottom shelf. "I'm just about finished."

"Okay, take a few more minutes while I make us a cup of tea."

"I'd like that. I'll be with you soon."

Nina had hoped for more time, but when she looked at her wristwatch, she saw the time was already 3:00. Not surprising, though, because the hours always slipped away when she was occupied with books. She quickly sorted through the last of the volumes on the shelves and then moved to Gwyn's desk. A laptop computer sat on the top. Perhaps she would find something relevant in Gwyn's files. Nina lifted the lid and pressed the power button. The machine powered up but needed a password to open the files. Although disappointed, she was not really surprised.

She turned off the computer and opened the desk's center drawer. A search yielded the usual pencils, pens, and other office necessities. The side drawers held files. Ah, here might be something of interest. Folders were labeled with names such as *Expenses, Lesson Plans,* and *Budget.* Behind those, however, was a large, taped manila envelope marked *Save.* Nina slipped a forefinger under the tape, popping it loose. Opening the flap, she peeked inside to find a sheaf of typewritten papers. They appeared to be submitted student assignments. Why had Gwyn kept them? They must be important and therefore needed further examination. Checking the doorway to make sure Cassandra had not approached, Nina added the envelope to her box of books. Moving to the file cabinet, she was almost through the first drawer, which so far contained prior years' income tax returns, when she heard sounds in the hallway.

In the next moment, Cassandra appeared. "Tea's ready." Her brow wrinkled. "Why are you looking in the file cabinet? I doubt any books are in there."

"Oh, you never know." Nina kept her voice casual as she closed the drawer and backed away. "I finished with the shelves and had a few extra minutes."

Cassandra's eyebrows peaked. "So, did you find anything I should know about?"

With a guilty twinge, Nina thought of the envelope she put with her books. "Ah, no, I didn't. Just the usual household records." She gestured toward the file cabinet. True enough, since she hadn't yet examined the envelope's contents.

A few minutes later, Nina and Cassandra were settled in the living room, drinking tea. Gwyn's selections included Nina's favorite Earl Grey, which she sipped from a china teacup decorated with pink roses.

"Have another cookie." Cassandra held out a plate holding the treat.

"Thanks, I will." Nina selected a shortbread cookie, inhaling the sugary aroma, and bit into it. "Did you bake these? They're delicious."

Cassandra shook her head. "Heavens, no. I don't like to bake, or cook anything, for that matter. I found these in the freezer. Gwyn must've made them. She was such a homebody at heart."

Ah, here was an opening that might yield important information. "Too bad she didn't have a family."

Cassandra shrugged. "Neither of us does. We've both been too involved in our careers."

"Gwyn mentioned she followed someone here to the Northwest, but the relationship didn't work out. Still, she stayed and got at job at PNU."

"I don't know much about that." Cassandra sipped her tea. "She was teaching at Caldonia, and being quite a bit younger, I had just started college in Texas. I heard from our parents she was leaving Cal and coming here. When she and I did get together, I asked her what happened to the relationship, but she didn't want to talk about it. So, I dropped the subject, too." She looked away.

"The breakup must have greatly affected her." Could this person be the one to whom Gwyn had dedicated her poetry booklets?

"I suppose. I wish we'd been closer. But with our

age separation and our different interests, well, we just didn't have much in common. Going through her belongings, I feel as though I'm dealing with a stranger."

"I'm glad I could help today, if only for a couple hours."

Cassandra's countenance brightened. "You have been a big help, believe me."

They chatted awhile longer, and then Nina took her leave, loading her box of books into the car. "I'd be glad to come again."

"Thanks, Nina." Cassandra waved from the front door. "I'll keep your offer in mind."

Nina drove away, feeling her mission was a success. Even if the contents of the envelope she took yielded nothing of interest or value, being in Gywn's home gave her a more intimate picture of her former professor. She also had a different opinion of Cassandra, other than the self-important impression the woman gave at the Lit Fest Committee meeting.

Although Nina was an only child, she empathized with the two sisters' estrangement, due both to age separation and different interests. How sad they'd not enjoyed their relationship more. Perhaps if Gwyn had lived, the two would have found a chance in later life for more sisterly intimacy.

Nina turned her thoughts to spending the weekend with Stephen. Although they had activities planned, the matter of Gwyn's death and the upcoming Lit Fest undoubtedly would occupy much of their time. Solving the mystery was still a number one priority. Until she knew the truth, she wouldn't rest.

Chapter Fourteen

At her condo, Nina carried the box of Gwyn's books to the living room, placing it beside the sofa. She wanted to give the books a closer look and, of course, examine the papers in the taped envelope. First, though, she needed a break. Kicking off her shoes, she stretched out on the sofa, resting an arm over her closed eyes. She'd barely drifted off when her phone chimed. Sitting up, she saw, not surprisingly, the caller was Stephen. She quickly connected their video chat.

"How was your visit with Cassandra?" he asked.

"Good. I feel I know her better now. I brought home books from Gwyn's collection and other stuff to go through." She gestured toward the box at her feet. "What about you?"

Stephen held up his notebook. "I have info to share about Alexander Brightly."

"Ah, you checked him out."

He nodded. "As promised."

"We'll have a lot to talk about tomorrow night." The prospect of being together brought a smile to her lips.

"Looking forward to being with you." One eyebrow peaked. "Oh, what about dinner?"

She'd been so busy with Lit Fest she hadn't given thought to the menu. "I'll fix something. Maybe not as elaborate as your meals, but…"

He held up a hand. "Hey, I love your cooking. Have I ever complained?"

She tilted back her head and laughed. "No, you're too polite."

"The most important thing is our being together."

When the call ended, Nina stared at the empty screen, already missing him. They could be together every night, as he frequently reminded her. But they'd known each other just a little over a year. To her, their relationship had progressed quite a bit, with already spending the weekends together. After enduring two previously failed relationships, she didn't want this one to end badly, too.

She made a toasted cheese sandwich and a cup of tea and sat at the kitchen table where windows overlooked the condo village's spacious courtyard, with paths winding through the gardens. She liked living here, enjoying the coziness of her home, the friendly neighbors, and the hilltop location. But she liked Stephen's home, too. She was comfortable there, as well. She heaved a sigh. Such a problem. Would she ever solve this relationship dilemma?

Finished with her supper and cleaning up the kitchen, she returned to the living room. Time to direct her energies to the mystery. From the box of books, she took Gwyn's *Save* envelope and sat again on the sofa. "Here's hoping," she whispered as she tore the tape from the flap. Reaching inside, she pulled out a handful of papers, with some stapled together and others paper-clipped. A sticky note affixed to the top page immediately caught her attention: *Talk to them about this!*

Further examination revealed the papers were

photocopies of stories for the short story writing class Gwyn taught at Caldonia U. When Nina saw Portia Quinlan's name as the author, she gave a start. Alexander Brightly's Portia? Then she recalled Alexander mentioning he and Portia both were Gwyn's students. The stories had all been awarded A or A+ grades, along with glowing praise. However, each story had parts heavily underlined and with notations such as *Same* and *See p. 15*, or some other page number reference.

Nina frowned. What was this all about? Choosing one of the stories, she settled down to read. The prose was smooth, and the characters were well developed and engaging. She put aside that manuscript and selected another. This time, she focused on the underlined passages. One had the additional note: *Forever Our Spring.* Wasn't that the title of one of Alexander's books?

Nina looked at two other manuscripts and then the last one. The story's setting was a Caribbean island. More perusal brought the realization the plot was very similar to Alexander's latest book, *Island Dreaming.* Sure enough, flipping the pages, she spotted Gwyn's note, *Island Dreaming!*

Had Alexander copied Portia's ideas for his own books, which became bestsellers and brought him fame and fortune? How could he do that without Portia's knowledge?

Nina sat back, deep in thought. What if Portia had allowed Alexander to use her ideas to write the books he published? But, again, why, when he'd sold a story to a magazine that launched his career? Or did he write the initial story? Was that manuscript one of Portia's, too?

Another possible scenario was even more daring. What if, instead of just giving Alexander her ideas, Portia wrote the books and allowed him to claim authorship? What if Alexander Brightly, bestselling author, was just a sham?

Then, when Gwyn happened to sort through manuscripts she'd saved from her classes, she realized the books Alexander claimed to have authored were really Portia's. Nina could imagine the betrayal Gwyn felt upon learning she'd launched the career of a fraud. And then, she'd invited him to be the featured speaker at Lit Fest. Her note *Talk to them about this!* indicated she planned to confront Alexander and Portia with the evidence of their deception.

Had she had the opportunity? If so, what was their response? Had one or the other—or both—murdered Gwyn to silence her? Visualizing such a scenario in the bell tower sent a chill down Nina's spine.

Finally, she returned the stories to the envelope. Hopefully, she would discover more evidence to either prove or disprove her theory. Whatever the outcome, she could now assign a motive to both Alexander and Portia for murdering Gwyn.

Next, she pulled from the box a poetry booklet titled *Always and Forever.* When she discovered the book at Gwyn's and saw underneath the title the initials *T.L.*, she knew she must have it. Could this T.L. be the same person to whom Gwyn dedicated several of her own poetry booklets?

She opened the book and read again the dedication: *Dear Gwyn, the title of this book says it all. T.L.*

Tucked among the pages were several photos, all

showing a young couple in a photo booth. They clowned around, making faces and posturing. In one, they faced each other, nose-to-nose, forehead-to-forehead, while another had their faces scrunched up. All she could discern about the man was he had thick, dark hair and a square, masculine jaw.

Nina turned over the photos, hoping to find defining inscriptions but discovered only the date. After some mental calculations, she determined the photos were probably taken when Gwyn was in graduate school. She looked at the pictures again, focusing on the one featuring their profiles. Something about the man looked familiar. His straight nose? His high forehead? Had she seen him before? Certainly not when he was this young age, but perhaps as an older man?

Thinking Gwyn's poetry booklets might contain a clue to his identity, she climbed the stairs to her study and retrieved the books from a desk drawer. She glanced at her worktable where her Lit Fest project waited for completion. Her preoccupation with Gwyn's death and her program had resulted in Nina's neglecting her own presentation. She made a silent promise that this weekend she would remedy the situation. Settling into an overstuffed chair by the window, she took a few moments to admire the setting sun's reflection on the Sound and the town's buildings. Red and yellow leaves from nearby aspen trees also caught the glow.

Then, turning to Gwyn's books, she opened one and read, watching for clues to reveal the mysterious man's identity. Keeping in mind Gwyn tended to be cryptic, she reviewed each poem several times. She'd barely finished the first book when she noticed darkness had fallen. Also, her eyelids fluttered. Better stop and get some much-needed sleep. She wasn't giving up, though. Experience had taught her persistence paid off. Sooner or later—hopefully, sooner—she'd discover the answers to the mystery of Gwyn's death.

****

Friday at Seaview Library was especially busy. A new order of books arrived, which needed to be added to the collection. A group of realtors held a meeting in the conference room, and a preschool teacher brought in her class for a story hour. Not that Nina minded any of the activity. She loved her job and thrived on being busy. After her deep involvement in Lit Fest—and the mystery—focusing on her job at the library offered a welcome change.

Her tasks were confined to business hours, however, and when her time elapsed, she left the job behind and went home. Tonight, Stephen was coming to spend the weekend. She looked forward to being with him again and sharing all she'd found out about Gwyneth. Also, he promised to tell her the results of his research on Alexander Brightly.

"This clam chowder is excellent," Stephen announced later that evening.

Sitting across the kitchen table, she raised an eyebrow. "Probably because I used your recipe."

He laughed. "Okay, maybe the chowder tastes different because I'm eating it here instead of at my house."

She batted her eyelashes. "Or maybe you're just trying to get in good with the cook?"

He smiled and winked. "Could be."

The banter lasted through the meal and the kitchen cleanup. Then Stephen hung up his dishtowel and brushed together his hands. "Now, down to business. We have a lot to discuss tonight."

A few minutes later, sitting next to him on the living room's sofa, Nina pointed toward the envelope he'd earlier placed on the coffee table. "Your turn first. What did you find out about Alexander?"

Stephen picked up the envelope and pulled out a sheaf of papers. "I think you'll find his history very interesting. You can study the report in depth later, but here are the highlights." He pointed toward one of the papers. "As you know, Alexander was Gwyn's student in a short story writing class at Caldonia U. He turned in a story she thought had promise. She recommended he send it to *Upcroft*, the prestigious literary journal. He did, and they published it. That's pretty much the official word on him, isn't it?"

She nodded. "Your version matches what he told me."

"Okay, so, here's what's under that layer. First of all, Alexander's birth name is Axel Elwood."

"Axel?" Nina giggled.

Stephen held up a hand. "Truth. He was a football jock in high school and went to Caldonia on a scholarship. The hoped-for pro career tanked when he sustained a knee injury freshman year and was sidelined. Although he recovered, he never regained his status on the team."

"The setback must have been a terrible disappointment. How did he end up in a writing class?"

Stephen rubbed his chin. "He probably needed an English credit. Anyway, Gwyn took a liking to him and became his mentor." He pulled more papers from the envelope. "Here are some photos from Caldonia yearbooks that might be of interest."

The first picture showed Alexander dressed in his football uniform, assuming the classic pose with feet spread and football helmet tucked under an arm. Another showed him as a Zeta Mu Nu pledge. Still another was his senior portrait.

"I see he's Axel in all of these photos." Nina held up the pictures.

"Right. He didn't change his name until he became an author. Probably the publisher's idea, or his agent's."

"All this is very interesting and relates to something I found at Gwyn's house yesterday." Nina reached into the box sitting beside the sofa and retrieved the envelope containing Portia's stories. She sat back and shared them with Stephen.

Stephen gave a low whistle. "Wow, this discovery moves both of them up on your suspect list."

"It does. But I won't breathe a word of this to anyone, and I know you won't, either."

He raised a hand. "Of course not. But I'll continue to dig around and see if I find anything that might support your theory." Stephen stuffed the papers and photos into the envelope. "Tell me more about your visit to Gwyn's house."

Nina supplied details of her trip, describing Gwyn's cottage, sorting her book collection, and visiting with Cassandra Lightship.

"Find anything of interest besides the stories?" Stephen sat back and folded his arms.

"I did." Reaching again into the box, she pulled out the poetry booklet. "Remember those booklets of Gwyn's dedicated to a T.L.? Well, here's one from T.L.

to her." She handed him the book.

Stephen spent a few minutes examining the poems and then looked up.

"What do you think?" Nina leaned forward, eager to hear his opinion.

"Lots of clichés." He pointed toward a page. "*Your smile sparkles like a diamond*?" He flipped to another page. "*You're the cream in my coffee*?"

"Maybe because Gwyn was a poet, he wanted to impress her by being one. Too bad he wasn't more original."

"Too bad we don't know who he is."

"Maybe we do. I found photos in the book." She retrieved the pictures and held them out. "Here, take a look."

Stephen studied the photos and then shook his head. "I don't know this guy, but I'll do more research on Gwyn and her time at Caldonia, when she was a student and later a teacher. Hopefully, T.L. will turn up somewhere."

Nina leaned back against the cushions and heaved a deep sigh. "Everything I've discovered has possibilities, but nothing leads to a definite conclusion."

He patted her shoulder. "*Yet*. I have faith in you."

"Thanks, Stephen." She gave him a warm smile. "I've spent a lot of time on the mystery, but as you know, I won't rest until I find the answers."

"Right, and I'm glad to help. But now, there are two other people who need our attention."

She wrinkled her brow. "Really? Who?"

He grinned. "You and me." Reaching out, he pulled her into his arms and kissed her.

Stephen's kiss made her forget everything else, and

when it ended, she settled against his shoulder, content just to be there beside him and enjoy their time together.

****

On Saturday, while Stephen took care of business at the newspaper, Nina dove into preparing her lecture, making notes and gathering photos and other visuals for her slideshow presentation. That evening, she and Stephen joined his photographer, Earl, and his wife, Beverly, for dinner at Runyon's and then a movie at the Crest Theater.

Sunday morning found Nina and Stephen with Jessica and Joe, playing golf at Joe's club. Afterward, the group went to the clubhouse bar, selecting a window table overlooking the course.

Jessica turned toward Nina. "How's your investigation into Gwyneth's death coming along?"

"I've been wondering, too, Nina." Joe put down his glass and looked at her. "Have you learned anything more about her?"

"I visited her home the other day." Nina told them about her trip.

"What about the notebook of hers you found in the bell tower?" Jessica reached for the bowl of assorted nuts, added some to her napkin, and then passed the bowl to Joe. "Are you learning anything from it?"

Nina sipped her wine. "I found a poem that might relate to what happened, if I can figure out the meaning. I also plan to give the entries more study."

"I suppose you have a suspect list?" Joe passed the bowl to Stephen.

Nina nodded. "I do, and at this point nearly everyone connected with her is on it. How about you,

Joe?"

Joe sat back and raised his hands. "Don't look at me. I never knew the lady. Now, there's only one lady in my life." Smiling, he tipped his head toward Jessica.

"Awww, you're so sweet." Jessica leaned against his shoulder.

Nina hid a smile. They were a cute couple, and she was glad her grandmother had him as her companion.

"Speaking of suspects," Stephen said, "and Alexander Brightly in particular, isn't that his publicist?" He nodded toward a table across the room.

Turning, Nina glimpsed a woman typing on a laptop. Dark hair pulled away from her face revealed a familiar snub nose and rounded chin. "Why, yes, she's Portia Quinlan. What's she doing here—and by herself?"

"Only you can find out." Stephen laid a hand on her arm.

"Go for it." Jessica waved in Portia's direction.

"I think I will." Nina rose and headed toward the woman, quickly closing the gap between them. Portia's back was toward her, and over her shoulder Nina glimpsed the computer screen. A couple more steps and she would be close enough to make out the words.

Just then, Portia turned. "Nina!" In one swift gesture, she closed the computer's cover and folded her arms over the top.

What was Portia hiding? "Sorry, Portia. I didn't mean to startle you. I saw you sitting here and wanted to say hello. I'm with Stephen Kraslow—I think you've met him—and my grandmother and her friend." She pointed toward the others.

They all smiled and waved.

Portia nodded in return.

"You're busy, and I didn't mean to interrupt." Nina gestured toward the computer.

"I'm working on promo copy for Alexander. He's here with the mayor and his wife. They're out there somewhere." Portia tipped her head toward the window overlooking the course.

"You don't play golf?"

"I do, but I have a deadline." Portia tapped her pink-painted fingernails on the laptop's cover.

"You do a lot for Alexander." Hoping to learn something of importance to the mystery, Nina needed to keep the conversation going.

Portia lifted her chin. "Promoting him is my job."

"You've known him since college…"

The woman's eyes narrowed. "How do you know that?"

"Why, he told me you both were in Gwyneth's short story writing class."

Her eyebrows peaked. "Oh? What else did he tell you about us?"

"Just that she encouraged him to send his story to a magazine, which launched his career. Do you still write?"

"Just for Alexander—his promo stuff… Oh, look, there he is now. Alex, over here!" Portia straightened and waved.

Nina looked around to see Alexander, Mayor Fitzpatrick Heyden, and his wife, Tonya, enter the bar. With his coal-black hair and mustache and her brilliant red lipstick and high-piled blonde hair, the mayor and Tonya made a striking couple. As the group approached, Alexander's gaze lighted on Nina. "Well, look who's here. I didn't know you played golf, Nina."

"I do, on occasion." She greeted the mayor and his wife. "I'm here with Stephen Kraslow and my grandmother and her friend."

"I'd like to meet them," Alexander said. "Join us. We're staying for a drink, aren't we?" He looked toward the couple.

Mayor Heyden nodded. "Of course. We need to relax after that workout." He put an arm around his wife's shoulder. "Right, honey?"

Tonya flashed a smile. "You're always right, Fitz." She turned toward Nina. "Do ask your group to join us."

Nina returned to her table and issued the invitation.

"Sure," Stephen said. "Why not?"

Jessica nodded. "I'd like to meet this Alexander guy."

"Me, too," Joe echoed.

In the shuffle to claim seats, Nina expected Alexander to sit next to her. Instead, without so much as casting her a glance, he pulled out a chair and motioned toward Jessica. "How about this lovely lady sitting by me?"

Jessica sent a wink in Nina's direction and then smiled at Alexander. "Why, thank you, Mr. Brightly."

He waved a hand. "Call me Alexander, please."

Nina inwardly rolled her eyes.

After a waiter took their drink orders, Alexander quickly became the center of attention, telling one amusing story after another. When one particular tale brought a chorus of laughter, Nina happened to glance at Portia. Instead of laughing, she sat with her mouth turned down. Was she unhappy because she wanted to be more than his employee? What exactly was their relationship, anyway? Had she really been writing promo copy for Alexander when Nina first approached? Or something else?

Chapter Fifteen

After spending time with Alexander and his group, Nina and Stephen returned with Joe and Jessica to Marley Manor. In Jessica's apartment, Nina helped her grandmother make tea and arrange her home-baked brownies on a plate. She and Jessica carried the refreshments to the living room where they joined Joe and Stephen.

After a few minutes discussing the golf game, Nina turned toward Jessica. "What did you think of Alexander? He sure gave you a lot of attention."

Jessica sipped her tea. "Good thing I'm not twenty, um, better make that *forty,* years younger. I might fall for his line, which, I must add, was mostly about him— how he just loves our little town and how our golf course is one of the best ever." She pursed her lips and shook her head.

"Good to hear you weren't taken in, Jessica. I was worried." The corners of Joe's lips twitched.

Jessica lightly slapped his shoulder. "Uh-huh. What about you and Miss what's-her-name? Portia?"

Joe shook his head. "For a PR person, she was kinda sulky."

"I think she's upset with Alexander." Nina reached for another brownie. "They were at odds with each other the day I met him for lunch, too."

"Did you find out why she didn't play golf with the

others?" Stephen asked.

Nina finished a bite of the brownie, savoring the rich, chocolate flavor. "She said she had work to do. She didn't want me to see what it was, either, because when she realized I was behind her, she closed the laptop." Nina knitted her brow.

Jessica shook a forefinger. "Those two have secrets."

Stephen looked at his wristwatch. "I see it's almost time for dinner, but first, how about showing us your new boxes, Joe?" He turned toward the other man.

Joe snapped his fingers. "I almost forgot. Yes, I have new work I want you to see." Rising, he went to a nearby table and returned with a large cardboard box. Lining the inside were his wooden boxes, each with a carving on the lid. He unloaded them onto the coffee table.

Nina put down her cup and leaned to view Joe's wooden boxes.

Joe handed her one of the boxes. "What do you think of this?"

Nina focused on the lid's carving of a cardinal poised on a branch. "Very nice." She opened the box to find a velvet insert covering the bottom. As she handed back the box, she noticed one with a wide-centered flower encircled with narrow petals. "That looks like a sunflower."

"It sure is." Joe grinned and handed her the box.

"I love this one. Sunflowers are my favorite." She looked up just in time to see Joe aim a wink at Stephen. "What?" She looked from one to the other.

Joe waved a hand. "Oh, just that Stephen was helping me with ideas the other day."

"Are you thinking of learning to carve, too?" she asked Stephen.

He shrugged. "Maybe. I don't have the talent this guy has, though." He nodded toward Joe.

"These are all beautiful," she said, after examining the others. "Are you making them for another show?"

Joe nodded and straightened a row of the boxes. "This is the season for craft shows. I have one scheduled at the Richmond Senior Center and another at a local church."

After admiring Joe's boxes, Nina and the others went to the first floor dining room for the Sunday buffet. Pumpkins and autumn leaves backlit with yellow and orange lights gave the room a warm glow.

The servers filled the buffet table with prime rib, chicken, grilled salmon, and a variety of vegetables.

Delicious aromas filled the air. So many choices. Soon, however, her plate filled, she followed the others to their reserved table. Jessica's friends were already there. Nina and Stephen slipped into seats beside Selma Belari and Mabel Whiteside, while Jessica and Joe sat across from Lily Ciliano and Wally Anders.

Conversation skipped from the morning's golf game, to Lily's and Wally's visits with their relatives, to Selma's and Mabel's book club. During a lull, Lily leaned in Nina's direction. "Do you have the mystery solved yet?"

Nina sighed and shook her head. "I'm still working on the solution."

"That reminds me." Selma touched a napkin to her lips. "We found out who donated your professor's poetry booklet to the bazaar."

Nina looked up. "You did? Who?"

"Doris Dilmar." Selma turned toward Jessica. "You know her, Jessica. She lives on six and paints all those lampshades."

Jessica spread butter on her roll. "She sold a lot of those at the bazaar."

"I should learn to paint lampshades." Lily turned toward Wally. "What do you think?"

"Whatever you want to do is fine with me, hon." Wally patted her shoulder.

"Tell me more about Doris." Nina looked from Selma to Mabel.

"I'll let her tell you about herself." As she leaned forward, Selma's topknot shifted. "Here she comes now… Oh, Dorrr-iss!"

A tall, thin woman passing by looked around. Her brown bangs swirled over her high forehead. Dark pencil outlined her eyes, and pink lipstick created lips larger than they actually were. Her powder-blue sweater made a nice contrast to her navy slacks.

Mabel waved. "Come on over."

Doris returned Mabel's wave and made her way to the table.

The Marley Manor folks all exchanged greetings.

"This is my granddaughter, Nina Foster, and her friend, Stephen Kraslow," Jessica told Doris.

"Pleased to meet you both." Doris smiled and nodded.

"Doris, dear," Mabel said, "they want to know about the book."

"Book?" Doris's brow wrinkled. "Oh, yes, the poetry booklet I donated to the bazaar."

"Can you join us?" Stephen stood and pulled out a vacant chair.

Doris consulted her wristwatch. "For a few minutes. I'm meeting Casper for pinochle, and he's a fanatic about starting on time."

"We won't keep you long." Nina sent her a friendly smile.

Doris took the seat Stephen offered. "What did you want to know?"

Nina leaned toward Doris, catching a whiff of her lilac-scented perfume. "Where did you get the booklet?"

"I took a class in poetry writing Gwyneth Miller taught at the Richmond Senior Center. At the end of the session, she gave us each a copy. I just loved her. She was fun and bright and so, so generous." Doris clasped her hands. "I never would have given away her gift, but somehow, I ended up with two copies. I decided to donate one so someone else could enjoy her poems. I'm glad you found the book, Nina. I'm sure it will be a keepsake."

"Thank you, Doris," Nina said. "I am so pleased to have it. But did she happen to reveal the identity of the person in the dedication? T.L.?"

Doris laughed. "Oh, yes. She was quite open about the initials."

Nina held her breath. Was she about to learn the mysterious T.L.'s identity at last?

"The initials stand for True Love." Doris looked around the group. "Clever, don't you think?"

Nina expelled her breath and let her shoulders sag. She'd been so sure the initials were for a name.

"What?" Lily's eyes widened. "Not a person?"

"Apparently not." Doris shrugged. "No one thought to ask. But I'm so glad I took her course and so, so sad about what happened at the bell tower."

Nina gave a solemn nod. "We all are."

A silent moment followed, and then Doris straightened. "Well, I'd better get to our pinochle game. Casper and I have a bet going, and I want to win."

"Will we see you two at Monday Movie Night?" Selma asked. "The film is a Bogart and Hepburn."

Doris pushed back her chair and stood. "Oh, I love them. Yes, please save us seats."

After Doris left, the talk turned to movies. Nina joined in as best she could, given her preoccupation with Doris' news about the initials T.L.

Eventually, Nina and Stephen also took their leave, returning to Nina's condo.

"Busy day." Stephen hung his and Nina's coats in the hall closet. Then he approached her, grasping her shoulders. "But I can see your mind is still working."

She nodded and ran a hand over her forehead. "I do have a lot of new information to process, but if you want to kick back and watch some TV, I'll join you."

He slowly shook his head. "Uh-uh. Neither of us could focus."

"So…I could get my notes on the case." She raised an eyebrow.

He laughed. "Go, while I make coffee."

Fifteen minutes later, Nina settled beside him on the living room sofa. Mugs of steaming coffee sat on the coffee table.

Opening her laptop, Nina brought up the file on Gwyn. "I need to add what you found out about Alexander's background." She typed while she spoke. "I'm adding the big question, *What is going on between him and Portia?*"

Stephen rubbed his chin. "Hmm, I'd say she wants to be more than his employee. She's had a crush on him since college, but he's busy being Mr. Big Writer. She keeps hoping he'll eventually fall in love and promote her to Wife-of-Mr.-Big-Writer."

Stephen's humor brought a smile. "Could be. Or else the dissention has to do with the stories Portia authored that I found in Gwyn's office."

"Here's an idea." Stephen raised a forefinger. "What if, instead of swiping her ideas, he wrote those stories for her to put her name on? Then he wanted to use them for books."

Nina gave Stephen's suggestion some thought. "I suppose that could be the case. I'll add your idea to my notes."

"Whatever, I think you're on the right track about the two of them having an odd relationship. Maybe Gwyn noticed, too. Did she write about them in her journal?"

"Not that I've found so far. But, like the poem I read to you, she doesn't name names."

"Right. We learned that tonight from Doris' revelation about T.L."

Nina typed another sentence and then sat back. "Her news came as a disappointment. I was so sure the initials stood for a person."

"Even though they don't, the booklet from T.L. indicates a relationship with someone."

"I agree." Nina picked up the poetry booklets from the coffee table. They numbered five in all, four written by Gwyn and one by someone who, at this point, remained anonymous. She opened one of Gwyn's books and turned to the first page. "This dedication is just to T.L." She examined the next book. "So is this one."

"Which could be the generic True Love."

A check of the other two books revealed *My T.L.* in both. "Here, My True Love indicates a specific person." Nina showed Stephen the inscription.

He shrugged. "Maybe. But, without knowing the person's identity, we're back to square one."

"So frustrating." Nina ran a hand through her hair. Then, sorting the pile on the coffee table, she located the photos from the booklet she found in Gwyn's desk drawer. "I wish I knew this guy's identity." She studied the pictures, turning them this way and that. "Hmmm, maybe he's Desmond Desoto. They both have a high forehead and a long, thin nose." She passed the photos to Stephen.

He studied them and then looked up. "I've seen DeSoto only at the Marley craft show, but I suppose this younger man could be him."

Nina's thoughts spun. "What if he and Gwyn knew each other when they attended college? What if he's the one she followed here? He married someone else, but they found themselves working together and eventually began an affair. I do recall seeing them together a few times when I was a student. So then his wife found out and—"

"Decided to get rid of her rival, once and for all." Stephen's brows knit.

"Well, what's wrong with that scenario?" Nina threw up her hands.

"Ah, how about evidence?"

Nina put a finger to her lips. "I'm hoping evidence will be found in the bell tower. I planned to visit there again, anyway, before the Lit Fest program. I'll also see what I can find out about Desmond's past, including where he went to undergraduate school."

"I'll match you on that. I might turn up something not so public. And don't forget, I want to be with you when you go again to the tower."

"Okay, but I'll need Admin's permission."

Stephen handed her the photos. "Tell them I'm helping you with your setup."

"Good idea. I hope it works." Nina tucked the pictures into the booklet and added it to the others.

"What else is on your agenda?" Stephen asked.

"Lit Fest Committee meeting tomorrow. I want to visit Cara, too. I'm worried about her. I still think she knows more than she's told me, but she's defensive when I probe."

Stephen's brow wrinkled. "Do you think her boyfriend, Diego, might be mixed up in Gwyn's death?"

"I don't know. I hope not. So far, I feel as though I'm on a treadmill, working hard but getting no closer to the truth."

He put both arms around her and drew her close. "Hey, now, I guarantee that, eventually, you will know the truth. I have faith in you. So do a lot of other people."

Being sheltered in his arms and hearing his words of encouragement soothed Nina, but, still, doubt persisted. Would all the clues eventually fit together to reveal the truth? Or would she fail and Gwyn's murderer remain forever free?

Chapter Sixteen

The next morning, Nina once again drove out of town, first along the highway and then the secondary road leading to PNU and today's Lit Fest Committee meeting. Upon entering Bannon Hall's Faculty Room, she found the members already assembled, drinking coffee and eating doughnuts. She made a cup of tea and looked around for Desmond, intending to study him—surreptitiously, of course—to determine whether or not he was the young man in the photo booth with Gwyn. Ah, there he was, in conversation with Ambrose, doing most of the talking, as usual. His back was to her. Wanting to see his profile, she sidled around a couple chairs and craned her neck.

"Whatcha looking at?"

Nina gave a start and turned to find Jaz standing behind her. Nina waved a hand and thought fast. "Ah, just enjoying the sunshine beaming through the window. Autumn is such a beautiful season, don't you think?"

Jaz grimaced. "Yeah, when it's not raining. I knew when I moved here that it rains a lot, and I've already worn out several raincoats. I sure hope we have nice weather for Lit Fest."

"Me, too." Thankful to have successfully diverted Jaz's attention from her apparently blatant staring, Nina expelled a relieved breath.

"Time to start our meeting, everyone." Vivian's command boomed throughout the room.

"C'mon, let's sit." Jaz motioned toward the table.

So much for her plan to check out Desmond. Oh, well, she'd get a good look at him when they all sat. But that idea didn't work, either, because he took a seat at the opposite end of the table, next to Eldon, who with his bulk overshadowed him. Nina wished she dared take a picture of Desmond, but that was out of the question.

"We're coming down to the wire, so to speak." Vivian's gaze swept the group. "Just a couple more weeks until the big event, and we still have a lot to accomplish, as you can see by today's agenda." She tapped her paper with a forefinger.

"To match clichés, I'd say this is quite a laundry list." Desmond smirked.

Ambrose chuckled behind his hand. "We'd better get a move on."

Eldon turned toward Desmond. "There's another book idea for you, Des. You could title it *Clichés Are Us*."

Vivian frowned. "Okay, enough clowning around—"

That response brought roars of laughter from everyone, Nina included.

"Stop, please." Vivian held up a hand.

The laughter finally faded away.

Vivian cleared her throat. "The first item on our agenda is your venue assignments. A student assistant will help each of you set up equipment and troubleshoot any problems. You will meet him or her at the location sometime this week for a preliminary run-through."

Nina's assignment was a room in Bannon Hall, and she was to meet her student assistant there tomorrow afternoon. The bell tower was not listed. Was she on her own for that program? She hoped so. Then she could have Stephen help her.

"Don't forget the reception for Lit Fest participants and their guests this Saturday night, at President Olivera's home." Vivian beamed a smile around the table. "The occasion promises to be very festive."

Jaz raised a hand. "Does that mean we have to dress up?"

" 'Dress up'?" Desmond leaned forward and wrinkled his nose. "What does that mean these days?"

"You can use your own judgment," Vivian said. "But if you've been to Hollis and Mitchell's home, you know it's elegant. I wouldn't show up in jeans and a sweatshirt. Now, I'd like to hear a progress report from each of you."

Nina's turn came last. "I have all the authors and their books selected, but I still have work to do on the script."

"Maybe you shouldn't have taken on Gwyn's program." Eldon leaned around Jazmine to frown at Nina.

"We told you your program for Gwyneth was totally unnecessary," Desmond added.

Nina opened her mouth to defend herself but then decided not to encourage what would no doubt turn into an argument. She looked toward Vivian, expecting her to come to her defense.

However, the chairperson was busy writing on her agenda. When she finally finished, she looked up. "All right, everyone, it's time to—"

"Call it a day?" Eldon hid a snicker behind a hand.

Everyone laughed, even Vivian.

When the meeting was over, and the others were on their way out, Vivian beckoned to Nina. "Can you stay, please? I need to talk to you."

About the bell tower, she'd bet. "All right."

Sure enough, once the door closed on the last person and Vivian had delivered a few stray cups to the refreshment cart, she turned to Nina. "How was your visit to the bell tower? I didn't want to ask in front of the group. Such a touchy subject."

Nina strove to choose her words carefully. "Well, I familiarized myself with the tower layout. I climbed to the top and checked out where to put my equipment."

Vivian's brows drew together. "You were comfortable there?"

Nina turned up a hand. "As much as could be expected, given what happened to Gwyn."

"Did you...find anything?" Vivian turned away and stacked a few of the cups.

"Find anything? Like what?" Why was Vivian so curious about her visit?

"Anything of Gwyn's." Vivian shrugged. "I know the authorities searched the tower after her fall, but..."

No use avoiding the question any longer. "I did find something—a notebook of Gwyn's was stuck in the stairs' framework."

Vivian turned back to Nina, her eyes wide. "That pink book she carried everywhere?"

Nina nodded. "Her poetry journal."

"Do you still have it?" Vivian's tone rose a notch.

"I took the book with me when I went to visit Cassandra." Although her response was true, it was not the entire story. "Is there something particular of Gwyn's you want me to look for the next time I visit the tower?"

"Ah, no." Vivian waved a hand then studied her. "Won't the next time be the Lit Fest presentation?"

"I need to return once more before that." Anticipating Vivian's disapproval, she hurried on. "I've made arrangements with Wildon, the maintenance man. He was most cooperative and helpful."

Vivian frowned. "All right. I'll just be glad when you're safely on the ground to stay."

"Please don't worry, Vivian. I'll be very careful." Nina spoke the words sincerely.

A few minutes later, as Nina walked along the hallway toward the stairs, mulling over her conversation with Vivian, Desmond DeSoto suddenly appeared at her side. She expected him to give her no more than a cursory nod, but instead, he slowed and fell into step. "We didn't hear your report on the bell tower." He leaned to peer at her.

"The tower wasn't on the list. Perhaps Vivian just forgot. She has a lot to do, now she's our chairperson."

"Pssht! We're all extremely busy. So, what did you find in the tower?"

As she had with Vivian, Nina chose her words carefully. "The tower is very clean and well-maintained. Having Gwyn's program there shouldn't be a problem."

He flattened his lips. "I didn't say *how* did you find the tower, I asked, *what* did you find?"

Nina frowned. "I'm not sure I understand. Do you mean like the tables and chairs? The bell?"

"Of Gwyn's!" His voice rose a notch.

There, she'd made him admit what she surmised was his interest. Although she told Vivian of her find, she balked at telling Desmond. She wasn't sure why. Perhaps his rude manner put her off. Or their past history made her reluctant to share her discovery. "Ah, none of her equipment." Spotting the turnoff to the elevator, she headed in that direction. She'd planned to take the stairs, but the elevator offered a better escape—as long as he didn't follow her there, too.

She reached the elevator just as it stopped. The door swished open, and several people poured out. Nina rushed past them into the now vacant car. Turning, she punched the first floor button.

Just before the door closed, Desmond ran up and waved. "We haven't finished our discussion!"

Pasting a smile on her lips, she shrugged and returned his wave. Once the doors closed, she breathed a sigh of relief. My, but he was pushy. But, then, wasn't that how she remembered him? Pushy, bossy, arrogant, and egotistical, he really hadn't changed much in the ten years since she'd been his student.

Why had he asked if she found anything in the tower? Did he know about Gwyn's notebook? Probably. Gwyn made no effort to conceal it, and no doubt, most of her associates knew of its existence. Did he suspect she wrote something about him? About their affair—if they indeed had one. Nina must study the book. For all she knew, the pages were full of secrets disguised in Gwyn's cryptic verse.

Nina exited the elevator on the first floor, worrying she was all too obvious in her evasion of DeSoto's questioning. He might be self-absorbed, but he was no dummy. He would see through her vague answers to his questions and know she hid something.

Nearly everyone she encountered wanted to know what she experienced in the bell tower. Were they exhibiting only a natural curiosity? Or did they all have an ulterior motive? Surely not. She wished she knew who was only curious and who might have some other reason for inquiring.

Nina stepped outside into the bright autumn sunshine. Now, on to her appointment with Cara. The young woman had a break between classes and had agreed to meet Nina at the StuU. Here was another situation in which she had to be careful. She truly wanted to be friends with Cara and was concerned about her, yet her involvement in Gwyn's death prompted Nina to probe for information on that subject.

Nina strolled along the sidewalk, heading for the StuU. What a beautiful day. Not for the first time did she wish she were here under different circumstances, without the weight of Gwyn's death on her shoulders. She reminded herself that she was the one who took on the burden. No one told her she had to investigate. She thought ahead to how satisfied she would feel when she had solved the mystery. With that in mind, she quickened her steps.

As she passed the bell tower, she couldn't resist gazing first at the clock and then at the window and the bell. Today, glowing in the sunlight, the tower certainly didn't appear an evil place. Then she recalled being inside, surrounded by the stone walls, and then the panic, even though short-lived, of being imprisoned. The tower harbored secrets, not only Gwyn's but also others' as well.

I'll discover your secrets. She set her steps toward

the StuU and her meeting with Cara.

****

As always, the StuU was a busy place, not only as a haven for food and drink but also for meetings and individual study. Nina joined the stream of people gaining entrance through the double doors and stepped into the bright interior. She gazed around for Cara, thinking they might arrive simultaneously, but the young woman was not in sight.

Nina entered the cafe and again searched for Cara. When she didn't see her seated at a table or standing in line for a beverage, Nina joined the line herself. A few minutes later, balancing a tray holding a cup of tea and a paper plate with a sweet roll, she found a vacant table near the window overlooking the courtyard. She'd been seated only long enough for a couple sips of tea and a bite of the roll when she spotted Cara standing near the door talking to Diego. She hoped he didn't plan to join them. She wanted to visit with Cara alone, without the young man's interference.

Cara looked around, caught Nina's eye, and waved.

Nina smiled and returned the gesture.

Diego's gaze landed on Nina, too, and he frowned. Placing a hand on Cara's shoulder, he whispered in her ear, then turned and left.

Nina exhaled a relieved breath.

A few moments later, Cara reached the table. She put down her cup, pulled out a chair, and sat. Unwrapping the plaid scarf from around her neck, she shrugged out of her tan jacket, spreading it on the back of her chair. An orange sweater and dark brown slacks completed her outfit. "Sorry I'm late." Her brow wrinkled, and her mouth turned down.

Nina fluttered her fingers in a dismissive gesture. "Not a problem. I've been here only a couple minutes myself."

Cara's gaze strayed to where she had stood with Diego.

"Did Diego want to join us?" Nina sipped her tea, looking at Cara over the rim of the cup.

"Oh, no. He's meeting friends for a workout at the gym."

Nina tilted her head and studied Cara. "You look like you're feeling better." True, but not much better. Her eyes looked tired, with drooping lids and circles underneath.

Cara's brow wrinkled. "I am, a little. I have to get my mind back on my studies."

"What classes are you taking?"

"I'm majoring in Education." Cara's smile added brightness to her face. "I want to teach primary grades. I'm looking forward to your Lit Fest presentation on children's literature. Books and storytelling will be a big part of my teaching."

Pleased to find something in common, Nina named a few authors she would feature in her talk. She discovered she and Cara both were only children and that while growing up, reading occupied much of their time. They had favorite authors in common, too.

After a while, Cara looked at her wristwatch. "Oh, I've got to go. Almost time for my next class."

Nina nodded and took a last sip of tea. "I'm on duty at my library this afternoon, so I need to be on my way, too. I'm so glad to see you today and know you're feeling better."

Cara picked up her purse. "I liked getting together,

too, Nina. I'll have to tell Diego he was wrong."

Nina drew back and frowned. "Wrong? What about?"

"He said you just wanted to pick my brain about the bell tower and Professor Miller."

Why was Diego so concerned about her motives? "Is there a reason we shouldn't talk about what happened?"

Cara looked away. "Ah, no... He just doesn't want me to be upset."

Nina couldn't resist taking advantage of the opening Cara provided. "Have you had any more thoughts about the person you saw running away that night? Or thought you saw?"

Cara's lips pursed, and her eyelids lowered. "N-no."

Nina would bet Cara was lying. But if she pressed the issue, this meeting—that so far had been pleasant—might end on a negative note. She didn't want to alienate Cara when they were on their way to becoming friends. "Well, if you know or recall something you feel is important and want to talk to someone, I hope you'll call on me."

Cara looked up, meeting Nina's gaze. "But I don't know if I can trust you."

Cara's blunt statement hurt Nina. "All I can do is assure you that you can. I'm good at keeping confidences. I also have the feeling the truth is as important to you as it is to me. Am I right?"

Pushing back her chair, Cara stood. "I have to go. Really."

Nina slung her purse strap over her shoulder and rose to her feet, as well. "Me, too. But I'm so glad we

Linda Hope Lee

had this visit. I'll be in touch." After parting with Cara, Nina headed for the visitor's parking lot. When she reached her car, she pressed the remote to open the door. As she grasped the door handle, she saw a piece of paper flutter to the ground. At first, she thought the paper just a bit of trash. But then, remembering the other paper stuck in her window, she retrieved it. Sure enough, the paper held another message:

You've been warned. No more tower!

Nina shook her head. Did whoever sent this note— and the first one—really think she would back off so easily? If so, he—or she—was in for a rude awakening. The warnings spurred her on to continue her investigation. Of course, she'd be careful, but she wouldn't stop until she learned the truth.

Nina drove toward Richmond. Who was behind the notes? Today, both Vivian and Desmond wanted to know if she found anything of Gwyn's in the tower. One or the other could be the sender.

Or, how about Diego? Cara's comment he worried about what she might reveal to Nina indicated something important was still being kept secret.

Alexander came to mind. He was quite interested in her tower presentation. Why? Was something hidden there which would incriminate him?

Her suspect list continued to grow. Time grew short, though. Only a few weeks remained until Lit Fest. What if the event came and went without discovering the truth about Gwyn? No, Nina would not even consider failure a possibility.

Chapter Seventeen

Tuesday found Nina once again on the PNU campus, this time to meet with her student volunteer in the room where she would give her presentation. Although not finished preparing her program, she'd made progress during the past few evenings. She was excited about the event and looked forward to sharing her love of children's books with her audience.

Being assigned a room in Bannon Hall pleased her. As an undergraduate, she took many classes in Bannon and felt comfortable there. But, when she opened the door to Room 202 and stepped inside, she stopped and stared. She didn't remember the room being so large. Nearly a hundred seats were arranged amphitheater style. Would her audience fill the room?

Well, this was her assignment, and she'd make the best of the situation. Crossing to the desk, she set her tote next to the lectern. Pushing back her jacket sleeve, she checked her wristwatch. Ten-thirty. Where was her student helper?

"Hey, there, Ms. Foster."

She turned to see a familiar-looking young man wheel in a cart loaded with audio-visual equipment. "Hello. I met you last week at the StuU. You're…Jason…"

"Hopkins. Right. You were with Professor Blanchard." He grinned and ran a hand through his hair.

"I met your father, Lincoln, too. He's on our board of directors."

"Right again." Jason brought the cart to the desk. "I'll get this stuff set up, and you can do a run-through."

Jason was with Diego that day, too, exchanging the secret society's handshake. Plus, he was in the photo in Cara's room, posing with Diego and Benjamin Logarth, who was killed in the car accident and whose medal she found in Gwyneth's journal. Had Benjamin belonged to the secret society, too?

What good luck to have Jason as her assistant. Hopefully, conversation would yield something useful to her investigation. She'd have to be careful, though, not to obviously pump for information.

Jason approached the blackboard and pulled down a screen. "So, how do ya like this room?"

Nina grinned. "I had a debate class here, so the room is familiar, but I didn't remember it being so large."

"I had debate here, too, my freshman year."

"You're a senior now, right? As I recall, you're off to law school after graduation." Nina took her laptop from her tote bag.

"Yeah, law school..." His voice dropped a notch.

She slanted him a glance. "You don't sound very happy about your future plans."

"My dad's happy, and that's what counts...I guess." Jason grabbed a cord and headed toward the wall outlet.

Nina placed her computer on the cart. "What would you rather do?"

"Get me a little farm in eastern Washington. Raise

a few cattle, ride horses…"

"You could be a country lawyer." Nina hoped to be helpful.

"I wish, but Dad's pushing for the big city." Jason plugged in the cord and returned to the cart. "Let me see whatcha got, and we'll make a dry run."

For the next few minutes, Nina watched Jason set up her program. She gave similar sessions at the library, but in these unfamiliar circumstances, she appreciated help. Jason went about the task with a smoothness that spoke of confidence and experience, and the images she chose to illustrate her talk soon flashed on the screen.

Jason laughed at one book cover featuring a cartoon elephant. "Hey, I remember reading that story when I was a kid."

More covers flashed, which prompted more discussion. Conversation ceased when Jason stopped the projector to clean the lens.

Nina took out her notebook and jotted down points she wanted to remember.

"Professor Miller was always writing in her notebook, too."

The unexpected introduction of Gwyneth into the conversation surprised Nina. Did Jason's comment come from an ulterior motive? She glanced at him, but his face was turned away, hiding his expression. "Yes, I remember seeing her notebook often when I was a student. But she wrote poetry, while my notebook serves a more practical purpose."

He turned to look at her. "How'd you like the bell tower? Creepy, huh?"

She didn't bother to ask how he knew about her visit. "The tower might be intimidating at night, but I was there during the day. Have you been inside?"

"Everybody has, at one time or another. Okay, not *everybody*, but whoever wants to go there manages to get inside." He shook his head. "Don't know why they bother to keep the door locked."

"What do you think of the place?"

He shrugged and returned to polishing the projector's lens. "No big deal. But, hey, you climb to the top?"

"I did. That's where I'll broadcast Gwyneth's program. Have you been up that far?" She studied him for clues to his honesty.

He waved a hand. "Of course. You, um, find anything?"

Nina closed her notebook, giving her full attention to their conversation. "I'm not sure what you mean, Jason. Was I supposed to find something, other than what should be in the tower?"

Jason shrugged and bent over the projector. "Just talkin'. A friend of mine says he found some money there."

"Really?" That news surprised Nina. "Was it hidden? Or in plain sight?"

"I don't know. Wasn't much, anyway, but rumor has it there's more."

"Well, I didn't find any money during my visit." Nina was glad she could answer truthfully.

Jason straightened and pointed toward the projector. "Clean lens now. Pictures should be sharp."

From then on, their talk centered on Nina's presentation.

At last, Jason stood back and brushed his hands together. "You're good to go, Ms. Foster."

Nina tucked her laptop into her tote. "Thank you so much for your help, Jason."

"Sure. I'll be on hand for your program, too." He unplugged the equipment and rolled up the cords.

"Great. I'll look forward to seeing you then."

"If you don't need me for anything more, I'll take this stuff back to AV." He waved toward the cart.

"You go ahead. I have a few more details to work out."

Nina waited until Jason left, then she made a sketch of the room, marking where her book cover posters might be displayed. Finally, she turned out the lights and left the room. As she rounded a corner, she approached a classroom where the door stood ajar. Room 230. Desmond DeSoto's. Voices came from within.

"She doesn't know anything, I'm tellin' you."

Jason. Nina stopped and stepped behind the door.

"I don't trust her." A second person's comment drifted into the hallway. "She's so damn nosy. We need to keep her outa there."

Nina's cheeks burned. Were they talking about her?

The speakers drew closer. Uh-oh, were they about to exit the classroom? She looked around. If she ducked behind the door and they saw her when they came out, they would guess she was eavesdropping. Instead, she wheeled around and headed back the way she'd come. The next sound she heard was a door slamming. Without slowing her pace, she glanced over her shoulder. Whew! No sign of anyone, which indicated the two had stayed in the room.

Who was the second speaker? Since the classroom

was Desmond DeSoto's, he was the obvious answer. Still, the voice didn't sound like his. Diego Rivera might have been the one, but she couldn't be certain.

More importantly, were they discussing her? Even if they were, she wouldn't let Jason and his companion deter her. If anything, what she overheard made her even more determined to continue her investigation.

Jason said a friend found money in the tower and more might be hidden. Was that the tower's secret? If so, who owned the money, and how did it become hidden in the tower? Two more questions to be answered. This new possibility made visiting the tower again even more important than before. With time until the festival growing short, she needed to schedule the trip soon.

But what about the warnings to stay away from the tower? Should she heed those? Or forge ahead with her plan?

****

That evening, with much to talk over with Stephen, Nina eagerly awaited his video call.

Soon, his smiling face filled the screen. "I have free time Thursday afternoon. How about giving me a tour of the tower?"

Before responding, Nina considered his request. While she still thought sleuthing alone best, since Stephen would be with her the night of the program, he should familiarize himself with the place beforehand. "All right. Thursday is a good time for me, too. But you should know I received another warning note today." She held up the paper and read the note aloud.

Stephen frowned. "Shouldn't you report the incident to Admin?"

"Under other circumstances, I might. But in this instance, I'm afraid if I do, they'll cancel the program. I can't take the risk, not when I haven't yet solved the mystery. Does my not reporting mean you don't want to go to the tower, after all?"

His frown faded. "Of course not. In fact, I'm more determined than ever."

She gave him a warm smile. "Thanks, Stephen, for your understanding."

"We're in this together, Nina. Anything else new on the mystery?"

Nina settled back on the sofa and rested the phone in her lap. "I had an interesting meeting today with Jason Hopkins, my student volunteer. He asked about my being in the tower and if I found anything."

Stephen chuckled. "I bet you sidestepped the question."

"I did. But he said a friend found money in the tower, and there's supposed to be more."

"Interesting. We'll keep a special eye out on Thursday."

They decided on two o'clock, with plans to stop afterward for dinner.

After ending the call, Nina went upstairs to her study and retrieved Gwyn's pink journal from a desk drawer. Settling in her favorite wingback chair, she opened the book and reviewed the poem she discovered, but with no more understanding than she had on the first read.

Turning the page, she read on. As she previously learned, most entries were fragments consisting of words and phrases that only introduced ideas and imagery. At last, however, she found another completed poem:

A trust betrayed by both of you
Poses the question, what to do?
Keep silent and perpetuate
The lie?
Or blurt the truth and
Destroy the world you built?

Nina reread the poem several times to herself and aloud. Two people betrayed a trust, and now the author of the poem didn't know what to do. Were the words idle imaginings by Gwyn, or something more? Oh, how she wished her teacher were here to shed light on her journal entries. Nina missed her, too; she truly did. She would always regret that after knowing each other as student and teacher, they hadn't had the opportunity to renew their relationship as friends.

Rereading the poem brought no new insights. Best to let the words sink into her mind, and perhaps her subconscious would discover the meaning. For now, she would turn her thoughts to the upcoming trip to the bell tower. Did the tower harbor more secrets? If so, would she and Stephen discover them?

Chapter Eighteen

On Thursday afternoon, following a pleasant drive through the autumn countryside to the PNU campus, Nina and Stephen walked to the bell tower. Ready to explore the structure from top to bottom, Nina wore jeans, a sweatshirt, and sturdy shoes.

Stephen was similarly attired, with the addition of his camera slung over his shoulder. Should anyone inquire, he was covering the festival for *The Richmond Review*.

Reaching the tower's door, Nina stopped and gazed around.

Several students crossing the quad passed by at a distance.

However, no one gave them a glance.

Pulling out the key Wildon gave her, she unlocked the door and, with a deep breath, stepped over the threshold.

Stephen followed and then stopped. "What about the door? Shut? Or open?"

"Wildon said he'd fix the inside handle, but we'll make sure. You stay outside with the key, and I'll see if I can open the door from inside." She handed him the key.

"Good idea." Stephen stepped out and closed the door.

Nina grasped the handle, and when it turned readily

and the door opened, she whispered a silent *thank-you* to Wildon.

Stephen reentered the tower. "Now that issue is settled, what's today's plan?"

Nina swept her gaze over the two tables and several chairs, and the otherwise bare floor and walls. "Everything appears the same as when I was here before." She pointed toward the stairs. "We'll climb to the top and review what I've decided for the presentation."

"I'll take a few pictures, too." Stephen fingered his camera.

Gripping the railing, Nina started up the stairs. Soon the tower walls closed in. Shrugging off a shiver, she pressed on. Would today's visit to the top yield new clues to what happened the night Gwyn took her fatal plunge? Reaching the top at last, she stepped onto the platform underneath the bell.

A moment later, Stephen joined her. "Wow, this bell is huge."

Nina followed his upward gaze. "It is impressive."

"Do you really think Gwyneth rang it before falling from the window?"

"As a desperate call for help? Yes, I think she could have." She pointed toward the rope dangling from the bell's top. "The ringing got attention, but not in time to save her life."

Turning away, Nina approached the window. As she gazed at the impressive view, a brisk autumn breeze cooled her cheeks. In the distance, the mountains stood outlined against the sky, while forests dotted with colorful patches of red, orange, and yellow leaves marched along the foothills.

Stephen stood beside her. "The view is definitely worth the climb." Holding his camera to his eye, he snapped a picture.

After a few moments admiring the view while Stephen took photos, Nina stepped away from the window. "Okay, back to business."

"Right." Stephen captured his last shot and joined her. "Exactly how do you plan to present Gwyn's program?"

"She was scheduled for Sunday afternoon, the last day of the festival. From the information she submitted to Vivian and the committee, I learned Gwyn would stand in the window and talk to the audience assembled below. The only equipment she needed was a microphone and a loudspeaker, to be set up either in the window or on the outside ledge."

Stephen approached the window and leaned out. "Deciding how to place the loudspeaker on the ledge might have resulted in her fall."

"An accidental fall is still a possibility." Seeing his frown, she put out a hand. "But don't worry, I've already decided to mount the loudspeaker inside."

"That's a relief." His frown changed to a smile.

"First, I'll say a few words about her and then read her talk, including the poems she chose. Pretty simple, huh?"

"Yes, but something else bothers me." Stephen raised a hand. "You said she planned to present her program during the day. Why, then, would she come here at night? I'd think she would have plenty of time for day visits to get a feel for the place and decide how to set up her equipment."

"That question occurred to me, too." Nina shook

her head and shrugged.

"Maybe she was meeting someone."

"For a romantic tryst?" Nina laughed. "Hey, I sound like one of her poems. But seriously, if she were murdered, someone else would, of course, be here."

"The murderer could have snuck in after she came. He—or she—crept up the stairs and surprised her." Stephen pointed toward the stairs.

"Or forced her up the stairs at gunpoint." Nina folded her arms.

Stephen's forehead wrinkled. "If that were the case, why didn't she scream or do something else to attract attention?"

"The idea that she planned to meet someone here fits better. Then his or her presence would be no surprise. If only I knew who and why." Nina blew out a breath. "Without knowing the answers to those questions, the theory is useless."

"Lots of possibilities." A moment elapsed, and then Stephen waved a hand. "Okay, on with your program. We need to decide where to set up your equipment."

Nina took out her notebook and, with Stephen's help, made a map showing the placement of her recorder, microphone, and the loudspeaker.

"What else do we need to do today?" Stephen asked, when they had finished.

"Nothing more up here. On the way down, I'll show you where I discovered Gwyn's journal, and we'll keep an eye out for anything I might have missed."

Stepping forward, Stephen took the lead.

When they were halfway to the bottom, Nina stopped. "There's the spot where I found Gwyn's journal." She pointed toward a narrow space between the railing and the stone wall.

Stephen leaned over the railing. "That's another reason why someone might have come here—to steal her book. You've said several people are interested in it."

"Right, but I do have the feeling something more is hidden here in the tower." Nina waved toward the opposite wall.

"Maybe the money your student helper, Jason, mentioned."

"Maybe."

Nina and Stephen continued down the stairs, stopping here and there to examine a crevice or other irregularity in the wall. However, they found nothing. At the bottom, Nina gazed around. "I examined this area, but I'd like to give it another look today."

"Did you search underneath the stairs?" Stephen pointed toward the shadows behind the stairway.

Nina turned to survey the area and then shook her head. "No, I didn't. I'll do that now."

"I'll make sure nothing's hidden on the undersides of the furniture or in the tables' drawers."

Nina ducked underneath the stairs and, with the small flashlight she carried in her purse, searched beneath the steps as well as along the walls. Not finding anything, she joined Stephen, who was on his hands and knees, poking his pocketknife into a crevice between the wall and the stone floor. She bent over him. "What have you found?"

Stephen pulled out his knife and grasped his find between thumb and forefinger. Sitting back, he held up a piece of silver chain.

Nina studied the chain, which appeared about two

inches in length. "That fragment looks like it's from a bracelet or a necklace."

"I agree. Here's part of the clasp." He pointed his knife toward the ring on one end.

"I didn't see this chain when I was here before. Did I just miss spotting it when I searched, or did someone lose it since then?"

Stephen stood and handed her the chain. "It was stuck far enough in the crack to have been there for a while. I'd guess Wildon, or whoever sweeps the floor, didn't see it or did see it and, instead of bothering to pick it up, swept it into the crack."

"Maybe what the piece belongs to is still here."

Nina and Stephen spent the next half hour searching the tower's bottom floor for the missing section of the chain—or anything else that might turn up—but with no success.

"I just thought of something." Nina fingered the chain. "The medal we found in Gwyn's journal has a missing piece. Maybe this is it."

"Could be. We'll compare the two when we return to town. Meanwhile, how about some dinner?" He patted his stomach. "I've worked up an appetite. This sleuthing is hard work."

She laughed. "I agree. Any ideas where we should stop?"

"How about the restaurant at Pine Lake Resort?"

Nina nodded and slipped the chain into a side pocket in her purse. "I've seen their advertising. Let's check it out." Upon leaving the tower, Nina looked around for a familiar face but saw no one she recognized. Still, her failure didn't necessarily mean someone didn't lurk. She wasn't so naïve as to believe the notes warning her to stay away from the tower were a hoax. Until she solved the mystery and laid Gwyn's memory to rest, she needed to be on guard.

****

After traveling several miles and keeping an eye out while Stephen focused on driving, Nina spotted the turnoff to Pine Lake Resort. From there, a winding road led through dense woods that eventually opened to reveal a campground, a dozen or so cabins, and a restaurant with a deck overlooking the lake. A few minutes later, Nina and Stephen were seated at a window table in the dining room. Elevated booths around the room's perimeter offered those diners a view, as well. Enticing aromas drifted from the double doors leading to the kitchen.

Gazing out the window, Nina pointed toward several boats cruising the lake. "This is quite a place."

Stephen nodded. "We'll come here again when we have more time."

"I'd like that." Spending a relaxing afternoon at the resort sounded appealing.

Stephen picked up his menu. "Right now, though, eating dinner is a priority."

"Good idea." Nina took her menu, too, and perused the selections ranging from trout to beef to vegetarian cuisine.

After a few moments, Stephen looked up. "I'm opting for steak and baked potato."

"Sounds good to me, too." Nina closed her menu. After giving her order to the server, she excused herself to find the restroom. The path led her by the cocktail lounge. A cursory glance in the door revealed a semicircular bar, tables in the center, and booths lining the walls.

A few minutes later, on her way back to the table, she heard piano music coming from the lounge. She again stopped and peeked in, thinking she and Stephen might enjoy an after-dinner drink. She was about to turn away and continue on when voices caught her attention:

"Oh, Dezzy, you wouldn't…"

"You bet I would, Viv."

Dezzy? Viv?

Leaning farther into the room, she spotted Vivian and Desmond headed in her direction. Nina blinked and looked again to make sure she wasn't mistaken. But no, despite the room's dim light, the two were definitely her fellow Lit Fest Committee members.

Her first impulse was to step into the shadows so they would pass by with seeing her. But, on second thought, why should she avoid them? She had nothing to hide. But perhaps they did, and if so, she wanted to see their reaction when confronted. Nina stepped into the doorway just as Vivian and Desmond were about to leave. "Oops, sorry!" She stopped short of bumping into them, peering first at one then at the other. "Vivian? Desmond?"

"Nina?" Vivian squinted and leaned forward.

"Who?" Desmond dropped an arm from around Vivian's shoulders. "Oh, it's you. Nina Foster. What are you doing here?"

"My friend, Stephen, and I visited the bell tower today, and…"

"You went up in that tower again?" Desmond scowled.

"Honestly, Nina, wasn't one time enough?" Vivian's lips twisted.

"Then we stopped here for dinner." Nina folded her arms and leaned against the doorjamb. "What brings you two to Pine Lake?"

Vivian and Desmond gave each other wide-eyed looks.

"The resort is one of our Lit Fest advertisers," Vivian said. "We're—"

"Checking them out." Desmond waved a hand. "To see if they—"

"Deserve to have our endorsement." Vivian smiled.

Yeah, right. "What a good idea. What have you decided?"

Vivian sighed. "Fabulous place."

"Superb service." Desmond lifted his chin.

An awkward silence followed.

Then Desmond cleared his throat. "Well, we'd better be on our way. I'm due home soon." He tapped his wristwatch.

"I have an engagement this evening also." Vivian stepped forward.

"Of course. So nice to see you both." Nina straightened and stood aside.

Heads high, Vivian and Desmond swept by and down the hallway.

Nina watched the two weave their way through the dining room to the restaurant's front door. She waited until they exited and then returned to Stephen.

"I thought you were lost." He joked but then regarded her with raised eyebrows. "What's wrong?"

Nina slipped into her chair and related what she witnessed.

"The two who just walked through here?" He frowned. "Yeah, I saw them. I thought I recognized him from that day at Marley Manor, but I wasn't sure because the woman didn't look like the wife I met. So, those two are colleagues. Do you think they're having an affair?"

"I wouldn't be surprised, but they also could've been checking out the place as an advertiser, as they claimed."

Nina's and Stephen's meals arrived, and she turned her attention to enjoying her food. The steak was cooked to medium, just as she'd ordered, and came with a tangy sauce. The baked potato included garnishments of green onion, bacon bits, and grated cheese.

Conversation during the meal was light, confined to comments about the food or the campground activity they saw from the window.

When he finished eating, Stephen sat back and slowly shook his head. "If a feast like this follows every visit to the bell tower, count me in."

Nina laughed. "This meal was a well-deserved reward for our hard work."

Later, as Nina and Stephen continued on their way home, Stephen cast her a glance. "Okay, I can see you're again in sleuthing mode. Anything you want to talk about?"

She turned from the window to face him. "One theory I've been mulling over is that either Desmond or Vivian murdered Gwyn. Desmond because he wants the department chair, and Vivian because she saw Gwyn as a threat to her and Desmond's affair—assuming they are having one. For example, let's say Gwyn threatened to tell Desmond's wife he was carrying on with Vivian. One or the other lured Gwyn to the bell tower and pushed her out the window."

"Maybe they both lured her there."

Nina held up a forefinger. "Ah, I hadn't considered that scenario. Good thinking, Mr. Kraslow. If that's the case, they're both afraid they left evidence to incriminate them. That's why they keep asking me if I've found anything on my visits."

"Why don't they search the tower on their own?" Stephen slowed to navigate a curve.

"They have no valid reason to be there, while I do have a reason." Nina sat back and folded her arms. "Sneaking in at night might be too risky for either of them."

"Judging from their behavior today, they don't appear to be worried about being seen together."

"True, but they had a legitimate excuse for today. Explaining why they were in the bell tower might pose more of a challenge. Anyway, I'll add today's sighting to the data I'm collecting."

When Nina and Stephen arrived at her condo, she turned toward him. "Why don't you come up and we'll check out the chain fragment you found? I'd like to have your opinion."

"Of course. I'm curious to know if it belongs to the medal."

A few minutes later, sitting beside Stephen on the living room sofa, Nina examined the medal and the fragment. "The clasp pieces fit together." She showed him how she joined the two links.

"Okay, but clasps on chains are pretty generic."

"I'll count the beads on each side and see if they match." After completing the task, she looked up. "Exactly the same number."

He shrugged. "Still not proof."

"You're right, and I'm glad you keep me from jumping to conclusions. But let's say the pieces do belong together to make a complete necklace and see where that leads us."

Stephen folded his arms and sat back. "All right. Go for it."

Nina took a deep breath. "We found the fragment in the bell tower. The rest of the necklace was in Gwyn's pink journal. Why?" She snapped her fingers. "What if she found the medal part in the tower, too, when she practiced her presentation?"

"If so, why would she keep the medal and not return it to the owner? With a little research, she could discover it belonged to Benjamin Logarth."

"But Benjamin was dead—killed in the car accident."

Stephen folded his arms. "Then why didn't she return the medal to his parents? Wouldn't she think they would want it?"

"Good questions, Stephen. Let's backtrack a bit." Nina stood, crossed the room to the window, and gazed at the darkening sky. "If Gwyn found the medal in the tower, then Benjamin must have been there. Why?"

"Isn't it common knowledge kids break in from time to time?"

She turned to face him. "That's my understanding."

"Maybe Gwyn didn't want Ben's parents to know he'd been trespassing."

A soft smile tilted her lips. "That sounds like Gwyn. She would want to protect their feelings. But what did she plan to do with the medal, eventually? I think she kept it for another reason. If only I knew what the reason was."

Stephen put out a hand. "I'm sure you'll find the answer to that question, as well as to the other parts of the puzzle."

His words made her feel warm inside. "Thanks, Stephen. I appreciate your confidence."

But would she solve the mystery of Gwyn's death? Right now, that goal appeared as elusive as ever.

Chapter Nineteen

Two days later, on Saturday evening, Nina and Stephen were again on the road leading to PNU, this time to attend the Lit Fest Reception, held at the home of the university's president, Hollis Olivera.

"Any special investigation plans for tonight?" Stephen asked, after they'd traveled a few miles in silence.

Nina shifted in her seat to face him. "Just to keep alert to conversation and behavior that might be clues."

"I'll take pictures, too. Anyone you'd like me to capture on film?"

"All the Lit Fest Committee members would be helpful, especially Desmond DeSoto. I still need to determine whether or not he's the one in the photo booth with Gwyn. Also, Alexander Brightly and his crew."

"Sounds like an easy assignment."

"I'm so glad you're with me, Stephen." She patted his arm. "I feel I'm on the brink of something important. I might not have the case solved yet, but with so many suspects gathered under the same roof, I'm sure to learn new information."

Nina turned her attention to the landscape. The night sky was still pale from a brilliant sunset, but, one by one, the stars popped out. Thankfully, the forecasted rain had held off.

When the sign to the university appeared, Stephen turned, and soon, the familiar buildings came into view. President Olivera's home was on campus property but about a mile from the main buildings. A winding road took them through woods to a pair of iron gates.

Once inside the grounds, an attendant waving a flashlight pointed the way to parking places in a graveled area. The sounds of car doors opening and closing filled the air as Nina and Stephen and other arrivals exited their vehicles.

The attendant approached. "Right this way." He shined his light on a stone sidewalk leading to the front door.

Nina recognized him. "Hello, Diego."

He peered at her. "Hey, there, Ms. Foster."

Stephen stood beside Nina. "Hello, Diego. How're you doing?"

Diego straightened his shoulders. "Good. I'm good."

"Nice you could help out tonight." Nina gave him a smile.

Another car pulled in just then, and Diego ran to assist with the parking.

"Well, here we go." Taking Nina's elbow, Stephen led them up the stone walkway to the front door. In keeping with the university's Gothic architecture, the president's home had a steeply pitched roof with a decorative gable that came to a point. Chatter from the people ahead floated on the airwaves, along with the sweet smell of fir trees in the surrounding woods.

At the door, Nina admired the stained glass window while she and Stephen waited for those ahead to enter. Then, peeking over people's shoulders, she glimpsed Hollis Olivera greeting the new arrivals. In her fifties, she wore her salt-and-pepper hair short and framing her round face. The navy-blue dress she wore had a flared skirt and silver sequins decorating the neckline.

When Nina's and Stephen's turns came, Nina introduced herself and Stephen, adding that he was from *The Richmond Review*.

President Olivera's dark eyes lighted. "Ah, Nina, you're the one who's paying tribute to Gwyneth. How nice to meet you. And you, too, Stephen." She turned toward the man beside her. "This is my husband, Mitchell."

Dark-complexioned like his wife, but with more white in his hair and nearly a foot taller, Mitchell nodded and extended his hand, first to Nina and then to Stephen. "Welcome to our home."

"I hope you don't mind if I take a few photos." Stephen patted the small camera hanging at his side.

"Please feel free," Hollis said. "We'd love the publicity for our festival."

Stephen nodded. "Of course. I've already planned a feature for the *Review*."

Nina and Stephen moved on to the home's interior. The room they stepped into was obviously a place to receive and entertain, with furniture groupings conducive to conversation. Browns and neutral colors with gold accents dominated. One wall of sectioned glass looked out on a garden, illuminated with soft lights amid the foliage.

Nina turned from admiring the furnishings to studying those in attendance.

Jason Hopkins appeared holding a tray with glasses

of champagne.

Nina reached for two glasses, handing one to Stephen. "Jason, my, you are a busy volunteer." She introduced Stephen. "Jason is the student who's setting up the equipment for my presentation."

Stephen appraised Jason with a smile. "I heard what a big help you were."

"We saw your friend Diego when we parked our car." Nina sipped her drink, enjoying the fruity flavor. "You two belong to the same society, right?"

"Society?" Jason frowned.

"I meant fraternity." Nina kept her tone casual.

"Ah, yeah, we're both Omicron Alphas."

Leopold Manus joined them. With a nod to Jason, he picked up a glass of champagne.

Jason nodded in return and then stepped away to serve another group.

Nina turned toward Leo. "So nice to see you here." With his neatly trimmed, white mustache and beard and wearing a dark blue suit and contrasting red bowtie, Leo appeared as dapper as ever. She introduced Stephen, and the two men shook hands.

"All ready with your presentation?" Nina asked Leo.

Leo shrugged. "As ready as I'll ever be. How about you?"

"Just about. I had an equipment setup session with Jason the other day. He seems very active in campus activities."

Leo shifted his weight from one foot to the other. "I suspect a lot of what he does is encouraged by his father. You know him, don't you? Lincoln Hopkins, president of our board of directors?"

The image of Jason's father, who so much resembled his son, came to mind. "I've met him."

"Linc does everything for that boy. Always looking out for him." Leo took a swallow of champagne.

"Jason's frat brother, Diego, is parking cars tonight," Stephen said. "Are all the student volunteers Omicron Alphas?"

Leo gave a short laugh. "They all belong to a fraternity, but not that one."

Nina raised her eyebrows, putting together Leo's oblique statement with what she knew of other fraternities. "Oh, you mean…"

Leo's eyes narrowed, and he put a finger to his lips. "Shhh. You didn't hear it from me."

They talked more about the program, and then Leo took a step back. "Well, I'd better let you two visit with the other guests. Nice meeting you, Stephen."

Stephen lifted his glass. "You, too, Leo."

Once Leo moved out of earshot, Stephen turned toward Nina. "Why was he so mysterious about the fraternity?"

Nina glanced around to make sure no one was near enough to overhear. "I think he meant tonight's student volunteers belong to the Spearheads."

Stephen's eyes widened. "Ah, the secret society."

"Yes. I haven't quite made up my mind about the group, but seeing them here tonight speaks in their favor."

Nina and Stephen circulated among the guests.

Eldon was with his wife, Susan, a petite blonde who hung onto his arm and laughed loudly at his jokes.

Jazmine brought her friend, Maconel, a professor from the History Department. Dressed conservatively in a black suit and wearing rimless eyeglasses, he looked every inch the academic and made quite a contrast to Jaz, who wore a long skirt and matching shawl with a bright pink-and-lavender design.

Ambrose Grandstrom, who Nina had learned was a widower, had his son in tow, a man in his forties with his father's stoop-shouldered posture and soft smile. Vivian Blanchard sailed by clutching the arm of a man Nina didn't recognize. Vivian caught Nina's eye and waved but didn't stop.

Looking around for the remaining member of their committee, Nina finally spotted Desmond DeSoto surrounded by several women, none of whom was his wife. He was doing all the talking while his audience listened with rapt attention. Nina shook her head. What was the man's appeal?

Across the room, Alexander Brightly entertained his own groupies, also all female but younger than those drawn to Desmond. Were Alexander's associates here, too?

A sweep of the room revealed his publicist, Portia Quinlan, loading her plate with goodies from the buffet table.

Alexander's manager, Cab Feraro, surveyed the crowd from over the rim of his wine glass, as though deciding whom to approach.

Otis Lindstrom, the literary agent, handed a woman a small card, probably his business card, and talked non-stop while the woman maintained a pasted-on smile.

Nina and Stephen continued to mingle, eventually working their way to the buffet. Nina eagerly sampled the selections, discovering a salmon pate that was to die for and a fruit salad with a tangy dressing. Then, while Stephen compared notes with the journalism professor, she looked around for someone new to talk to.

A woman sitting alone on a sofa caught her attention. Ah, there was a guest who needed company. Nina reached her side, and when she took in the woman's gray hair and face devoid of makeup, recognition dawned. "Aren't you Jane DeSoto? Desmond's wife?"

The woman looked up, tilted her head, and squinted. "I am. Do I know you?"

"We met at the Marley Manor Fall Collectibles and Crafts Show. My grandmother lives at Marley, and I understand your mother's a resident."

"Oh, yes, the show…" She looked away and took a long swallow of her wine.

Despite not receiving an invitation to join her, Nina sat at the opposite end of the sofa. "I was in your husband's freshman composition class." She hoped to generate discussion and learn more about the woman.

Jane turned toward Nina and lifted her chin. "He's written a book, you know."

Nina nodded. "I've heard about his publication."

"When he's department head, we'll move into a bigger house. One like this." She smiled and made a sweeping gesture to include the room.

"Do you know when he will be appointed?"

Jane leaned forward and shielded her mouth with a hand. "Soon as this stupid Lit thing is over."

Hearing Jane's derogatory opinion of the festival, Nina winced. "Department head is quite an honor. Does he have any special plans for when he takes over?"

"I don't know. You'll have to ask him." She

hiccupped. "Think I need some fresh air." Clutching her glass, she scooted to the edge of the sofa. She stood, wobbled, and then plopped down again.

"Why don't I bring you a cup of coffee?" Nina leaned toward her, ready to catch her if she toppled sideways. "Or something to nibble on. Have you visited the buffet?"

"Never mind. Just need air." Jane pushed to her feet again and managed to stay upright. Not giving Nina a glance but instead facing the door leading outside, she lurched toward her destination.

Thinking the woman was in no condition to wander alone, Nina stood and prepared to follow.

"Hello, there."

The speaker's low, sexy tone was all too familiar. She turned and looked into Alexander Brightly's brown eyes. "Hello, Alexander." Nina stepped back, putting distance between them.

He shuffled forward, closing the gap. "I've been waiting all evening to talk to you, but you're always with someone."

"Really? I'm with someone now, too." She turned toward the door, expecting to see Jane, but the woman had disappeared. Peering through the glass to the garden outside, Nina saw guests strolling the walkway, but Jane was not among them. "Did you see a woman go out this door just now?"

"No, I was looking only at you. You look absolutely stunning tonight." He swept his gaze over her from head to toe. "We haven't had the dinner I promised you."

"I don't recall dinner was a promise, and we did have lunch. I saw the rest of your crew here." Craning her neck, she looked over his shoulder.

He waved a hand. "Yeah, they're working the room. Otis is always looking for the next big star, and Cab always needs new clients."

"And Portia's singing your praises to everyone she meets."

"Of course." One eyebrow quirked. "But how about you and your people? I see your newspaper buddy's on the job."

Knowing Stephen would not appreciate the term "buddy," Nina hid a smile.

"But about that dinner…"

Just then, the sound of silverware tapping glass reverberated throughout the room. Glad for the interruption, Nina turned to see Hollis Olivera standing in front of the fireplace.

"I'd like to welcome you all to our Lit Fest Reception." Hollis beamed a smile around the room. "We have a fabulous program." She held up a booklet with a cover design featuring the school colors of red and blue. "Please take these and give them to friends and family." She gestured toward stacks of the programs on a nearby table.

"Now, I'd like to introduce our Board of Directors. We couldn't do without them. Lincoln Hopkins is our president. Come on, Linc, say a few words." She gestured toward Lincoln, who stood nearby.

With Hopkins was a woman Nina guessed was his wife. In her forties, she had a salon-perfect hairstyle and wore a cocktail dress of a flashy silver fabric that caught the light when she moved.

Leaving the woman's side, Lincoln strode to Hollis and then turned to face the room. "I've been a director here for over ten years and watched this program grow each year to what it is today. I'm proud to be associated with PNU and to have my children, Jason and Jill, attend. Jason is here tonight. Jase, where are you?" He craned his neck. "Oh, there you are."

Standing at the edge of the group, still holding a tray of champagne, Jason smiled and gave a salute.

Once again, Nina took note of the father's and son's resemblance to each other. Both were tall and thin, with square-jawed faces and thick hair combed straight back from a high forehead.

After Lincoln finished, a few more officials spoke.

Then Hollis again took charge. "On to the performers. We are honored to feature best-selling novelist Alexander Brightly. Alexander?" She looked around. "Ah, there you are."

"Good to be here." Stepping forward, Alexander rotated his wave to include all corners of the room.

"Although we celebrate, we also mourn the loss of one of our own." Hollis's voice took on a sad note. "We dedicate this year's Lit Fest to Gwyneth Miller. I'm so pleased the program she planned to present from the bell tower will go forward, thanks to a member of our committee and former student, Nina Foster." She gestured toward Nina.

Nina waved to the group. "I'm honored to give Gwyn's program and hope to see you all there."

Hollis picked up her champagne glass and held it aloft. "Again, thank you all for coming, and here's to a successful Lit Fest."

"Lit Fest!" everyone chorused and raised their glasses.

When the noise died down, Alexander, his brow

furrowed, turned toward Nina. "Seriously, you're going ahead with Gwyn's program from the bell tower?"

Nina straightened her shoulders. "I certainly am. I've been planning the presentation along with my own lecture."

"Spooky place."

She studied him. "You've been there, then?"

"I, ah, the tower *looks* spooky. From the bottom... I mean from the...*outside.*"

Alexander's stumbling over his words surprised Nina. He was always so glib.

His eyes narrowed. "You're not gonna be there alone, are you?"

"Maybe. But the program's in the afternoon, and people will be assembled outside. What could happen?" She shrugged.

"Why, only your sweet voice ringing across the quad. Sweet voice ringing, get it?" He grinned. "Now, about our dinner—"

"Say, 'Cheese,' you two."

Nina turned to see Stephen aiming his camera at them.

Alexander gave a salute. "Sure, Mr. Cameraman. My pleasure." He sidled up to Nina and put an arm around her shoulder.

Nina stiffened and pasted on a grin.

Stephen took a couple pictures and then held out a hand to Alexander. "How're you doing?"

Alexander accepted the handshake. "Good, good. Say, I'd like a copy of the picture."

"No problem. I'll shoot you an email. I'm sure Nina has your address." With one eyebrow arched, he looked toward Nina.

"Of course she does." Alexander grinned. "We've been emailing a lot… Oh, I see someone waving at me. Talk later." He hurried off.

Stephen slung his camera over his shoulder. "That guy is something else." He slanted her a glance. "I hope I didn't interrupt anything important."

Thinking of Alexander's persistence about a dinner date, Nina shook her head. "No, you came along at just the right time."

The party soon ended, and guests took their leave.

After picking up several Lit Fest programs to give to family and friends, Nina joined Stephen to head for the front door, saying their good-byes along the way.

Hollis caught up. "Nina, wait a moment. I almost forgot—"

"Yes, President Olivera?" Nina faced the woman, wondering what she could possibly have forgotten. Something to do with Gwyneth?

Hollis held out a small, brown-paper-wrapped package. "Here's a tape recorder of Gwyn's the police found in the bell tower the night of her accident. Included is a tape of her reading her poems, which I thought might be useful. You probably have her program all planned, though."

Surprised, Nina stared for a moment at the package before accepting it. "Why, ah, my presentation can always be changed, and, yes, I'm very interested in hearing the tape."

"I've had the recorder in my office, but I brought it home, so that I might give it to you tonight. When you finish with it, give it to her sister, Cassandra. Too bad she couldn't be here, but she had a stargazing event."

"I'm keeping in touch with her, and I'll see that she

gets the recorder and the tape." Nina tucked the envelope into her purse.

Later, on the way home, a rising moon illuminated the dark landscape. Although an impressive sight, for Nina, thoughts of the party took precedence.

"Quite an evening," Stephen commented after a while. "Did you learn anything to help your investigation?"

"The party gave me a lot to think about. But the tape recorder was certainly a surprise." She patted her purse where the recorder was safely stowed. "I hope the tape yields something important." Actually, Nina spoke with more confidence than she felt. Time grew short. Only one week remained until Lit Fest. After the event, she would no longer have a reason to be on campus. Could she solve the mystery before then?

Chapter Twenty

The morning following the Lit Fest reception, Nina claimed her favorite spot on Stephen's sofa, facing the picture window. The morning sun shone on the waters of Puget Sound and reflected from the tops of the Olympic Mountains. She gave the view a few moments of appreciation and then focused on her computer.

Stephen appeared and sat beside her. "How're you doing with your notes from last night?"

"Just about finished." Nina made another entry and sat back. "Now we'll put them together with your photos and see what we discover. First, though, I'd like to listen to the tape President Olivera gave me."

"I'm eager to hear it, too."

Nina picked up the small cassette recorder from the coffee table and pressed the Play button. Gwyn's melodious voice filled the air. "*Although the snow lingers, when the crocuses appear, I know Winter's over and Spring is near...*" At the end of the poem, Nina pressed the Stop button. "I recognize the verse from one of her poetry booklets."

"Are all her poems in rhyme?"

"All the ones I know of. She was really big on rhyming. Sometimes, she even spoke in rhyme."

Nina and Stephen listened to a few more poems, then Nina turned off the recorder. "So far, I haven't heard anything to help us know what happened. This tape seems to be just what President Olivera said it was, Gwyn recording the poems she planned to present at Lit Fest."

Stephen shrugged. "We might as well listen to all of them, though, don't you think?"

Nina checked the tape. "Okay, only a few minutes remain."

Gwyn's voice once again filled the room as she read another poem. Then the tape was blank.

"That must be all she recorded," Stephen said.

Nina held up a hand. "Wait. I thought I heard sounds of movement, like feet shuffling and maybe someone talking." She rewound the last couple minutes of the tape, turned up the volume, and pressed Play. Again, she heard noises, although she couldn't identify them.

Then, Gwyn launched into another poem.

"So comes the time to make a choice. I know you'll do what's right. No matter what the future holds, you'll always be a light—"

More shuffling sounds followed, and then someone spoke but with the words being indiscernible. Then a sharp clatter, as though the recorder fell and hit the hard floor. Soon after, the tape ran out.

Nina punched the Off button. "What do you make of all those sounds?"

Stephen sat back and folded his arms. "Hmmm, the noise sounded like something interrupted the recitation of another poem."

"Something? Or someone?"

"I don't know. I couldn't tell whether or not the muffled voice was hers or someone else's."

Nina shook her head. "Me, neither."

"Plus, we don't know where the recording was made. She could have been in her PNU office, or her home, or—"

"The tower?"

"Maybe. But we don't know for sure."

Nina played the tape's ending several more times, struggling to make sense of what she heard. Finally, she threw up both hands. "I'm at a loss. What's on the end of the tape might be important or might mean nothing. Let's move on to the reception. Hopefully, with my observations and your photos, something significant will turn up." Nina put aside the tape recorder and turned toward her computer.

"I have the photos downloaded." Stephen pulled his computer from the coffee table onto his lap.

Nina positioned her screen for him to view. "Okay, here's my list of suspects and my observations from last night. Let's look at Desmond DeSoto first. Under Motivation, I put two possibilities: *eliminate Gwyneth as his competition for Department Chair, and Gwyn threatened to expose his and Vivian's affair.*

Stephen frowned. "Would he commit murder just for a promotion?"

"Maybe. He does have a big ego."

"As for having an affair, he doesn't hide his interest in women. Check out these pictures I took." He showed her several photographs of Desmond placed side by side on the screen.

Nina studied the photos, each showing him with a different group of women who gave him their rapt attention. "Not one of these includes Vivian. I saw her with another man in tow, who was someone I didn't recognize."

"Maybe Desmond and Vivian avoided each other on purpose, so no one will suspect they are having an affair. Wasn't one of our theories that together they murdered Gwyn?"

"Or Vivian could have been on her own as the murderer."

Stephen scrolled to another photo. "Here's one of Desmond with his wife. I recall meeting her at Marley's craft show."

Nina viewed the picture. Jane leaned close to her husband, with a hand on his arm. In contrast, Desmond had his arms folded and was turned away, looking off into the distance. "She wants something, and he's rejecting her request." Nina pointed toward the couple.

"Maybe she doesn't like his flirting." Stephen's nose wrinkled. "Why does she put up with him?"

Nina told him about her conversation with Jane. "She's waiting for all the perks he'll have as department chair—more money, bigger home, more prestige. She lives in his shadow."

Stephen nodded. "So Gwyn would be a threat to her, too, as well as to Desmond."

"Right. She's already on my list. What I saw last night just adds to her being a suspect."

"Who do you want to see next?"

"How about Alexander Brightly?"

"Sure. Here's the photo of the two of you." Stephen scrolled to the next set of pictures. "He's wearing a big grin, but you look like you just ate a sour pickle." He laughed.

Nina made a face. "You caught me just before I pasted on my best smile. But go ahead and send him the picture, anyway."

Stephen showed her a few photos of Alexander surrounded by women.

"I wonder if he ever gets tired of putting on a show." Nina waved a hand. "Okay, enough of him. What about his crew?"

"I have a few shots of them, as well." He showed a photo of Portia Quinlan loading her plate at the buffet table.

"The buffet is where I saw her, too," Nina said. "Maybe eating satisfies the frustration of dealing with him."

Next were pictures of Cab Feraro and Otis Lindstrom, each in a different part of the room talking to a guest.

Nina studied the photos, searching for clues. "Alexander said they were working the room, but I don't see anything suspicious. How about Jason?"

Stephen held up a forefinger. "Ah, I have one very interesting picture of him and his friend, Diego. When I went into the kitchen, I heard voices near the back door and saw two people standing in the shadows. I couldn't get too close, because I didn't want them to see me. But I heard one say, 'Professor Miller didn't know anything. Quit worrying.' And the other person answered, 'Soon as Lit Fest is over, we're home free.'

"I turned off the flash and snapped this picture." Stephen brought up a new photo. "The result is dark, but you can make out some details."

Nina leaned closer to peer at the photograph. A ray of light from the open door shone directly on two young men's right hands, both doubled into fists with their forefingers linked. "They're making the secret handshake of the Spearheads. Remember when I asked

Leo Manus if Jason and Diego were Omicron Alpha fraternity helpers, and he said, 'No, not *that* fraternity'? I believe he meant they were at the party as Spearheads."

"So, is the group good? Or bad?"

Nina sat back and folded her arms. "According to Leo, both. They help out, like at the reception, and donate money for special projects, such as the ceramic stones in the StuU courtyard and the aquarium in the library. Leo said he'd wanted an aquarium for years, and then one day, the tank and all the fish appeared. Anyway, will you print those photos, please? I'd like them for my files. And thank you for being on the job yesterday."

"My pleasure." Stephen planted a kiss on her cheek. "Nothing I'd rather do than help my favorite sleuth." He looked at his wristwatch. "Hey, it's almost time for our Sunday call with David."

The three shared a video call once a week, usually on Sundays, with Stephen and David texting on the days in between. "Good. I'm ready to take a break." Nina closed down her computer and cleared the coffee table.

Stephen positioned his computer so they both could participate in the call. The phone trilled, and soon David's smiling face filled the screen. "Hey, buddy." He gave David a salute. "What's going on?"

"We won our football game last night. Gotta brag a little and say how my touchdown put us over the top."

"Congrats." Stephen made a thumbs-up. "Wish we coulda been there."

Nina clapped her hands. "Good job, David."

David nodded. "Thanks. I'll send you the video a

friend took."

They talked about the football team and David's classes.

Then David looked directly at Nina. "Got that mystery solved yet?"

Nina shook her head. "Still working on it."

"Wish I was there to help you."

Stephen laughed. "Oh, boy, another sleuth in the family. But, hey, we could set up our own detective agency."

"Cool." David grinned.

The banter went on for a while longer until David pointed toward his wristwatch. "Okay, gotta go."

"Looking forward to seeing you at Christmas," Stephen said.

"Me, too." David nodded.

Stephen ended the call and then turned toward Nina. "He's a good kid. Thanks for being his friend. I know getting used to the situation was difficult."

Nina placed a hand on his shoulder. "Having David in our lives has helped me to know what family means."

"Speaking of family, I wonder if he'll ever call me Dad? The DNA test we took made my status official."

"I know, but Dad means much more than a biological relationship. Besides, the two men he called Dad left him. I can understand his reluctance to use that title again. When he's secure with you, I'm sure you'll be Dad."

"I hope so. But now, back to our Sunday. What's next?"

Nina sat back and stretched her arms above her head. "I'm ready to take a break. How about a walk on the beach?"

"Good idea." Stephen shut down his computer, then stood and offered her a hand.

Five minutes later, wrapped in coats against a brisk autumn breeze, Nina and Stephen strolled along the beach bordering the Sound. Low tide offered a wide stretch of sand between water and higher ground. Seagulls swooped, landing in tide pools and perching on pieces of driftwood. A couple tugboats chugged by, hauling logs to the northern lumber mills, and a ferry made its way across the Sound to Kingston. Both the walk and focusing on topics other than Gwyn's death restored Nina's energy.

After a light lunch, Nina and Stephen prepared for their Sunday trip to Marley Manor for their visit with Jessica and Joe. Since the couple had expressed an interest in attending Lit Fest, Nina made sure to tuck into her purse one of the programs she picked up at the reception.

Nina always found Marley Manor an interesting place with plenty of activities to entertain residents and their guests. Today, she and the others attended a musical program featuring a string quartet. A buffet in the dining room followed, in which, for a nominal donation, visitors were invited to partake. Joined by Jessica's and Joe's friends, the occasion was always filled with lively conversation and, of course, the chef's wonderful array of food. Afterward, Nina, Stephen, and Joe gathered in Jessica's apartment for coffee and more conversation. The talk jumped from one subject to another.

During a lull, Stephen turned toward Joe. "How are you doing with your carved boxes?"

Recalling the appeal of Joe's project, Nina gave the two her attention.

Joe nodded and set down his cup. "I've finished several more. They're at my apartment. You want to come take a look?"

"Sure, I'd like to see them."

Nina was about to chime in that she'd go along.

Just then, Jessica leaned toward her. "While they're gone, I want to show you my latest potholders." Reaching into a large wicker basket next to her chair, Jessica pulled out a half-completed crocheted potholder and held it up. "What do you think?"

Nina studied the blue and green pattern. "Very colorful." Then, seeing the men had left, she frowned. "I would've liked to examine Joe's boxes, too."

Jessica made a dismissive wave. "Oh, let them do their guy stuff. Gives us a chance to talk." She took another potholder from the basket.

The men returned eventually, talking not about boxes but about the upcoming football game. "We're having a big party here," Joe was saying. "You're invited, of course."

"Wouldn't miss it," Stephen said.

Shortly after that, Nina and Stephen prepared to leave. When Nina picked up her purse, she remembered the Lit Fest program inside. Pulling out the colorful booklet, she extended it to Jessica. "Here, I almost forgot to give you this program. You can mark the sessions you want to attend."

"Yours, for sure." Jessica accepted the program and flipped through the pages. "That Alexander guy's, too." She grinned and cast Joe a sideways look.

He leaned to put an arm around her shoulders.

"He's got all you women's attention, doesn't he?"

Nina didn't want to tell them Alexander might also be a murderer, but the mention of his name reminded her she still had questions about him and his crew and their relationship to Gwyn.

Back at Stephen's house, Nina settled on the sofa, scrolling through the TV's channel guide. Outside, the sun had dropped behind the mountains, casting a silver glow over the water.

Stephen built a fire in the fireplace. He put a last log on the fire and then sat beside her.

Nina snuggled against him. "We had a nice visit with Jessica and Joe."

He patted her arm. "We did, but being back home again with just the two of us feels good."

Home. Could Stephen's home be hers, also? Permanently? She let her mind drift to what such an arrangement might be like. She would wake up in his bed—no, *their* bed—every morning, come here from work to have dinner, and then they would spend the evening together. The work she'd done with the therapist had helped her to understand and deal with her fear of commitment, but still— She heaved a sigh and laid her head on his shoulder. She didn't want to think about the issue now, not when she was so comfortable.

With Stephen's input, she picked out a TV program and barely settled down to watch when her phone chimed.

"Let it go to voice mail." Stephen tightened an arm around her.

"Just let me check—" Pulling away, she picked up her phone from the coffee table and read the screen. "It's Gran. I'd better see what she's calling about."

Stephen nodded and then used the remote to pause the TV show.

Turning to her phone, Nina connected the call, and soon Jessica's face filled the screen. "Hey, Gran. You okay?"

"I'm fine. But I just made a discovery I thought you should know about. I realize it's late, though, and I've probably interrupted—"

The excitement in Jessica's voice brought Nina to full attention. "Never mind, Gran. What have you discovered?"

She held up the Lit Fest program. "I was reading this program, and I suddenly saw something that rang a bell." She shook her head and gave a short laugh. "Uh-oh, bad joke. Sorry. Anyway, do you have a program handy?"

"I have one here somewhere." Nina sifted through the stack of paper and envelopes on the coffee table. Spying the program, she pulled it out. "Okay, ready."

"On a page near the back is a list of sponsors, including university people. Find Board of Directors."

Nina turned to the indicated page and ran down a forefinger. "Got it."

"Look at Hopkins. His name is T. Lincoln Hopkins. T. Lincoln. T.L. I know Doris said Gwyneth told her group that T.L. stood for True Love, but what if that was just a cover to protect the person?"

As Nina stared at the name, her thoughts whirled. "You just might be right, Gran. I'll check out Mr. Hopkins and see if he could be the man in Gwyn's past. Wow. Good eye, and good sleuthing. Thank you."

Jessica chuckled. "Never thought I could be a detective, but it's kinda fun."

After ending the call, Nina turned toward Stephen. "Gran might have made an important discovery." She reached for her computer.

One eyebrow peaked. "You're researching now? Tonight?"

"I must follow up this clue." She kissed him lightly on the lips. "Just a short delay, I promise."

He laughed. "I'll hold you to that. Meanwhile, count me in on the clue hunt."

As she booted up her machine, excitement filled Nina. Was she about to make an important discovery?

Chapter Twenty-One

"So, you plan to confront Lincoln Hopkins to see if he'll admit to being Gwyn's mysterious T.L." Stephen turned from stirring a skillet of scrambled eggs to give Nina a raised-eyebrow look.

"Don't worry; my approach will be low key." Nina finished buttering a piece of toast. "I'll show him the poetry book and tell him why I believe he's the poet. Then I'll offer him the book—if he wants it."

The previous evening's research had indeed turned up interesting information about T. Lincoln Hopkins. The T stood for Thaddeus. He and Gwyneth attended the same undergraduate and graduate schools, which gave them plenty of opportunity for association. When she and Stephen compared the photos he took of Hopkins at the Lit Fest Reception to the snapshots tucked into the poetry book, Nina was convinced Lincoln was indeed Gwyn's mysterious lover.

Stephen dished up the eggs and placed the platter on the table. "What if he doesn't want the book and denies everything?"

Nina shrugged. "I will have followed up a clue to the best of my ability." She set the toast next to the eggs.

When the meal preparations were finished, Nina and Stephen sat at the table.

Stephen held out the platter of eggs. "When will

you talk with Hopkins?"

"The board of directors meets on campus this morning, ending in lunch at the StuU." Nina added eggs to her plate. "I'll catch him on his way out of the building and ask for a moment of his time. We'll be in public. Nothing bad will happen."

Stephen's eyes narrowed. "I hope not. I still think any kind of confrontation is risky. Even if he is T.L., that doesn't prove he murdered Gwyn."

"Of course not, but the proof solves one mystery. A lot of little puzzles contribute to the big one. The more of those I solve, the closer I come to discovering the truth about Gwyn's death."

"I hope discovering T.L.'s identity brings you closer to the big mystery's solution." Stephen sipped his coffee. "Give me a call tonight, and let me know what you learned from your meeting."

"Of course." Nina spread strawberry jam on her toast and took a bite, enjoying the jam's sweet yet tart flavor, and then helped herself to more scrambled eggs. She needed a hearty breakfast for the busy day ahead.

****

That afternoon, sitting on a bench in front of the StuU, Nina checked her wristwatch. The time was almost two o'clock and still no sign of Mr. Hopkins. The group must have a big agenda. Maybe catching him on his way out wasn't such a good idea, after all. But she didn't want to phone. She wanted to observe his reaction when she presented him with the poetry booklet.

Nina focused again on the building's front doors. Two older women emerged, followed by several men. More people appeared, with some stopping to talk in small groups before moving on. However, none was Lincoln Hopkins. Just when she thought he hadn't attended the meeting and chided herself for wasting time, she saw him step out the door. He wore a dark blue suit and carried a briefcase. Without pause, he strode briskly ahead.

Nina jumped up and hurried to waylay him. "Mr. Hopkins!"

He stopped and turned. "Yes?"

"I'm Nina Foster."

He frowned. "I know who you are. What can I do for you? Make it quick because I'm meeting my wife."

Nina lifted her chin. "I want to talk about Gwyneth Miller."

"Something about the bell tower program?"

"No...I have a book to give you." Nina pulled from her purse the poetry booklet and showed him the cover. "Here are the poems you wrote for Gwyneth. I believe she would want you to have them." She kept her gaze on his face, ready to study his reaction.

He stared at the booklet and then looked up. "I don't know what you're talking about."

"The booklet is autographed by T.L. Those are your initials, and you and she knew each other in college." Nina held her breath. Would he take the poems? If he did, would his acceptance prove her theory that he was indeed Gwyn's former lover?

"Dad!"

Jolted from her thoughts, Nina turned to see Jason Hopkins running toward them. Uh-oh, she hadn't planned to share this meeting with anyone—least of all, Lincoln's son. Quickly, she stuffed the book into her purse.

Jason reached them, stopped, and huffed a breath. He wore his letterman's jacket and had a book bag slung over one shoulder. "Hey, Dad. Hi, Ms. Foster."

Stuffing down her irritation, Nina forced a smile. "Hello, Jason."

Jason faced his father again. "Sorry to interrupt, but Mom's waiting." He pointed toward the parking lot.

Scanning the area, Nina spotted a woman leaning against a car's fender. Her blonde hair and stylish brown slacks suit identified her as the same woman who was with Lincoln at the reception.

Lincoln placed a hand on Jason's shoulder. "You're not interrupting, son. Miss Foster and I have finished our business."

Just then, a young woman appeared. She wore jeans and a wool jacket and had her blonde hair in a single braid. "Dad. Jason. Sorry I'm a bit late. Is Mom here? Oh, I see her." She waved toward the woman standing by the car. Then she turned toward Nina. "Hello."

"This is my daughter, Jill." Lincoln's chest puffed up. "She's sophomore class president, honor roll, cheerleader—"

"Dad!" Jill rolled her eyes and then faced Nina again. "He's always bragging about us. But, you're one of the Lit Festers, right?"

Nina nodded. "I'm giving a talk on Children's Literature."

"I'll be there." She nodded. "I love Kiddie Lit."

Lincoln stepped between his son and daughter, grasping each by the elbow. "We must go. Madeline— my wife—is waiting."

"Of course. Nice seeing you, Mr. Hopkins. You,

too Jason. Good to meet you, Jill."

Jason gave Nina a wave.

Jill offered a smile. "I'm looking forward to your talk, Miss Foster."

The three turned away and headed toward the parking lot.

Stepping out to meet them, Mrs. Hopkins planted a quick kiss on her husband's cheek, patted Jason's shoulder, and brushed an errant lock of hair from Jill's forehead.

They all climbed into the car and, with Mrs. Hopkins at the wheel, drove away.

Nina waited until they were out of sight and then continued to her car. Along the way, her thoughts spun. If the children hadn't interrupted, would Lincoln Hopkins have accepted the book? Or would he continue to deny authorship?

Upon reaching her car and after making sure she'd received no more threatening notes, Nina climbed into the driver's seat. Opening her purse, she took out the booklet and stared at the cover. What should she do now? She and Hopkins were interrupted before she had a chance to study his reaction to the booklet. Should she make another attempt to give him the poems? Or should she offer them to Cassandra? Heaving a sigh, she tucked the booklet into her purse. Then she started the car and drove away, leaving the campus behind. The dilemma haunted her all the way home.

****

The following day at the Seaview Library, Nina selected books for a high school science class's visit.

Arlette joined her in the stacks. "Phone call for you, Nina."

"Thanks, Arlette." Nina pushed her cart into her office and picked up the phone. "Hello, this is Nina Foster."

"Miss Foster, Lincoln Hopkins here."

Nina gave a start. After the finality of yesterday's conversation, she never expected to hear from him. "Yes, Mr. Hopkins. What can I do for you?"

He cleared his throat. "I need to clarify issues raised yesterday."

"I'm listening." Her heart beat faster. Was she about to learn something important?

"Over the phone is not the best place for our discussion. Neither is the campus. I'll meet with you here at Arkone. Our plant is only a few miles farther up the main road from the school."

How clever of him to suggest a meeting on his territory. Did she want to accept his challenge? "All right, I'll come to Arkone. Is tomorrow convenient? I'll be on campus for a committee meeting at two."

"Let me check my schedule." A couple moments passed. "Tomorrow's convenient. Be here at four. Do you need directions?"

"No, thank you. I'm familiar with the area."

"I'll leave word at the gate you're expected."

After hanging up, Nina wasted no time calling Stephen. "I think Mr. Hopkins's conscience bothers him, and he wants to be honest."

"Or he wants to get you on his territory where he's in charge. I don't trust the guy, and I don't like the idea of your going there alone. I'll rearrange my schedule and accompany you."

"I appreciate your concern, Stephen, really, I do. But I want to deal with him on my own. With all his employees, we won't be alone."

"All right. But be careful, and call me when you get home."

"I will," she promised. But Stephen's warning lingered. Would she be safe at Arkone?

****

On Wednesday, Nina attended the Lit Fest meeting as planned and then, after leaving Bannon Hall, hurried toward her car, anxious to meet with Lincoln Hopkins.

Huffing to catch up, Vivian joined her. "How are you coming with your inquiry into Gwyneth's death?"

Was Vivian making polite conversation? Or did another motive lurk behind her question? "I'm always open to new information. Have you heard anything?"

"Some of the committee are still rumbling opposition to your presenting Gwyn's program from the bell tower."

Nina wrinkled her brow. "Who, exactly?"

"Desmond grumbles a lot. But, then, Des complains about practically everything." She gave a short laugh.

"My presentation has been approved and included in the program. I have no intention of backing out now." Nina made her tone firm.

"I do admire your determination. Say, do you have time for coffee at the StuU?" Vivian gestured toward the building's entrance.

"I wish I did, but I have another appointment at four. The location is a bit of a drive, so I'd better be on my way."

"An appointment? Something to do with Lit Fest?" Vivian's eyebrows peaked.

"Ah, no. A personal matter."

"Sorry. Didn't mean to pry. I just thought if your appointment was Lit Fest related, I might be able to help. Don't get caught in the storm." She pointed toward the sky and frowned. "Those dark clouds look nasty."

Nina surveyed the sky, which had indeed turned a deep gray. "Hopefully, the rain clouds will pass without dumping on us." The prospect of rain held little appeal for driving either to Arkone or home to Richmond.

"Doubtful. You know this country. We could be socked in with rain for days."

Nina laughed. "True enough."

After parting from Vivian, Nina reviewed their conversation. Was the woman warning her to abandon the bell tower program, after all? She also expressed interest in Nina's plans for the afternoon. Why? Was she just making conversation, or did something more sinister lie behind her inquiry?

Chapter Twenty-Two

Leaving the campus, Nina drove along the winding road through farmlands with fields of ripening corn and orchards of apple and pear trees. Crossroads offered stores with fruit and autumn flowers on display, adding to the landscape's color.

Passing one such area, she spotted a sign that said *Annie's Antiques*. Outside the door sat an old spinning wheel and a rack with colorful quilts and vintage clothing. What really caught her eye was a shelf of books. Should she stop and take a look? Books on sale were always difficult to pass up. But she had no time now. She'd stop on the way back. Pressing on, she drove several more miles until she finally reached the Arkone factory.

A uniformed guard at the gate provided Nina directions to the visitors' parking lot and Building A, where Mr. Hopkins had his office.

Inside the building, a tall, blonde woman stepped from behind a counter and approached. In her thirties, she wore black slacks and a yellow jacket with *Arkone* embroidered on the pocket. "You must be Nina Foster. I'm Betty, Mr. Hopkins's assistant. I'll take you to his office."

"Thank you, Betty." Nina fell into step beside her.

Keeping up a brisk pace, Betty led Nina along a hallway and into an elevator. On the second floor, another hallway led them to Hopkins's office. Betty opened the door and motioned Nina inside.

Lincoln Hopkins sat behind a desk while talking on a cell phone. "I'll expect my orders carried out by tomorrow. Don't bother to call back. Just do it." He punched off the call and laid the phone on the desk. "Have a seat, Miss Foster." He waved toward several leather-upholstered chairs.

"Thank you." Nina sat. The sound of the door closing behind her told her she was now alone with him. Shrugging off a sudden unease, she concentrated on her goal—learning more about this man and his relationship to Gwyn.

Lincoln leaned back in his chair. "What do you think of Arkone—what you've seen so far?"

"Very impressive." Nina spoke the truth. "I knew Arkone was a big outfit, but not this big." She made a sweeping gesture to include the windows behind his desk, which offered a view of nearby buildings.

"Our electronic products are distributed worldwide. I'd be willing to bet at least ten items in your household have our footprint."

"Perhaps so, but you didn't summon me here to gain my admiration for your company."

He tilted his head. "Why don't you tell me why I invited you here?"

Nina gave an inward sigh. So, he wanted to play games. Was this behavior how he conducted business? "All right. Gwyneth told me she originally came to the Northwest because of a man she was involved with. She named no names, but I believe that person was you." Nina paused to gauge his reaction.

His expression remained impassive.

Nina lifted her chin. "Anyway, the relationship didn't work out."

"Because…?"

She wanted to say, *Because you were offered a deal you couldn't refuse—marry the boss's daughter and eventually become the boss yourself.* Instead, she shrugged. "I don't know. But Gwyn remained here and was hired by PNU. She had other relationships, but none lasted. Maybe because she never got over you."

Hopkins turned away to look out the window.

Following his gaze, Nina noticed the cloud-covered sky had turned even darker than before. If she didn't leave soon, the drive home could be challenging.

He faced her again. "Sometimes, a person grows out of a role and leaves the old life behind."

Was he referring to the scenario she described? "But you became involved with the university where she worked. Was that because you couldn't quite let go?"

"Sometimes, little bits of that old life cling. Or guilt rears its ugly head."

She had trouble imagining this arrogant man ever feeling guilty. He would be right, all the time, and offer no excuses for his behavior. Still, they were having this conversation, weren't they? Strange though it was.

He leaned forward, his gaze intense. "Did you bring the book? The one you think I wrote?"

"I did." Reaching into her purse, Nina pulled out the booklet, laid it on the desk, and drew back her hand.

Instead of reaching for it, he only stared at the volume. Then he looked up. "What do you plan to do with this if I don't accept it?"

"I'll offer it to her sister, Cassandra. If she doesn't

want it, I'll add it to the books of Gwyn's poetry that I've collected." She tilted her head and eyed him. "What will *you* do with it—if you choose to keep it?"

"Burn it—just in case someone else would find it and make the same mistake you have about its authorship."

Hearing an option she hadn't considered, Nina frowned. "I'd hate to see the book destroyed. The poems have a certain charm and heartfelt emotion."

One eyebrow peaked. "So, you're a judge of poetry?"

"That opinion is purely subjective. Like I told you the other day, I brought the book to your attention because I truly believe you are the author, and Gwyn would want you to have it."

"I'm surprised you don't want to keep the poems as evidence."

"Evidence?" Nina widened her eyes.

"I know you're investigating what you believe is foul play in Gwyn's tragic death. I know all about you."

Of course, he did. He'd probably had her investigated more thoroughly than if she were applying for a job. The idea of being under such scrutiny made her nervous.

He folded his hands on the desktop. "I recall your involvement in the death of another alum a couple years ago."

She found the term *involvement* offensive, but then the memory of her good friend, Wildeen Bergman's, tragic murder tugged her emotions, bringing a wave of sadness. "I lost a good friend."

"Then a mysterious death at your grandmother's retirement home caught your fancy. Now, you're focusing on Gwyn's accident." He tilted his head and narrowed his gaze. "Are you so eager to solve mysteries that when none presents itself, you make up one?"

Fearing an explanation about her intuition would fall on deaf ears or else elicit derisive laughter, Nina remained silent.

He picked up a pen and tapped it on the desktop. "So, tell me, what makes you so sure Gwyn met with foul play in the bell tower?"

He hadn't included the mystery she solved at Stephen's high school reunion, so, thankfully, he didn't know about that one. "I'm not sure, Mr. Hopkins."

"Then why are you pursuing the matter?" He tossed down the pen and sat back.

Nina leaned forward. "Most important is honoring Gwyneth by presenting her program at Lit Fest."

"Ah, yes, the *program*. As I told you on campus the other day, such a presentation is a bad idea." He slowly shook his head.

Nina gave an inward sigh. Not the first time she'd heard that same opinion. "Why?"

"The reason should be obvious. Gwyn had an accident there that took her life. The bell tower is a dangerous place. I don't know what purpose it serves, anyway."

Nina straightened her shoulders. "The tower is a campus landmark. The bell was brought from Italy by the man who donated the land for the university."

He waved a hand and shook his head. "I know the history. But, still, the tower itself is unsafe. The stairs in particular need repair."

She tilted her head. "So you've been inside the tower?"

"Not lately." He frowned and rubbed the bridge of his nose. "But when I had a tour years ago, the stairs were faulty, and to my knowledge, they've never been repaired. I'm surprised Admin agreed to Gwyn's request to present her poetry there."

He no long referred to her as Professor Miller, or even Gwyneth. Now she was simply Gwyn, which indicated if not intimacy at least more than a casual acquaintance. "But Admin did agree, Mr. Hopkins, and I will honor their wishes. Did you have anything more you wanted to tell me about your relationship with Professor Miller?"

His eyes narrowed. "I don't recall using the word *relationship* to describe our association."

"Then there was an association between the two of you."

Hopkins folded his arms and sat back. "I think we've finished our interview."

Interview? Nina inwardly shook her head. The man was impossible.

He opened a drawer and, in one swift motion, swept in the booklet and slammed it shut. Turning to his desk console, he pressed a button. Then he picked up a file folder, opened it, and bent his head toward the contents.

Reluctant to dispute his rude dismissal, Nina instead gathered up her purse and scooted forward in her chair

Betty soon appeared. "Yes, Mr. Hopkins?"

Hopkins looked up. "Please show Miss Foster out." His gaze swung to Nina, and his lips curved into the barest of smiles. "Thank you, Miss Foster, for coming today. I'll certainly give your grant proposal my immediate attention and get back to you soon."

Nina nodded and stood. "I'll look forward to hearing from you." She played along, alternating between amusement and disgust at his blatant lie.

Betty led Nina along the hallway and down the elevator, retracing their steps to the front door. "I hope you get home before the storm hits."

Putting aside her annoyance with Hopkins's abrupt dismissal, Nina strove to be courteous. "Me, too. Thank you for your help today, Betty."

"My pleasure."

She gave Nina a perfunctory smile. Nina stepped outside, pausing to take a deep breath of fresh air. Gazing at the sky, she saw the clouds were still dark and hovering. She needed to start on her return trip. On her way to the parking lot, she encountered Hopkins's son, Jason, walking toward the factory's entrance.

He stopped and frowned. "Ms. Foster, what are you doing here?"

"Hello, Jason. I found a book I thought your father would like, and since I was on another errand in the neighborhood, I dropped it off." There, she'd only slightly stretched the truth.

He glanced toward his father's office and then back. "Oh. Okay…"

"So, I'd better be on my way if I want to beat the storm." She pointed toward the dark clouds.

"Sure. See you on campus."

Nina continued on, but then on impulse, she stopped and glanced over her shoulder. Jason stood where she encountered him, watching her while talking into his cell phone. Was he discussing her visit?

Once in her car, Nina followed the guard's wave

through the gate. She stepped on the gas, driving as fast as the speed limit and the winding road allowed, while mulling over her visit with Hopkins. Would she ever know the truth about his and Gwyn's relationship? He dismissed her today without ever admitting a relationship existed. Plus, he strongly advised she cancel her program in the bell tower. Had he issued a veiled threat? She needed to know more about T. Lincoln Hopkins.

The first raindrops hit the windshield just as she rounded a corner and came upon Annie's Attic. A woman and a man were moving the outdoor merchandise inside. Anticipating the pleasure of hunting for books, Nina lifted her foot from the gas pedal. But what about the impending storm? She really should continue on home. Still, she found herself turning into the store's parking lot. Okay, five minutes, and then she'd be on her way again.

Half an hour later, Nina finally stopped browsing and paid for her purchases. As far as books were concerned, the store turned out to be a treasure house. She found several vintage children's stories, a history saga for Stephen, a young adult mystery for David, a book on crocheting for Gran, and one on wood carving for Joe. Not surprisingly, proprietor Annie, a middle-aged woman with a friendly smile, loved to talk, especially about books, and the two had a lively discussion.

When Nina left and stepped outside, rain pelted her in the face. Startled, she'd all but forgotten about the storm, and what a storm it was. Rain poured as though the sky had opened up.

"Drive carefully!" Annie called from the doorway.

"I will." Nina waved and ran to her car.

Fortunately, few cars were on the road, other travelers having the good sense to either seek shelter or to stay sheltered to begin with. Even with the windshield wipers at full power, visibility was poor. A car passed her traveling in the opposite direction. She slowed, careful to keep to her side of the road. Another vehicle came up behind, close on her tail. She resisted increasing her speed. If the driver was in such a hurry, let him pass—if he dared. Then the car dropped back, putting distance between them. Still, the headlights kept her glancing in the rearview mirror. Why didn't he just pass and go on his way?

Maybe she should pull off the road and let him drive by. However, her side of the road had only a narrow shoulder before dropping off. She had no idea how deep the drop-off was but knew for certain she didn't want to chance finding out.

The car behind her sped up, its headlights looming through the darkness, growing bigger and bigger, like staring eyes. What was wrong with the driver? She pressed the gas pedal as much as she dared, but the other car stayed close behind. Just when she thought a collision was imminent, her pursuer swerved to the left and passed, coming dangerously close. To avoid being sideswiped, Nina jerked her steering wheel to the right. The car's wheels skidded on the soaked pavement. Despite pumping the brakes, the car veered onto the shoulder, crunching over gravel and heading straight for the drop-off.

Chapter Twenty-Three

Gripping the steering wheel, Nina braced herself to plunge over the cliff, but instead, the car jolted to a halt.

Her pursuer sped down the road, disappearing into the gray curtain of rain.

She turned off the ignition and then, breathing heavily, leaned her forehead against the steering wheel. When her pounding heart slowed, she straightened and peered through the rain-soaked windshield. What exactly was her situation? She needed to leave the car to find out.

Opening the door, she crawled out and, her legs shaking, stood on the ground. Rounding the front of the car, she saw that the right wheel was jammed against a fallen log, which had prevented her from plunging over the embankment. Stepping to the edge, she looked down—and gasped. Huge boulders and trees lined the chasm. Not likely her car would've survived, and she didn't even want to think about her own chances.

Turning away, she focused on what to do now. She didn't want to summon a tow truck, not without attempting to drive on her own first. No other cars were in sight traveling in either direction.

Returning to the car, she turned on the ignition, put the car in Reverse, and stepped on the gas pedal. The rear tires spun, spewing water and mud as high as the rear window. She rested a moment and then tried again.

Several attempts later, she backed up enough to allow the car to rock back and forth. Her efforts were finally rewarded when the car rolled far enough to turn the front wheels toward the road.

Several more twists and turns aimed the car in the right direction. Taking a deep breath and gripping the wheel, she stepped on the gas and guided the car onto the road. Giving an inward cheer, she drove on, her success fusing her with new energy and purpose. She'd be okay now.

A few miles down the road, her cell phone rang from the depths of her purse. The special ringtone indicated the caller was Stephen, checking on her visit with Lincoln Hopkins. If she didn't answer, he'd worry. At the next intersection, she pulled into a gas station's parking lot. Retrieving the phone, she pressed the screen to return his call.

"Where are you? I've been worried."

"I was delayed on my way back from Arkone." She briefly sketched in the details.

"Sounds like you had a really bad time. Do you need me to come and get you?"

The concern in his voice brought tears to her eyes. "I'm okay, Stephen. Really. I'm almost home."

"Come to my place. Then we'll decide what to do."

"All right. I'll be there soon." An hour later, Nina sat on Stephen's sofa, sipping a cup of her favorite Earl Grey tea. After arriving, she'd first changed from her wet clothing into jeans and a sweatshirt. Then, while enjoying a bowl of chicken noodle soup and freshly baked rolls, she related her near-disastrous trip.

From the kitchen came the sounds of running water and clinking dishes, and from the adjacent laundry room, the hum of the dryer restoring her wet clothing. She gave thanks for having this refuge after her ordeal. Being here tonight with Stephen was so much better than being alone in her condo.

Stephen entered the room, carrying a cup of coffee. He joined her on the sofa, placing the cup on the coffee table. "How're you doing? Warm enough?" He hugged her shoulders.

She snuggled against him. "I'm fine. Thank you for taking such good care of me."

"My pleasure. Good to have you here, even under the circumstances—which we need to further discuss. You still don't want to report the incident to the police?"

She shook her head. "I don't have a license plate number or even a description of the car, except it was a dark color."

"Do you think you were targeted by whoever put the notes in your car?"

Nina shivered and hugged her arms. "I don't know. Maybe."

Stephen's eyes narrowed. "Or did Hopkins lure you to Arkone to have someone follow you on the way home?"

"Again, I don't know. But suppose the incident is related to seeing Hopkins. He didn't tell me much, and I was guarded in what I told him. I still think he's hiding something. If I'm a threat to him—or to his family—he might be desperate."

"What about his son, Jason? You said you saw him at the factory. Maybe he ran you off the road."

Nina rubbed a hand over her forehead. "I suppose he could be the one."

"Did anyone else know you were going to Arkone?"

"Vivian knew I was headed somewhere but not the exact location. She could have followed me. Or maybe the person in the car was a stranger and just a very bad driver." She heaved a sigh. "Everything's a maybe at this point."

Stephen took a drink of his coffee. "So you returned Hopkins's book, even though he didn't acknowledge authorship."

"I did."

"Don't you think you might regret giving it up? What if you need to refer to the poems in the future?"

She gave him a sly grin. "No problem. I made a copy of the entire book."

Stephen tossed back his head and laughed. "Of course, you did. Why didn't I think of that?"

"If he doesn't have something to cover up, why would he lie about being the poet?"

"Maybe he fears exposing his poetic side will tarnish his reputation in the business world. He's an important man now. He has to be tough on the job."

"You're probably right." Nina leaned against Stephen's shoulder and heaved a deep sigh. "I'd like to talk to him again. Don't know if I'll get a chance, though, with Lit Fest only a week away."

****

The following day, in typical Northwest fashion, the rain vanished, and the sun shone in a cloudless sky. After yesterday's unnerving interview with Lincoln Hopkins, followed by her harrowing near-accident, Nina welcomed the return to her job at Seaview Library.

Still, thoughts of Gwyn's tragic death and all that occurred since then hovered in the back of her mind. That evening, after a light dinner of tomato soup and a grilled cheese sandwich, Nina took a cup of tea upstairs to her study. Booting up her computer, she accessed the notes on her investigation. Then she took out the box of the information and clues she'd collected and lined up the items on the table.

First came Gwyn's pink journal, the medal and separate piece of chain, and the copy she'd made of T.L.'s poetry booklet. To those she added Gwyn's booklets and the tape recorder and tape Hollis Olivera gave her. From the bottom of the box, she took the manila envelope marked *Save,* containing the stories Portia Quinlan wrote for Gwyn's class.

To her computer notes, she included the discovery that T.L. was Thaddeus Lincoln Hopkins and then summarized her visit to Arkone. She described her accident on the way home, including as many details as she could recall. At this point, she had no proof the incident was related to Gwyn's death, but she would add it to her notes, anyway.

Then she turned to the items from the box. Picking up the medal, she ran a finger over the engraved words. She still didn't know why Gwyn kept the prize instead of returning it to Benjamin's parents. "Do you hold the secret to Gwyn's death?" she whispered.

If Gwyn discovered the medal in the bell tower, wouldn't that fact indicate Benjamin was there before being killed in the car accident near Sattoo Pass? Were the two incidents related? If so, how?

She thought of the photo in Cara's room, of Benjamin with Jason Hopkins and Diego Rivera. Were

Jason and Diego connected to the loss of Benjamin's medal? Would Cara know? Nina hadn't wanted to risk upsetting her with questions. But now that Lit Fest was almost upon them, she needed to follow up every possible clue. She reached for her cell phone and texted Cara.

****

The following afternoon, after traveling the now-familiar route to PNU, Nina stood on the steps of the Mu house and rang the doorbell.

After a short wait, Midge Cornell opened the door. A smile lit her face. "Nina! Good to see you!" Her hair in a ponytail, Midge wore her usual slacks and blouse, today adding a sweater with the sleeves tied around her neck.

"Hello, Midge. I'm here to visit Cara, as you probably guessed."

"Sure, sure. Come on in." Midge led Nina into the Greeting Room and waved toward a chair. "Are you all ready for Lit Fest?"

Nina nodded and sat, placing her purse on her lap. "Just putting the finishing touches on my presentation."

"What about Professor Miller's program?"

"I'm prepared for that, too."

Midge tilted her head and eyed Nina. "Still convinced her death wasn't an accident?"

"I'm not convinced either way, Midge, and I'm always looking for more information." She leaned forward. "Do you know something?"

Midge took a step back and raised both hands. "I hear talk here and there."

"Have you heard anything you think might help me?" On alert now, Nina sat straight.

Midge bit her lip and looked away. "Word has it the prof might have discovered something somebody didn't want known."

"Could you be more specific?"

"The discovery concerns some of her colleagues. That's all I know. Honest." Midge's eyes widened.

"Hey, you're here."

Nina turned to see Cara enter the room. "Hello, Cara. I just arrived and was about to give you a call. Are you ready to take in the exhibit?" During the previous evening's texting, Cara suggested they visit the art show at Compton Hall. Especially, she wanted Nina to see the painting she had on display.

Cara buttoned her brown wool jacket and adjusted the plaid scarf around her neck. "I am, just as soon as I sign out." Approaching the desk, she picked up a pen and wrote in the sign-out book.

Nina grasped her purse and stood, prepared to leave.

"You two have fun." Midge accompanied them to the door. "Come back for tea. We have some yummy pumpkin scones."

On the way to Compton Hall, Nina carefully kept the conversation light, questioning Cara about her classes and activities at the Mu house. However, when they passed the bell tower, Cara's grimace and visible shudder told Nina she still harbored deep emotions about witnessing Gwyn's fall.

At Compton Hall, Nina and Cara took the elevator to the second floor art gallery, a long room with white walls and small lights affixed near the ceiling. In addition to paintings were sculptures and other three-dimensional art.

Halfway through the exhibit, Cara pointed toward one of the pictures. "Here's mine."

Nina studied the watercolor painting of a woman and a child walking hand in hand through a field of red, yellow, and orange tulips. A barn and snow-topped mountains formed the background. "Cara, what a charming picture."

Cara beamed. "Thanks. I was inspired by a trip to Skagit Valley's tulip fields last spring."

Farther on, Nina noticed an oil painting of cars on a racetrack. The informational card identified the artist as Benjamin Logarth. Ah, here was the perfect entry into a conversation about the young man and his relationship to Jason and Diego. She turned toward Cara, who had fallen a few paces behind. "Take a look at this painting, Cara. The artist is Benjamin Logarth."

Cara caught up and nodded. "That picture is Ben's."

"Was he in your art class?"

"He was, but for only a week or so before he died. Our professor wanted to honor him by including his painting in the show."

Nina thought the work well executed, with swirls of color suggesting the speed of the cars traveling along the track. "He must have been a skilled driver to participate in races. Hard to believe he would have an accident that cost him his life." She cast Cara a sideways glance.

Cara frowned and fingered her scarf. "I don't know anything about his accident."

"Ben was close with Jason and Diego, wasn't he? Was he a frat brother?"

"If you mean Omicron Alpha, no, he wasn't." Cara

turned away and approached another painting. "Look at the roses in this still life. Aren't the colors beautiful?"

Nina responded, and she and Cara continued on. But she couldn't help wondering if Cara resisted further discussion about Ben because his death was such a sad event, or because she was afraid she might reveal secrets.

After viewing the exhibit, Nina and Cara returned to the Mu house and, as Midge suggested, enjoyed tea and pumpkin scones. The scones were delicious, redolent of pumpkin and other spices, and baked to perfection. Nina made no more mention of Ben, Jason, or Diego.

Although Cara attended to their conversation, she occasionally looked away, or her speech trailed off.

Taking the last sip of her tea, Nina put down the cup and checked her wristwatch. "Three o'clock. I'd better be on my way. Besides, you probably have studying to do."

Cara touched her napkin to her lips. "Always. Studying never ends."

Nina picked up her purse and slung the strap over her shoulder. "I remember those days. But today has been fun, and I'm glad we got together. I really enjoyed the show. I hope you'll keep painting. You're good."

"Thanks, Nina." Cara's lips curved into a soft smile. "Your encouragement means a lot." Cara walked with Nina to the front door.

Nina gave her a hug and then headed down the walk.

"Oh, Nina!"

Nina stopped and turned to see Cara standing in the doorway. "Yes, Cara?" She held her breath.

Cara's eyelids lowered. "Oh, nothing. Just thanks for coming today."

"Of course."

"'Bye." Cara waved then disappeared inside and closed the door.

Nina waited, but when the door remained shut, she continued down the walk. The art show proved a compatible activity for her and Cara, and Benjamin Logarth's painting provided an opening to talk about the young man. Cara's evasiveness indicated she knew more than she shared, which only made Nina more determined than ever to learn about Benjamin. The name of another person on campus who might help popped into her mind. With new determination, she turned her steps toward where she would find him.

Chapter Twenty-Four

When Nina entered Herkimer Memorial Library, she quickly spotted Leopold Manus, the person she'd come to see, disappearing into the stacks with a couple students in tow. While she waited for his return, Nina approached a display case. The exhibit advertised Lit Fest, with descriptions of the various sessions. She was pleased to see hers included. However, the display also served as a reminder that the festival would soon be upon them, and she hadn't yet solved the mystery of Gwyn's death. Seeing Leo emerge from the stacks, Nina waved.

His face lit with a smile, and he stepped up his pace. "Hello, Nina. Good to see you."

"You, too, Leo."

"To what do I owe this visit?"

Nina took a deep breath. "I have a huge favor. I want to talk about the Spearheads."

His smile faded, and he raised both hands. "Now, wait a minute. What makes you think I know any more than I've already told you?"

"Please, Leo. I believe I'm close to finding out what happened to Gwyn. I just need to know a little more to put together all the pieces."

He pursed his lips and slowly shook his head. "All right, let me alert my assistant, and we'll go into my office."

A few minutes later, Nina sat in Leo's office, talking not about the Spearheads but about his latest acquisition of a medieval manuscript discovered in a church basement. Under other circumstances, she would have listened with interest, but today, her purpose in coming made concentration difficult.

Finally, he placed his treasure in its box, sat back, and folded his arms. "All right. What do you want to know about the Spearheads?"

"Was Benjamin Logarth a member?"

Leo shook his head. "He would have been, but he suffered his tragic accident before he could be initiated."

"Initiated. So the Spearheads have a ceremony?"

"Yes, just like the Greek organizations."

Nina took a moment to digest the information. "Would they have had the ceremony in, say, the bell tower?"

Leo gave a short laugh. "I suspected, sooner or later, the infamous tower would appear in our conversation. But, I can't answer your question because I simply do not know. All sorts of shenanigans have gone on in that place."

"And a tragedy, as well."

Leo bowed his head. "Rest her soul."

Nina let a moment pass while acknowledging Leo's sentiment. "Can you think of anything else about the Spearheads that might help me?"

"No, my knowledge is limited. But, Nina, take my advice and let the matter go. Accept that Gwyneth died accidentally. Concentrate on Lit Fest, on your program, and on honoring her with your presentation. Stop wasting time and energy on queries that lead nowhere."

Nina shook her head. "I can't rest until I know exactly how her death occurred."

He leaned forward and eyed her solemnly. "Well, if the Spearheads had something to do with that night in the tower, they won't like you poking around." A few minutes later, he walked her to the main entrance. "When Lit Fest is over, I hope we can get together and just talk books. We haven't had any book discussions yet."

She laughed. "We will find a time to discuss books. I promise." As she drove home, Nina mulled over her meeting with Leo. Was she imagining intrigue? She wanted to believe she was on solid ground with her suspicions, but doubts nagged. Maybe she should take his advice and accept Gwyn's death as accidental.

****

Later, when she was in bed, Nina reviewed what Leo told her about the Spearheads, and her imagination spun a scenario. Benjamin wanted to be a Spearhead, but he died before he could be initiated. Yet Gwyn had his medal, and Stephen found the medal's missing section in the tower. Was that where Gwyn found the medal itself? If so, Benjamin was there. Why? Had he been with the Spearheads? Or on some other mission?

Despite Gwyn's possession of Benjamin's medal, perhaps neither he nor his prize had anything to do with her death. Nina still had other suspects and possible situations to consider. She needed more information to come to any conclusions, but with Lit Fest only a few days away, time was fast running out.

In the week remaining prior to the big event, Nina put aside her sleuthing and concentrated on her Lit Fest programs. For her own presentation, had she included all she wanted to share about children's literature? Did she have enough books to show, in addition to those depicted on the screen? Would the audience be entertained, as well as educated?

For Gwyn's program, had she included all her observations about poetry as well as the poems she wanted to share? So many questions to consider in so little time.

****

"There they are!" Nina stood and waved toward Jessica and Joe, who had just entered the PNU auditorium. Today, Thursday, was the opening of Lit Fest, and the first event was Alexander Brightly's keynote talk. The room was fast filling. Sitting next to her, Stephen turned and also waved toward the couple.

Gran and Joe returned the gestures and then headed down the aisle to settle into their seats.

They all chatted for a few minutes.

Then Vivian appeared on the stage. She approached the microphone, and with a "Welcome, everyone!" the event officially began.

Upon being introduced, Alexander ran out, dressed casually in slacks and a blue sports shirt.

The audience applauded and cheered.

After a few jokes, he settled down to talk about his writing.

Or, as Nina now suspected, Portia's writing, which made her regard what he said in a whole new light.

When his talk was over, Stephen turned toward Nina, Gran, and Joe. "Is the guy really sincere, or does he just put on a show? What do you think, Joe?"

Joe shrugged. "Full of himself, but entertaining."

"I thought he was great," Gran said. "You men are

just sour grapes because he's so charming."

Joe rolled his eyes. "Uh-huh."

Stephen placed a hand on Nina's arm. "What's your opinion, hon?"

"He certainly knows how to entertain an audience." She meant the compliment, too, which made her wonder, had Alexander missed his true calling?

Since her talk was scheduled for the following day, for the remainder of Thursday, Nina attended other sessions. Two she especially enjoyed were Eldon's Famous Speeches in History, with his students dressed in costume, and Jaz's Folklore Tales, acted out by drama class students.

On Friday, although her presentation was in the afternoon, Nina arrived early enough to catch Desmond DeSoto's talk on idioms. She expected a dry speech delivered in his pompous manner. Instead, he surprised her with an amusing lecture enlivened with illustrations showing literal interpretations. Then, at the appointed hour, Nina stepped into her assigned room.

Jason was already setting up the equipment.

"Jason, thank you for being so prompt." Placing her tote on the desk, she took out her computer and added it to the cart.

Jason gave a salute. "No problem, Ms. Foster, although all the programs keep me hopping."

"Are your frat buddies helping, too?" She cast him a glance. Would he slip and reveal something about the secret society?

"You mean the Omicrons?"

She raised an eyebrow. "Do you belong to another fraternity?"

"Uh, no, not to speak of. I mean, no." Jason

unwound the projector cord and plugged it into the wall outlet.

"Well, I'm sure everyone appreciates the Omicrons's help. I saw Diego at the reception, too."

Jason's scowl and the set of his jaw discouraged any more questioning. She'd best devote herself to her preparations. But in the back of her mind lurked the nagging reminder that her time at PNU grew short, and she must take advantage of each opportunity to gather information.

The audience arrived, filling the seats.

Then Stephen appeared. They'd come together this morning but parted while she attended sessions and he conducted interviews for his newspaper.

Gran and Joe soon joined Stephen.

Nina recognized several librarians from the regional group she belonged to.

Cara appeared, along with a few other Mu sisters.

So many people. Nina was no stranger to public speaking, but most of her talks were to small audiences in the library or occasionally to a professional group. Never had she faced an audience this large. Her heart beat faster, and her hands were cold and clammy. Could she do this? Then she thought of Gwyneth and recalled her words of praise and encouragement when she recruited her for the festival. Straightening her shoulders, she strode to the podium and picked up the microphone. "Welcome, everyone..."

An hour later, judging by the enthusiastic applause, her talk was a success. Several people stayed to engage in conversation and ask questions. Then, with Stephen at her side, she left the campus, tired but in good spirits.

Saturday presented a bright and unseasonably

warm autumn day. As the time for her bell tower performance neared, Nina and Stephen headed for the quad. Per her instructions, Wildon and his crew had set up the loudspeakers and microphone. Today, she brought the notes for her personal remarks and also Gwyn's tape recorder and the tape of her poetry readings. Although the bottom floor was cold and damp, as always, when Nina climbed the stairs to the top, she stepped into bright rays of sunshine beaming through the open window.

"Looks like you'll have a spotlight." Following her, Stephen nodded toward the sunshine.

Nina moved into the sun's path. "Just like being on a stage." Gazing below, she saw several students setting up the rows of chairs on the lawn. Not surprisingly, Jason and Diego were among them.

Stephen made sure the loudspeaker was anchored in place. Then he tested the microphone. "All systems go," he reported.

Nina took out her notes for a last-minute review.

"Ms. Foster!" called a voice from below.

She went to the landing and leaned over the railing. "Is that you, Jason?"

"Yeah, it's me. I came to help you set up."

Nina descended the stairs until he came into view. He was not looking up toward her, as she expected, but instead he was bent over, walking along the room's perimeter. "Are you looking for something, Jason?"

He jerked upright. "What? No. Well, okay, remember I told you about the money that's supposed to be hidden here?" He gave a short laugh. "Whenever I come, I always look for it. Maybe one day I'll get lucky."

"So, you come here often?"

He waved a hand. "No, of course not. I'm here now to help with your equipment."

"I appreciate your offer, but Wildon already took care of that job. Today, my friend, Stephen, is with me, in case adjustments are needed." Aware Stephen had descended the stairs, too, she gestured over her shoulder.

Jason frowned and propped both hands on his hips. "Setting up is supposed to be my job."

"You need to see Wildon, Jason." She expected him to leave.

But he stood his ground.

Stephen took another step down the stairs. "Thanks, Jason. We'll see you after the program."

Jason mumbled, wheeled around, and marched out the door.

"I've never seen him so upset." Nina followed Stephen to the top of the tower. "He's always been polite and helpful."

"He's probably used to getting his own way, or else he has some other agenda. We'll keep an eye out for him."

The time arrived to begin her program. Nina put Jason and his odd behavior to the back of her mind. Stepping to the window, she surveyed the audience.

Gran and Joe, among the first to arrive, had claimed front row seats.

All the Lit Fest Committee members congregated together, chatting with one another—except Desmond DeSoto and Vivian, who wore frowns and sat with arms folded. Oh, well, what else could she expect when they'd opposed this venture from the beginning?

Cara, Diego, and Jason were with a group of students, most of them focused on their cell phones.

Midge Cornell, seated behind the students, looked up and waved.

Nina returned the gesture.

President Olivera, her husband, and several other school officials, including Board President, Lincoln Hopkins, filled the back rows.

Then Alexander Brightly arrived, accompanied by half a dozen fans. They crowded around him while Portia, Cab, and Otis tagged along behind.

Gwyn's sister, Cassandra, dressed in a blue skirt and matching jacket, her hair piled atop her head, hurried across the grass to plop into a chair.

Suddenly realizing all her suspects were in attendance sent a frisson of fear through Nina. She shrugged off the feeling, telling herself she was perfectly safe. Besides, Stephen was with her. She turned her thoughts to Gwyn and imagined how thrilled she would be to have such an audience.

Stephen came to stand beside her. "Time to begin."

Taking a deep breath, Nina picked up the microphone. "Good afternoon, ladies and gentlemen. Welcome to this tribute to Gwyneth Miller, esteemed colleague, beloved teacher, poet, and friend. Fortunately, before leaving us, Professor Miller had today's talk prepared, and I am pleased to share it. It includes her thoughts on poetry and its place in our lives, with examples from renowned poets as well as from her own works, some of which she wrote in this little book she carried everywhere." Nina held up Gwyn's pink journal. "She told me she never knew when a poem might spring to mind. With her book handy, she was always ready."

Nina launched into Gwyn's program, reading from her notes and when appropriate switching to the tape recording of her poems. When she finished, a round of hearty applause greeted her. Nina remained at the window waving to the audience as they drifted away.

Stephen put an arm around her shoulders. "Judging by everyone's rapt attention and applause, I'd say you are a big hit. Your professor would be proud."

Tears burned Nina's eyes. "I wish she were here."

He pulled her closer. "I know. But take a moment to be thankful you honored her."

Leaning into him, savoring his warmth and strength, Nina did as he suggested. Then, she pulled away gently. "Okay, time to go. We can leave the equipment here for someone to pick up, probably Wildon."

"Or Jason. He seemed determined to do his job."

"Or to look for the lost money he talks about. Say, maybe we should search."

Stephen grimaced and shook his head. "I've had enough of this place, haven't you?"

Nina nodded. "I just wish I could have solved the mystery of Gwyn's death."

"Maybe there is no mystery, Nina, and her fall was accidental, after all."

"I'm not convinced." She gazed around. "I think the clues are all here. I just haven't figured out how to put them together."

"Meanwhile, how about hitting the authors' autograph party?"

"Good idea. I have a list of books I want to buy."

He laughed. "Of course, you do. Seriously, though,

I have a list, too." He patted his jacket pocket.

Nina and Stephen soon joined the other Lit Fest attendees in the auditorium. The participating authors sat at tables behind stacks of their books, autographing and chatting with fans. Not surprisingly, Alexander Brightly's table had the longest line.

While he autographed, Portia placed the books in bags decorated with his photo.

Wondering what Portia thought about her role, Nina studied her. Was she resentful and angry because as the true author, she received no recognition? Or had she accepted the arrangement? Nina was pleased to see that the PNU Press had copies of Gywn's poetry booklets for sale and that business was quite brisk.

A party in the StuU marked the festival's final event. The sun was setting as Nina and Stephen joined the group streaming into the building. Although today especially had taken its toll, she did not want to miss this last celebration.

A huge banner that said *PNU LIT FEST*, plus balloons and bouquets of flowers decorated the facility. Nina and Stephen joined the buffet line and after filling their plates with baked salmon, mashed potatoes, a vegetable medley, and an assortment of salads, they joined Nina's committee members at their reserved table.

"We can congratulate ourselves." Jaz clapped her hands.

"We sure can." Eldon made a fist and pounded the table. "Lit Fest rules."

Even Desmond Desoto wore a smile. "I sold all my books," he announced, in a voice loud enough to be heard by everyone. "Whoever was in charge should have ordered more."

Looking around, Nina spotted President Olivera sitting with other university dignitaries, professors, and board members, including Lincoln Hopkins. Cassandra, Gwyn's sister, was a part of their group. Nina smiled to herself. How nice they included her.

Alexander and his followers sat with some of the other speakers, people Nina knew only by their names in the program.

Everyone was in a festive mood, and the air rang with the sounds of talk and laughter.

Still, Nina found joining the festivities difficult. Despite the successes of both her presentations, she hadn't solved the mystery of Gwyn's death, and the chances of succeeding diminished with each passing minute.

"Do you mind if I leave you for a while?" Stephen's voice interrupted her thoughts. "I want to interview a few of the speakers." He pointed toward a table nearby.

"Go ahead. I'll be fine."

"Are you okay?" He leaned closer. "You look a little down."

She mustered a smile. "I'm just tired."

"Understandably. We'll go in a little while, okay?"

"All right."

After he left, Nina listened to nearby conversations, but thoughts of Gwyneth intruded. So many clues pointed to foul play in the tower, but nothing she'd discovered established proof. The answer eluded her. She would read Gwyn's journal again, and the poems she published, and the book to T.L. What about the tape recorder President Olivera gave her? She would listen to that one tape again, especially where it sounded as though Gwyn had been interrupted.

After the bell tower presentation, Nina put the recorder and tape in her coat pocket. Hadn't she? Honestly, she couldn't remember. She slipped her hand into her right coat pocket. Nothing. In the other pocket, she found only a handkerchief. She searched her purse but found no recorder.

Could she have left the device in the bell tower? Or had she lost it elsewhere? At the autograph party. Or here in the StuU? Closing her eyes, she pictured the recorder where she last saw it, at the top of the tower near the window. She must search that location first. Now. Before Jason or whoever collected the equipment arrived. She'd glimpsed Jason earlier here at the party, helping people to find seats. Looking around, she didn't see him. She didn't see Stephen, either.

She put on her coat and gathered up her purse. "I have to leave for a few minutes," she said to Jaz, who sat next to her.

Jaz's brow wrinkled. "Is everything okay? You look stressed."

"I'm fine." Nina waved a hand. "Just a quick errand."

She hoped.

Chapter Twenty-Five

Outside, except for a few lights here and there, the campus lay in darkness. The moon was on the rise but had not yet cleared the tops of the trees. The bell tower would be dark. No matter. Nina had in her tote the small yet powerful flashlight she brought in case she needed it for the presentation. Plus, she'd be in and out of the tower in no time. Stepping aside to avoid a group just arriving, she took out her cell phone and texted Stephen:

Left recorder in tower. Back soon.

The bell tower was a couple blocks away. Globe lights along the streets provided some light, but the night prevailed. The temperature had dropped, too. Nina buttoned her coat and turned up the collar. She encountered no one on the way. The campus was deserted, with Lit Fest attendees and speakers either having departed or gone to the StuU.

She reached the tower, but before approaching the door, she stopped and gazed at the top. Cold and forbidding. Did she really want to do this? Why not wait until tomorrow? No, if the tape recorder was there, she couldn't risk someone else finding it and taking it away.

Nina put her key in the lock and opened the door. Switching on her flashlight, she stepped inside. The light did little to illuminate the entire room but shone brightly enough for tonight's purpose. Should she close and lock the door? Or not? What if someone saw the door ajar and took advantage of the easy access? She'd best not provide such a temptation. But after she locked the door, she felt imprisoned and shut off from the world outside. Never mind. Just find the recorder and get out of there.

Sweeping around the flashlight's beam, she saw the room was just as she and Stephen had left it. The microphone and loudspeakers were still on the table. For all Jason's intensity about setting up the equipment, he certainly wasn't in any hurry to collect it. She aimed her light at the stairs. The beam illuminated only the bottom few steps. The remainder of the ascent lay in darkness.

She would climb the stairs, collect the recorder, and return to the StuU party. Very likely, this visit to the tower would be her last. Putting one foot on the bottom step, she started up. Guided by the flashlight, she made her way, one step after the other. Tonight, though, the stairs seemed longer and steeper than on any previous visit. Still, she plodded on and at last reached the top. She stood on the platform a moment to catch her breath and then turned toward the window. Yes, there on the ledge, outlined in the dim light, sat the cassette tape recorder. A sigh of relief escaped her lips. Grasping the recorder, she slipped the machine into her coat pocket. Now, to descend the stairs and leave.

She had just placed a foot on the first step when she heard a noise below. The door opening? Probably Jason. Sure enough, when she peered over the railing, she glimpsed a tall, thin figure, just Jason's height and build. Did she want to interact with him? Not really.

She'd stay put until he gathered the equipment and left.

But, instead of taking the equipment from the table, he pulled out a flashlight and shone it around the room. *Oh, great. Looking for the lost money again.* She didn't want to wait while he conducted his search. No telling how long he would be. She crept back up to the platform. *Hurry up, Jason, and leave!*

Peering over the edge of the stairs a moment later, she saw the light moving upward. Oh, no, he was climbing to the top of the tower. Now what? Well, she'd just have to face him. Her heart beat faster.

He reached the top of the stairs and stepped onto the platform.

"Hello, Jas…" Nina stared, and the name died on her lips. "Mr. Hopkins. I—I thought you were Jason."

One eyebrow quirked. "We do look alike. But this is my mission, not my son's."

Keep cool. You can handle him. "Mission? Don't tell me you're after the lost money, too."

He snorted. "No, something much more valuable than money."

"You don't seem surprised to see me here."

"I saw you leave the StuU party and followed you. I didn't know you were coming here. But when you did, I took advantage. Your locking the door didn't keep me out. I have my own key."

In the dim light, his features appeared sharper than she recalled, and…*evil*. Nina shivered. Being alone with him was dangerous, but how could she escape when he blocked the stairs? She glanced at the window. No, not *that* way.

Still, sensing she was on to something important, she slipped a hand into her coat pocket. Grasping the tape recorder, she located and pressed the Record button and then turned up the volume. *Please let there be enough blank tape to capture this conversation.* Nina lifted her chin and made her tone firm. "What do you want, Mr. Hopkins?"

"I'm looking for a medal that was lost here. Very valuable."

She frowned. "Medal? Do you mean the one Benjamin Logarth won in a drag race?"

"That's the one." His voice rose. "Did you find it?"

"Why would he lose the medal here?"

Hopkins shrugged. "You know kids come here. So, do you have it? You found Gwyn's pink journal here, so I'm betting you have the medal, as well."

Nina narrowed her eyes. "How do you know I found her journal here—unless you were with her when she lost it?"

He clamped his mouth shut and glared.

"You were with her the night she died." Nina's thoughts whirled as the missing pieces to the puzzle of Gwyn's death finally fell into place. "Jason isn't looking for lost money; he's searching for Ben's medal. Ben lost it when…when he was being initiated into the Spearheads. But then he died in a car crash. Wait." She held up a forefinger. "Maybe he didn't die in the crash. What if he died here…and Jason and Diego took his body to Sattoo Pass and sent him and his car over the cliff? That's what really happened, isn't it?"

Hopkins waved a fist. "Why did you have to stick your nose into something that wasn't your business?"

Not about to be intimidated, Nina lifted her chin. "Because I had to find out the truth."

He looked away. "Sometimes, the truth isn't the

best for everyone."

The cover-up sparked Nina's anger. "Don't Ben's parents deserve to know what really happened?"

He turned to face her again, his eyes blazing. "His death was an accident. Yes, the Spearheads were initiating him, making him climb to the top of the tower and ring the bell." He gestured toward the bell hanging overhead. "They didn't know he was afraid of heights. He made it to the top, but when he reached for the rope to ring the bell, he must've become dizzy. Okay, the drinking didn't help. He fell down the stairs and hit his head on the cement floor. His death was an accident! Did you hear me? An *accident!*"

Finally learning the details of Benjamin's tragic death made Nina feel sick inside. "Why didn't Jason and Diego and the others tell the truth?"

"And ruin all their lives? The Spearheads do good around campus. Jason's going to Harvard. Do you think they'd still accept him after such a scandal?"

"So, you and Gwyn were here the night of her death. Why?"

"She wanted Jason and Diego to tell the truth about what happened to Ben. But instead of going to them, she wanted me to convince them to come forward." He poked a thumb toward his chest. "Okay, so we met in this tower at night a few times over the years. But there was nothing between us anymore, not as far as I was concerned. Maybe she thought being here together again would make me change my mind about keeping secret what happened to Ben."

"And you wouldn't change your mind."

"Of course not!" Hopkins glared. "Do you think I'm crazy? Risk everything I've worked for, sacrificed for, all these years, just because a Spearheads' initiation went bad?"

"Ben lost his life." The man's lack of empathy appalled her.

"His death was an *accident*! Don't you get it?" He waved a fist.

She lifted her chin. "I suppose now you'll tell me Gwyn's death was an accident, too."

"It was! When I asked her to prove she had Ben's medal, she pulled it from her journal and waved it in my face, taunting me. I reached for the medal, but she jerked it away and stuck it back in the journal. We locked arms and struggled…"

"Go on." Nina steeled herself against what she feared would come next.

"She went into a rage and pushed me aside. I got my fingers around the book, but she held on. Somehow, we both let go at the same time, and the book disappeared down the stairs. I started for the steps, but she tackled me and pulled me back. We struggled again until I finally broke free. She grabbed the rope and rang the bell. I knew I had to get out before someone came. I headed for the stairs again, but then I saw the rope slipping from her grasp. Before I could reach her, she fell backward out the window, and then she was gone."

She was gone. . . .

His last words hung in the air.

Nina shuddered and hugged her arms. Finally, she had learned the truth about Gwyn's fall from the tower.

He took a step toward her. "But since you have the journal, I'm betting you have the medal, too. They're probably in your purse."

Instinctively, Nina gripped her purse strap.

"Give me that bag!" He lunged and grabbed the strap.

Nina flinched but kept a tight hold on the purse.

He pushed her.

With her free hand, she pushed back.

He tugged on her purse.

Still, she managed to hold on.

"Nina! Nina! Are you up there?" Stephen's voice came from outside the tower.

"I'm here!"

"What the hell!" Shoving Nina aside, Hopkins headed for the stairs.

Arms outstretched, grabbing only air, Nina stumbled toward the window. Eyes wide, gasping for breath, she watched as the opening came nearer and nearer... Just when she decided all was lost, her fingers caught the ledge. She gripped the cold surface, feeling the rough cement dig into her flesh. "Stephen! Get Hopkins!"

Nina crumped into a heap on the floor. Seconds passed while a roaring filled her head and the room spun. *Get up... Don't let Hopkins escape...*

She crawled to the top of the stairs. Grasping the railing, she pulled herself to her feet. Fighting a wave of dizziness, she looked down. Where was Hopkins? Waiting at the bottom? But Stephen was here now. Hopkins wouldn't dare attack her again. Would he? He was a desperate man. Who knew what he would do. Suddenly, she feared for Stephen's safety, too.

Her legs shaking, her hands gripping the railing, Nina crept down the stairs, alert for sounds of Hopkins's presence. She heard nothing. Then came a pounding on the door. "Nina! Nina!"

Stephen's voice.

Was Hopkins lurking in the shadows and waiting to assault her? Nina went down a couple more steps—and saw her attacker. He lay on his stomach, with his face turned to the side, his eyes closed, and his mouth open. A pool of blood trickled from a gash in his forehead. Was he dead? Or only unconscious? She descended the remainder of the stairs and ran to the door. Fumbling with the lock, she opened the door—and fell into Stephen's arms. "Call the police, Stephen!"

"I already have," he said, holding her close.

Nina leaned against him, relief washing over her. Thank God for Stephen.

Chapter Twenty-Six

The following day, thoroughly exhausted from her ordeal, Nina rested on the sofa at Stephen's house.

He stood nearby, talking on his cell phone, learning the latest news from one of his sources.

As Nina waited for him to finish, her mind reeled with memories of last night's events.

Shortly after Stephen summoned the police, both the campus patrol and local officers arrived, along with an aid car. Spreading the word didn't take long, and soon, a crowd of onlookers gathered around the tower.

Still alive, Hopkins was attended to and subsequently taken to a hospital.

Nina and Stephen sat with an officer in his patrol car while she related what had taken place in the tower. Her emotions ran high, and more than once, she had to stop and take deep breaths in order to continue. Fortunately, despite the struggle with Hopkins over her purse, the tape recorder remained secure in her coat pocket. She gave the device to the officer, and a test revealed the tape had indeed captured her and Hopkins's conversation.

Stephen finished his call and came to sit beside her.

She looked up, eager to hear what he'd learned. "Did you find out how Hopkins is doing?"

"Still in the hospital." Stephen tucked the phone into his shirt pocket.

"Have the police questioned him?"

"Some. My guy will call again when he has more news. Meanwhile, can I get you anything? Tea?" He gestured toward her cup on the coffee table.

Nina shook her head. "No, thanks. I'm okay. I should have gone to work today."

"After only a few hours sleep?" He frowned. "You need to rest."

"What will happen to Hopkins?"

He shrugged. "Depends on the prosecutor. If he agrees Gwyn's death was not premeditated, he'll probably go with manslaughter or second-degree murder. Or acquittal."

"I don't believe Hopkins went to the tower that night with murder in mind. Even though he said there was nothing between them, I think he still cared for Gwyn."

Stephen adjusted the pillows at her back. "Then why did he marry someone else?"

"She was the boss's daughter. He chose advancing his career over love."

"Would Gwyn want to get back at him by destroying his son's future?"

"I doubt revenge was a motive." Nina settled against the cushions. "Like me, she wanted the truth to be known. I'm just sorry she had to pay such a high price."

Stephen moved closer. "Was Hopkins the person who interrupted Gwyn when she called to invite you to Lit Fest?"

"I don't know for sure, but I am guessing he was the intruder, because she told him they would meet later, which they did, that fateful night at the tower."

"I'm betting this tragedy will blow apart the Spearheads."

"I suppose. Which is too bad, because the group was also a positive presence on campus."

"Then they had the bad judgment to initiate Benjamin in the tower." Stephen tilted his head and eyed her. "They must've been behind the threatening notes you received, and I wouldn't be surprised if one of them—most likely, Jason or Diego—drove the car that ran you off the road."

"I told the investigators about both incidents, and they promised to question the two." Full of mixed emotions, Nina fell silent. Then, gathering her thoughts again, she looked at Stephen. "If the Spearheads hadn't tried to cover up Benjamin's death, or, if he hadn't lost his medal in the tower, this story might have a different ending. Whatever, when all the investigation is over, I hope Benjamin's medal will be given to his parents."

Stephen put an arm around her shoulders. "I'll use whatever influence I have to make that happen."

Nina gave him a fond smile and snuggled closer. "You're the best, Stephen."

He planted a kiss on her cheek. "So are you, sweetheart. So are you." Stephen left shortly, to attend to newspaper business.

Nina continued to rest. Sort of. Her phone rang continuously with calls, first from Jessica and Joe, then Vivian, Cassandra, and Midge. Even Hollis Olivera called to express her concern.

"I'm so sorry about what happened, Nina. I know you can't discuss the matter until the investigation is completed and all the facts are revealed. But I want you to know we at PNU are here to help if you need us."

Her words brought tears to Nina's eyes. "Thank you, President Olivera. I really appreciate your support. I'm so, so sorry for any problems that arise for PNU as a result of anything I've done, but I just had to find out the truth about Gwyn's fall from the tower."

"Put your mind at ease, Nina. We at PNU want the truth to be known, as well, and we will survive any adverse results."

Although reassured by President Olivera's call, after hanging up, Nina still wrestled with her emotions. She'd done what she set out to do—solve the mystery of Gwyneth Miller's death. But in the process, many lives were altered. Was the revelation of truth always the best? Were some secrets better left buried? In this case, only time would tell. Right now, the best way to get her life on track was to return to her job at Seaview.

****

"Books on the Civil War? I'll show you where those are shelved." Nina smiled at the elderly gentleman who had approached her at the library's reference desk. Leading him through the stacks, she stopped at the appropriate shelf, pulled out a book, and held it up. "This one is popular."

The man took the book and peered at the cover through his thick eyeglasses. "Hmmm, this looks interesting."

She showed him a few more volumes and then left him to continue searching on his own. On the way to her desk, she put a spring in her step to show how glad she was to be back on the job assisting patrons. Later that afternoon, she helped to set up the reading room for Alexander Brightly's appearance. Now that she knew he wasn't involved in Gwyn's death, hosting his talk would be easier. Still, that he wasn't the true author of his books troubled her.

At the appointed hour, he swept in with only Portia in tow.

Nina looked from one to the other. "Cab and Otis aren't coming?"

Alexander made an offhand gesture. "They found other ways to spend this evening." He tilted his head and gave her a solemn look. "How are you doing? Heard about your ordeal in the tower. What a scandal. Poor Gwyn. Did Hopkins really push her out the window?" He grimaced.

Portia shivered and hugged her arms. "What an awful man."

"Sorry, I can't discuss Mr. Hopkins's actions." Nina shook her head. "The investigation's ongoing, and I don't want to spread rumors before the official word is released."

"I understand." Alexander nodded, his expression sober. "But, still, I am so sorry about Gwyn. She was my teacher, my mentor, and a good friend."

But did she also confront you with her knowledge of exactly how your books were written? She had no opportunity to ask the question—not that she would—because just then, his fans arrived, filling the library with their enthusiastic chatter.

Alexander broke away to greet them. "Welcome to my event, ladies." With a sweeping gesture, he guided them to the area set up for his performance.

Portia followed in their wake.

"Performance" was an appropriate description because, like his Lit Fest appearance, Alexander presented more than just a talk. First, he shared amusing experiences he'd had as an author. Then, when he turned to his books, instead of reading various passages, he acted them out.

The applause at the end indicated the audience's hearty approval.

Glancing at Portia, Nina saw the smile on her face. So, Alexander's showmanship pleased her, too.

After the autographing and socializing over coffee and cake provided by the Friends of the Library, Portia escorted the fans to the front door.

Nina approached Alexander. "Your talk was very entertaining."

Alexander tucked his pen into his shirt pocket. "Thanks, Nina. I do get a charge out of these programs."

"I suppose you're already planning your next book? Or maybe you've even begun writing it." She studied him, interested to hear his response.

He came from behind the table to stand beside her. "I'll tell you my news if you promise to keep it a secret until the official announcement."

News? Her interest piqued, Nina nodded. "Of course."

"I'm not writing a next book."

"What?" She widened her eyes.

"I just signed with Pilmore Pictures—as an actor."

"But you've been so successful as a writer."

"I know. But I'd rather express myself on the stage than on paper. I'll still have my hand in the literary arts. I'll be mentoring Portia." He nodded toward the door where she bid good-bye to the fans.

Although the news came as no real surprise, Nina kept an element of surprise in her voice. "So, Portia wants to be a writer?"

He nodded. "Ever since we were in college. Now, it's her turn to see if she's got what it takes."

Nina gave him a smile. "What a...*generous* gesture."

He grinned. "I know. I'm a generous guy." A few minutes later, Alexander and Portia left the library. He had an arm slung around her shoulders, and they appeared deep in conversation.

Would such a partnership be successful? Only time would tell. "Good luck to you both," Nina whispered, as she watched them climb into his car. "Don't worry, Alexander, how you really wrote your books will be a secret safe with me."

A few days later, at Cara's request, Nina traveled to the PNU campus to meet her in the StuU. After purchasing their coffee, they chose a table looking out at the garden. Autumn leaves decorated the flagstone path winding among patches of chrysanthemums and dahlias, while the nearly bare branches on the trees overhead admitted rays of muted sunlight.

"I'm so sorry if anything I did contributed to what happened to you in the tower." Cara pressed her lips together and shook her head. "I just couldn't tell you everything I suspected."

Nina nodded and sipped her coffee. "I understand your loyalty, Cara. But, did you know about the Spearheads' initiation in the bell tower?"

Cara's forehead wrinkled. "I didn't know about any of their secret meetings. But I thought the person I saw running from the tower was Jason. I was afraid to tell because he's friends with Diego."

"I can see how you would mistake Jason's father

for him. They look so much alike. You can still tell the police what you saw, though."

Cara gave a solemn nod. "I will. I want to do what's right." She looked down and fingered her napkin. "I'm breaking up with Diego, too."

"I'm sure that's for the best, as well. I'm proud of you, Cara."

Nina and Cara chatted awhile longer and then parted with plans to keep in touch. Nina was thankful the meeting ended on a positive note. She looked forward to their friendship and, hopefully, to being a constructive influence in the young woman's life.

Another week passed, during which Lincoln Hopkins's future was still undecided while those in charge debated the case. Nina knew if a trial were held, she would be called to testify, but for now, she would concentrate on her own life.

"Thanksgiving's coming soon," Stephen said, a few days later, pointing toward the date on his kitchen wall calendar. "I know we're having dinner at Marley Manor, but how about having a pre-holiday party here? I've done enough remodeling for us to entertain."

Nina clapped her hands. "What a great idea. I'm sure Gran and Joe and our friends would love to come."

"Can I count on you to help decorate?"

"Of course. And to cook, too, as much as I can without interfering with the head chef." She laughed and gave him a hug.

Nina eagerly prepared for the occasion, choosing flower arrangements and a new tablecloth and matching napkins for the buffet. Trips to the grocery store stocked the cupboards and refrigerator with the needed food.

At last, the day arrived. When everything was ready to receive their guests, Stephen approached Nina and placed an arm around her shoulders. "We've both been working hard. How about a walk on the beach?"

She smiled and nodded. "I could use a break."

Nina and Stephen put on jackets and headed outside for their favorite beach walk. Holding hands, they strolled the hard-packed sand near the surf, the sun shining brightly overhead and the mountains across the water etched against the blue sky.

Nina took a deep breath of the fresh air. "Ahh, this is great, and what a perfect day."

Stephen pointed toward a bench. "Let's sit for a while."

Once seated, Nina and Stephen focused on the view, including the passage of several tugboats and a ferry headed toward Kingston.

Then Stephen turned to face her. "I planned to wait until Christmas for this moment, but after all you've been through, I decided now is the right time." Slipping a hand into his coat pocket, he brought out a small wooden box.

She recognized the sunflower carving on the lid. "Joe's box."

"Yours, now." He placed the box in her hands.

She ran a forefinger over the carving. "The design is beautiful."

"Joe's a talented guy. But look inside."

Nina opened the lid, and there on a bed of black velvet laid another sunflower, this one with petals of gold, a center filled with sparkling diamonds, and attached to a silver chain. "Oh, Stephen! How beautiful. I love it."

"I thought you would. My mother loved this pendant, too, and wore it often. When you and I were in Parker's Landing last summer, and my sister, Judy, learned you favor sunflowers, she showed this necklace to me. We both agreed Mom would want you to have it."

Tears sprang to Nina's eyes. "I'm so honored."

"Here, let me put it on." Stephen picked up the necklace.

Nina turned and held up her hair while he fastened the clasp around her neck. Then she faced him again. "What do you think?"

Stephen nodded. "Perfect. Just perfect."

"Thank you, Stephen. I'll treasure this gift always."

He grinned. "I know what I'll always treasure—you. Come here, honey." He opened his arms.

Full of emotion, Nina went into his embrace and gave herself up to his kiss. Long, delicious moments passed before they finally drew apart.

Stephen patted her arm. "Since we have a party to host, we'd better go home."

Home. She liked the sound of that. "Yes, Stephen, I'm ready."

He stood and held out his hand.

Placing her hand in his, she rose and followed him onto the path. Happiness and contentment filled her as she looked forward not only to this day with family and friends but also to all the days ahead with the man she loved.

A word about the author...

A resident of the Pacific Northwest, Linda Hope Lee writes contemporary romance, romantic suspense, and mystery novels. She also enjoys watercolor paintings, photography, collecting children's books, and anything to do with wire-haired fox terriers.

www.lindahopelee.com

Other Titles by this Author
Dark Memories
Under Gemini

Nina Foster Mysteries
Murder Between the Pages
Secrets to Die For
Deadly Reunion

Red Rock Collection, boxed set of following titles
Finding Sara
Loving Rose
Marrying Molly

Thank you for purchasing
this publication of The Wild Rose Press, Inc.

For questions or more information
contact us at
info@thewildrosepress.com.

The Wild Rose Press, Inc.
www.thewildrosepress.com